# ELSA

## J. Douglas Lynn

PublishAmerica
Baltimore

© 2004 by J. Douglas Lynn.

All rights reserved. No part of this book may be reproduced, stored in a retrieval system or transmitted in any form or by any means without the prior written permission of the publishers, except by a reviewer who may quote brief passages in a review to be printed in a newspaper, magazine or journal.

First printing

ISBN: 1-4137-2171-0
PUBLISHED BY
PUBLISHAMERICA, LLLP.
www.publishamerica.com
Baltimore

Printed in the United States of America

# Author's Note

This is entirely a work of fiction. While there is a small community of Elsa in south Texas, its description is different than the town I describe. Neither the town nor the people bear any resemblance to the town or the people in this story.

# Acknowledgements

I wish to thank my wife Patricia and my daughters Susan MacMillan and Sarah Thompson for reviewing and editing the *Elsa* manuscript, and especially, for their unflinching support.

# PROLOGUE

SERGIO DOMINGUEZ OBSERVED THE scene with detached interest. Seated on the driver's side of his Chevy Malibu, the hardened bodyguard for an Austin drug dealer fit the image of an underworld "tough." He had a horizontal two-inch scar on his cheek from jawbone to mouth, a goatee, bald head, deep penetrating brown eyes, muscular torso, broad shoulders and the brown skin of an indigenous Mexican. Sergio watched as José Acuna and two fellow graduate students from the University of Texas attached a customized twenty-foot trailer to a hitch at the rear of a pickup truck. The bed of the trailer was packed with components of a proprietary system designed to extract precious metals from oil field brine that the students had meticulously built during the summer months. It looked like something Rube Goldberg would have put together.

Although José and his associates were upbeat about their task, joking and laughing, Sergio's normally crusty facial expression didn't change. Without taking his eyes off the students, he reached out with his right hand and tenderly caressed the package on the passenger seat, mumbling, "Enjoy yourself while you can, you little shit." The students locked the tow bar to the hitch, secured the safety chains, climbed into the truck cab, and left the parking lot of the Austin Airport Industrial Complex to begin the long journey south on Interstate 35.

It was easy for Sergio to keep the pickup and trailer in sight; the students drove slowly and stopped frequently. When they reached Falfurrias, they parked in front of a restaurant and went inside. Sergio hadn't eaten since dinner the previous evening, so he decided to follow them into the restaurant and gamble that he wouldn't be recognized. His decision fit perfectly with his macho attitude about everything; he relished the adrenaline rush he'd experience when he pushed danger to the breaking point. Dressed in a starched shirt and Levi's, boots, and a brimmed cap turned backwards, Sergio swaggered into the restaurant as if he owned the place. The students were fully engrossed in conversation, however, and didn't even look up when Sergio sat in a booth directly behind them. There was no hint of recognition, not even when Sergio turned around and asked for a bottle of ketchup.

After consuming a hearty lunch, the students renewed their southerly journey. They turned off State Route 217 onto Route 493, a road that featured miles of scrub brush and sand before passing through the postage stamp community of Elsa. The sun was positioned low in the sky when the pickup truck slowed as it approached a big sign attached to two 2-inch by 6-inch posts sunk into the ground at the side of the road. The sign read in large blue letters on a white background, *Hidalgo Brine Disposal Plant, Roy DeWitt, Proprietor*, followed in smaller print by a Railroad Commission permit number, and a telephone number. The truck turned onto the red clay entrance road, but Sergio continued on past the entrance, and pulled off the road into a secluded location under a tree.

Sergio checked the time on his wristwatch, 6:30 P.M. He grabbed a can of beer from a small cooler next to the package on the passenger seat, and in a series of gulps, drank the contents in a matter of seconds, and wiped his mouth with the sleeve of his shirt. He exited the vehicle, crossed the road and began the quarter mile trek around the disposal plant to a secluded spot that overlooked the prototype test site. The location provided Sergio with the cover he needed to observe the students' movements without fear of detection. As he approached Sergio heard voices in the distance. He crouched down and began to slither along the ground like an infantryman. The physical discomfort he experienced from crawling in the dirt on his elbows and belly, and the prospect of lying on his stomach in the tall grass for hours, were offset by thoughts of the sizeable commission he'd earn from fulfilling his assignment. The innovative technology that he'd overheard the students talk about during lunch didn't interest him at all; he just wanted to complete his assignment, get the hell out of there, and collect his $20,000.

When darkness began to frustrate the students' reassembly efforts, Sergio overheard Acuna announce, "We'd better quit before we make a mistake. I can hardly see my hands. If we come back around 7:00 A.M., we should be able to finish setting up and be ready for a demonstration before 9:00. It's been a long day. I'm tired and hungry. Let's drive into McAllen and find something to eat before we bed down for the night."

While the students packed their gear, Sonja Hyde asked, "Who'll be here for the first demonstration, José?"

"Martin Leary and Roy DeWitt. Dr. Gerba isn't scheduled to arrive until mid-afternoon. I think Dr. Robinson plans to come down with him."

Sergio rose from his prone position, stretched and brushed off his clothes. It was already too dark to see the face of his watch, but he guessed it was probably after 9:00 P.M. He began the circuitous route back to his vehicle to pick up the package. Although unsure of the footing, he was reluctant to switch on his flashlight for fear of discovery. Before he'd traveled fifty feet, he stepped in a hole, twisted an ankle, and fell to the ground. He lay on his face and groaned, stifling the urge to cry out.

Sergio sat up and rubbed his ankle for a few minutes before deciding that he'd better return to the test site by way of the entrance road rather than risk another fall. If he were to accidentally drop the package, it would be catastrophic.

The sky was clear and a three-quarter moon peeked over the horizon. Sergio opened the passenger door of his car and grabbed an empty backpack from the floor. He retrieved the package from the front seat and gingerly placed it in the pack, and then slid his arms under the straps. He looked both ways to make sure he was alone before beginning the short walk to the entry road.

Light from the moon enabled Sergio to step around the numerous potholes in the road and avoid falling a second time. At the top of an incline, he stopped and attempted to orient himself. Although he'd worked in the oil patch for a few years, he had never seen anything like the view off to his left: three large pits dominated an area about half the size of a football field. At that time of night, the fluid in the pits appeared to be an eerie jet-black.

Sergio recognized the outline of two buildings approximately one hundred yards straight ahead. The building on the right was obviously the manager's mobile home. *Must be asleep, all the windows are dark*, he thought. He knew from a previous visit that the smaller building on the left was the disposal plant's office. An outside spotlight illuminated the concrete dumping area. One light had been left burning inside the office so truckers could complete the required disposal forms after they'd unloaded. He crouched down and slid off to his right, making a broad ark around the mobile home, approaching the pits from the backside. He wanted to be far enough away from the mobile home so that the noise of a broken stick, or a kicked rock, wouldn't wake someone. When he reached the edge of the pits, he stopped, took a deep breath, and rested for a moment. Reluctant to use his flashlight, Sergio squinted toward a spot where he thought the trailer was located. After a few moments he recognized its outline and began to move forward again. He heard a sound, and froze. When he heard the sound again, he realized it was probably an animal scurrying around, and cautiously resumed his advance.

He carefully removed the package from the backpack and placed it in the middle of a long, waist-high laboratory table next to the trailer. The package was addressed to José Acuna in bold, black letters. He positioned it so the delivery instructions were on top and faced in the direction of a metal storage shed. *Ignore that, you shit-head.*

Satisfied that he hadn't left anything behind, Sergio cautiously retraced his steps and returned to his vehicle. He climbed into the passenger side, removed his shoes, reclined the seat and settled back for a few hours' sleep before daylight.

The vehicle was awash in sunlight when Sergio awoke the following morning and checked the time—6:15 A.M. He climbed out of the vehicle, stretched, and relieved himself. Reaching behind the passenger seat Sergio retrieved his binoculars and a plastic cushion, and began the return trip through the brush to the observation spot he'd occupied the previous evening.

Sergio sat down on the cushion Indian style, pulled a fingernail clipper from his pocket, and began to trim his nails. Shortly after 7:00 A.M. a compact automobile slowly make its way toward the small office building. Sergio dropped the clippers and grabbed the binoculars. He observed an older man, sporting a full head of gray hair, step out of the car, shake hands with another gentleman, and sit down. Sergio didn't recognize either man, but that didn't matter.

Less than fifteen minutes later, the students' pickup truck lurched over the top of the incline ahead of a cloud of dust and abruptly stopped at the office. The driver opened the window. After a brief verbal exchange, the truck continued on toward the test site, and parked under a carport. He watched the three students exit the vehicle and was confident the driver was José Acuna. To be certain, he referred to a photograph he carried in his pocket. The second young man climbed into the driver's seat, turned the truck around, and headed back toward the Farm Road. Sergio frowned when he realized that the female intended to remain with Acuna; he wanted to limit unnecessary collateral damage, but, if it was unavoidable, it was unavoidable.

Sergio watched as Acuna unloaded a large box from the bed of the trailer and move toward the shed. The female unlocked the door, stepped aside while Acuna carried the box inside. She followed him into the shed, but left the door open. Both remained inside for a few minutes before Acuna emerged carrying what appeared to be a rack of test tubes and a small scale. He set the equipment on the bench, and then reached for the package. Sergio muttered to himself, "Go for it, you little shit." Acuna turned the package over in his hands several times before he began to tear at the brown paper wrapping.

# 1

MARTIN LEARY SWORE AND slammed the newspaper down on the side table. "The dumb asses! When will they learn?" he mumbled. He'd just read a blistering editorial about the growing problem of ground water contamination. The author, a scientist with the Underground Injection Practices Council had used two examples of out-of-control abuses: strip-mining for coal in West Virginia and Kentucky; and, oil production in Texas and Oklahoma.

"Shirley, you've got to read the commentary in today's paper about ground water contamination. The problem's much bigger than I thought."

Shirley Leary stood next to a recently installed breakfast island in the center of her modernized kitchen. "I'll be there in a minute, Mart. Do you want anything in your coffee?"

"No thanks. I'll take it black. I need a good caffeine kick this morning."

Martin stood up and walked over to a large bay window that faced the Thames River. He was in deep thought. Not looking at anything in particular, he stood there running his fingers through a full head of silvery gray hair, and straightening the shirt under his belt, both unconscious habits developed over the years. His ebullient face and the ever-present twinkle in his Irish blue eyes conveyed the appearance of a man younger than his 62 years. A strict diet of healthy foods, coupled with a physical conditioning program at a Norwich gym, enabled him to remain fit and trim.

Martin said in a loud voice so that Shirley could hear him in the kitchen, "The problems we're having with our ground water aquifer can't compare with the problems rural Texans are having. You know, I'm glad I agreed to represent the County at the Houston conference. If the author's information is correct, we should have some lively discussions."

When he heard Shirley enter, Martin turned around. She was dressed in black pants and one of Martin's sweatshirts. The sweatshirt seemed to hang off her frame like it would a child. Shirley held a cup of coffee in each hand. She handed one cup to her husband, and said, "Let's face it, ground water issues are not the same across the country, Mart. The ground water problems in rural Texas undoubtedly are different from the problems here in Connecticut."

"You're right. Our major problem here is a dwindling supply. The problems in Texas appear to be a dwindling supply, but mostly growing contamination."

Martin's interest in ground water contamination didn't result from a general concern for the environment. Rather, it was the direct result of his water well becoming contaminated. Six months earlier Martin detected a metallic taste in his well water and decided to have the water tested for impurities. Unfortunately for the Learys, the tests showed traces of arsenic, mercury and lead. Laboratory technicians theorized that the impurities might be seeping into Martin's well from the Thames River, less than two hundred feet from the well. In their report, the water quality technicians warned Martin that the impurities might represent a health risk. More importantly, the impurities might expose the Learys to some potentially serious liability issues. The lab recommended Martin shut in his well until a remedy could be found. Shutting in the well, however, left the Learys with only one expensive option: connect to a County owned water pipeline that paralleled the road in front of their property.

Based on what he'd experienced with his own water well Martin Leary, Norwich, Connecticut's leading commercial Realtor, became a champion of ground water protection initiatives overnight. County Commissioners were impressed with his newfound advocacy and appointed him to a committee of concerned citizens to advise them on issues affecting the community at large. The Commissioners also asked him to represent the County in Houston at the annual conference of the Underground Resource Council, a watchdog group dedicated to protecting the nation's ground water reserves.

Shirley reached out with her free hand and tousled Martin's hair, and then kissed him on the cheek. "I hope you don't embarrass yourself by getting in over you head while you're in Houston."

"Come on, Shirley. Give me a break. I won't embarrass myself. I'm going to Houston to listen and learn." Shirley smiled knowingly, hugged him and then gave him a weak punch to the midsection. She'd been love punching him like that for over thirty-seven years. Martin knew from experience that, even though Shirley was a wisp of a woman, weighing less than 110 lbs., she still had one hell of a punch. In Martin's mind Shirley was prettier than when they dated in high school; well-proportioned facial features, movie actress teeth, sparkling blue eyes, and long lustrous black hair. She possessed an extraordinary personality and a fantastic sense of humor. Her smile lit up her face and her laugh was contagious. You just felt good when you were with her.

"Let's go out to dinner tonight to celebrate our anniversary."

"Why, Martin Leary, I believe you just asked me out on a date."

"Why wouldn't I? You happen to be the prettiest girl in this house, and I know you're available."

Shirley smacked him on the arm. "Don't be a smart ass."

Martin turned away and laughed. "I know just the place. I'll make a reservation at the Grist Mill in Brookdale for 7:00. We can go a little early, walk around town, and maybe visit the museum."

"Good idea. I never tire of visiting Brookdale."

Brookdale was Shirley's favorite town in all of Connecticut. The community had done a good job of maintaining its old New England charm, a charm that one is apt to find in a coffee table picture book. Large trees planted over two hundred years ago lined both sides of a half-mile long main street. Elevated concrete sidewalks were set back from the road approximately twenty feet. Except for a small central retail area, the balance of Brookdale's main street area featured old, restored eighteenth and nineteenth century mansions built in a line about fifty feet from the road which helped create a park-like atmosphere. The Learys theorized that the original residents of Brookdale were probably more concerned about road dust, than space and zoning.

Martin parked on the street in front of the old Hotel Benedict, home of the *Grist Mill* restaurant since 1898. As they strolled up the broad sidewalk toward the ornate front entrance to the hotel, highlighted by a hand carved door rimmed by light fixtures of lead and glass on each side, Shirley reached for her husband's right hand. "Happy anniversary, Mart. I still love you, you know." Shirley reached across her body with her right hand and tenderly clasped his upper arm.

Martin squeezed Shirley's hand, and said, "We're lucky. Not only have we been happily married for thirty-seven years, we're best friends to boot."

Martin and Shirley arrived a half-hour early for their 7:00 reservation. They wanted to relax in front of the massive fireplace in one of their favorite rooms, the restaurant's small, intimate cocktail lounge.

While sipping drinks, they reminisced about previous visits to the *Grist Mill* with friends and shared humorous stories about some of the stupid things they did when they were in high school.

The Learys' love affair began at *Toland's Drug Store* in Derby, Connecticut, while both attended Derby High School. Toland's was a throwback to earlier times: vintage chairs with metal seats and backs; table bases made of forged steel with marble tops, rounded at the edge; and, an authentic, turn of the century soda fountain with a gray, thick marble counter. The interior walls were painted white, the ceiling was a gray decorative sheet metal, and the floor was solid oak tongue and groove. When the place was filled with teenagers, the noise would ricochet off the walls, especially when one sex was calling to the other, giggling or generally attempting to impress.

Shirley fell in love with Martin the first time she saw him working as a soda jerk behind the counter at Toland's. She was new in town, and had to ask a friend who the boy was. The friend whispered, "That's Martin Leary. He's probably the best athlete in school. Isn't he good-looking?" Shirley nodded and asked her friend to introduce her.

What began as an adolescent crush, was to develop into a full-blown teenage romance, and finally into a loving relationship.

The following morning, Shirley lectured her husband. "I don't want you eating a bunch of junk food while you're in Houston. And make sure you bring your vitamins." Shirley was pleased that Martin kept his weight in check and was reasonably well conditioned. He weighed only ten pounds more than he did when they married. Shirley didn't belong to Martin's health club, but she walked at least one mile every weekday before heading off to the offices of the Norwich Board of Education where she was completing her second term as chairperson. Shirley's diminutive stature hadn't impeded her ability to lead; she continually challenged both administrators and teachers to improve student performance on state and federal assessment tests. She was also a strong advocate for extra curricular activities, especially music and drama. Martin delighted in admitting that his wife was better known within the community than he was, in spite of his having owned a successful real estate business in Norwich for over thirty years.

"If you'll lay out the vitamins for me, I won't forget to bring them. I wish you could come with me. We could make a mini-vacation out of it."

"Next time, Mart. The parents planned the award ceremony a month ago. I have to be there." Shirley added, "This will be the fourth award we've earned from the Connecticut State Commissioner's office. I'm proud of the board's accomplishments."

"You should be. Thanks to you, the board deserves every accolade it receives from the State."

"Ruth and Adam are coming to dinner tonight, Mart. Do we have enough vodka?"

"I'll check." Martin looked under the bar and responded, "Yeah, we're okay. I'm glad the kids are coming over. I want to talk to Adam about the recommendations I got from that County transportation guy. Did I tell you that he recommended a north/south route to minimize the possibility that a driver might be blinded by the sun? He also said the route he was recommending had wide shoulders and minimal traffic."

"Yes, you mentioned it the other day. I'm glad you looked into that. I've been nervous about his training route ever since he was hit." Shirley smiled and added, "I have a feeling the kids intend to make an announcement tonight."

"What kind of an announcement?"

"I think Ruth is pregnant."

"How can you tell?"

"Ruth has been asking me a lot of questions about nutrition lately, a subject we've never discussed before. Women tend to be more sensitive to things like that, Martin."

That evening, Adam and Ruth confirmed Shirley's prophecy. Ruth announced she was three months into the pregnancy, and that an ultrasound procedure had indicated the child would be a girl. The senior Learys were ecstatic; little Katherine would be their first grandchild.

# 2

IT WAS DARK AT 6:00 A.M. when Martin looked out of his bedroom window at the four to five inches of snow on the ground. He'd slept well and was unaware that a storm had passed through eastern Connecticut during the night. The decision to hold the January ground water conference in Houston in January had been planned months ago to avoid the very problem he was faced with now: bad weather. Martin didn't want to miss the start of the meeting scheduled for 2:00 in Houston the next day.

Although he watched the snow begin to accumulate and drift in his front yard, Martin was confident county crews would keep the roads clear. Late in the morning Shirley heard a weather forecast on the radio that predicted additional snowfall during the next twenty-four hours. When she suggested that Martin might have difficulty getting to the airport, he decided to leave at once and stay overnight in a motel near the Hartford airport.

Martin took a shuttle bus from Houston's Intercontinental Airport to a downtown hotel, and walked to the Petroleum Club to join with other attendees for a get-acquainted lunch. He was pleased to learn that he and Dr. Ely Gerba had been assigned to the same table. Dr. Gerba, Chair of the Chemistry Department at the University of Texas at Austin, had earned a reputation as an oil industry expert, and Martin wanted to query him about the commentary he'd read in the Norwich newspaper about ground water contamination in Texas.

Martin's interest in the conversation peaked when Ely began to describe his growing concern about the indiscriminate disposal of waste oil and brine.

"Waste from oil production is a serious threat to our ground water table, Martin. That's a major concern of my associates and myself at the university. If you drive around rural west Texas, you'll find large waste oil pits called evaporation pits. Before pit liners became mandatory, waste oil was dumped indiscriminately in the unprotected pits, and the sludge would seep into the ground water table from the top.

"We've determined that the natural contaminants in brine are also a serious threat to ground water, especially when the brine is injected into formations under the water table. One would think, after all these years, the industry would have developed a more scientific method for disposing of oil field sludge and brine. So far, only the ground water aquifers in a few remote, rural and sparsely populated areas have been affected. But as time goes on, larger and larger areas will be contaminated. Since clean ground water is essential to life, it's incumbent upon us to do something."

Lunch completed and with a half-hour to kill before the start of the general session, Martin and Ely moved to comfortable upholstered lobby chairs to continue their spirited discussion. Martin asked, "Why hasn't the federal EPA done something about the contamination, Ely?" Martin asked. "Aren't they responsible for regulating the oil industry?"

"They are in most states, but not in Texas. Years ago the Federal government delegated direct oversight of the oil industry in Texas to the Texas Railroad Commission."

Martin leaned back in his chair. "What in the world is a railroad commission doing regulating oil production? It sounds like political maneuvering to me."

"You could be right. It depends on who's telling the story. The political maneuvering, as you call it, goes back one hundred years. In my opinion, the Railroad Commission has been an ineffective regulator for a long time."

"It's interesting that you'd say that, Ely. I read a guest commentary in our local newspaper just the other day that was very critical of the Texas oil industry. Apparently the industry has demonstrated little regard for ground water contamination. What can the general public do to stop the contamination?"

"My colleagues and I are asking the same question, Martin. However, we're considering chemical solutions, not political solutions. We're asking ourselves, can chemicals be used to remove contaminants from the brine? Maybe brine can be treated like a sewage treatment plant treats human waste. If harmful chemicals can be removed and the brine cleaned up, it's conceivable that farmers could use the treated water for irrigation. Unfortunately we don't have the funding to undertake needed research; the subject of oil field waste generates little interest outside the oil industry. The subject of oil field waste has, for the lack of a better phrase, little sex appeal."

Ely leaned forward and in a confidential tone of voice, added, "My colleagues and I believe we may have stumbled onto something that does have sex appeal—the recovery of precious metals from brine water."

Martin stared at Dr. Gerba. "Precious metals? Do you mean the brine contains gold and silver?"

"Oil field brine contains more than that, Martin. It contains the entire platinum group of metals, PGM for short: platinum, palladium, rhodium, ruthenium, iridium, and osmium, as well as gold and silver. The university's business department told me that there's a growing demand for PGM in high technology and defense-related industries, and because of that, PGM may be considerably more valuable than gold and silver."

"Wow!" Martin exclaimed. "That does have sex appeal. Do you have a plan?"

"My colleagues and I are addressing the subject as we speak. We raised a little seed money to begin laboratory tests of a proprietary process. The initial results are encouraging. We'll have to find additional funding to continue our lab work, and build a small mobile prototype to test the process in the field."

Martin remained silent for a few moments as he digested what he'd just heard. His facial expression changed and his mind seemed to switch into overdrive. "That could be one hell of a business opportunity, Ely. How much capital do you need?"

"Our preliminary estimate is about half a million. We're considering selling stock in a closely held corporation. When the technology is proven, we'd like to take the company public, or sell it to a major oil or natural resource company."

Martin looked at his watch. "It's 1:50, Ely. The general session starts at 2:00. We'd better get moving." As they rose, Martin said, "Ely, I'm really interested in what you and your colleagues are doing. May I have one of your business cards?" As they exchanged cards, Martin added, "Maybe I can help. I'll talk with some of my friends and associates in Connecticut to see if there is any interest. Do you have a business plan?"

"Yes. I'll send you a copy later this week."

"Intercontinental Airport, please." Martin threw his overnight bag across the back seat of the cab, slid in and sat with his briefcase on his lap. His mind was consumed with thoughts of extracting precious metals from oil field brine and the potential financial rewards. When the cabbie asked, "What airline, sir?" Martin was jolted back to reality. After muttering an answer, he smiled when he realized that he'd been riding for over ten miles, but hadn't observed a thing outside the cab.

Martin's flight wasn't scheduled to depart for another hour, so he found a comfortable chair near the departure gate. He opened his briefcase and retrieved a few of the documents he'd collected while at the conference. He attempted to read, but was unable to concentrate; his mind kept returning to a conversation he'd had with the president of the Tamarack Country Club the day before he left Connecticut for the Texas conference. The president had told Martin that the club had too many real estate members already. "Sorry. The board will reconsider your application again in six months." In spite of being a successful entrepreneur in Norwich for over thirty years, his membership application had been rejected because the business was real estate. The news had been a terrible disappointment. The more Martin thought about it, the angrier he became. Martin stood up and began to pace.

His mind slowly began to return to thoughts of Dr. Gerba's technology. *Those bastards at the club will change their tune once they learn about the precious metals technology.* He stopped pacing, and sat down again. He made a list of the things he needed to do when he returned home: check the validity of Dr. Gerba's comments about the limited sources of supply of precious metals; confirm Gerba's claim that the military has classified the platinum group of metals as strategic; learn more about brine, and why it needed to be disposed of by underground injection; and talk with Shirley about who might be candidate investors.

# 3

Dr. Gerba was upbeat when he encountered his colleague in the hallway on the third floor of the chemistry building. "Jim, I ran into someone over the weekend who may be able to raise money for the precious metals project. Martin Leary, a commercial Realtor from Connecticut, sat next to me during lunch. After I described what we were attempting to do, he appeared to be very interested."

"I have good news also, Ely. I talked with your old friend Roy DeWitt yesterday. He tried to call you first, but you were in Houston, so he called me. He wants to be involved, said he'd make a personal investment. He also offered to contact friends and business associates to see if they'd be interested in investing. You'll also like his next offer: he suggested we use his Elsa disposal facility as a test site. How about that? He said he needs details about the project. Have you finished with the business plan? We should send Roy a copy to him as soon as it's ready."

"I've completed every section except the executive summary. I can finish that in a couple of days."

"What's the latest on the prototype design?"

"My best doctoral candidate, José Acuna, finished the first design iteration and is working on a cost estimate. He has to make a few more calls to vendors before he can give me a firm figure."

"I'd like José to be the point man and supervise construction of a prototype. He's the logical choice since he's the one that's designing it. José's a bright young man, Jim. I have great confidence in him. He's the best student in the graduate program. We have one major problem, however. I'll need additional funds to pay José and the other graduate students who are working with him on the project, and I don't know where I'll get the money."

"Don't worry, Ely. I have enough in reserve to front those expenses."

A few days after returning to Norwich, Martin arranged his work schedule so that he could spend the morning at the Norwich Public Library. He wanted to learn more about platinum group metals, and about the supply limitations. A Department of Commerce publication confirmed that nearly all of the world's supply of PGM was extracted from lode deposits in just three countries—South Africa, Russia, and Canada. He was particularly impressed by a Department of Defense publication that stated, "The heavy dependence on imports of the critically important industrial metals could have strategic implications if supplies were to halt."

Reinforced by his research, Martin began to promote the technology whenever he talked with friends and business associates. His enthusiasm was infectious, especially when he described how the technology would provide a domestic source for a group of scarce metals needed by industry and the military, and that a business built on a proprietary technology could result in substantial monetary returns for investors.

The following week, Martin received a Federal Express package from Dr. Gerba containing the business plan. The more Martin studied the plan, the more enthused he became; the new, innovative and proprietary precious metals extraction technology might be the once-in-a-lifetime opportunity he'd been dreaming about. It could be the vehicle that would vault him into the financial elite of eastern Connecticut, and help him secure a membership in the Tamarack Country Club.

"Good morning, Claire."

"Morning, Martin." That familiar greeting had been repeated without significant deviation for over fifteen years. Claire Wilson managed the administrative side of Leary Realty, while Martin supervised the sales agents. Martin had acquired the agency from Greg Orloff thirty years earlier. Under his leadership, the agency had grown into the second largest real estate business in metropolitan Norwich.

The reception area of Leary Realty had been the vestibule of the former Gulliver Mansion, built in 1790 by the Reverend Jacob Gulliver, an early pastor of the first Episcopal parish in Norwich. When a distant relative of Gulliver listed the Broadway property in 1958, Orloff jumped at the opportunity to purchase it. He was keenly aware of the importance of a business address on one of the most historically significant streets in all of eastern Connecticut. Orloff pushed to complete the purchase before the

Norwich Historical Society could gain control of the building, and saddle it with all sorts of restrictions.

Following the purchase, Orloff successfully secured a zoning change from residential to commercial/residential and established a new home for his real estate business. The mansion served as an excellent foundation for the subsequent growth of the business during the 1960's. The simple, straightforward Federal design provided an ideal floor plan for a real estate agency: eight large rooms, four on the first floor and four on the second, a spacious vestibule, wide staircase, and a fireplace in each room. While the interior needed extensive plumbing and electrical upgrades, as well as a little TLC, the exterior required only a few gallons of paint, and repairs to the two massive chimneys.

"Any calls, Claire?"

"We've had a few calls inquiring about Thurston property, but I don't think they were serious buyers. I left the messages on your desk."

Martin mumbled, "Damn. We can't seem to move anything lately." Martin moved toward his office, but stopped and asked, "Do you have Dusty Long's telephone number in Groton? I think I'll give him a call. He may know of someone who'd be interested in the Thurston place."

Claire gave Martin the number and watched him cross the reception area until he closed the door to his office. She looked around the spacious reception area, and for umpteenth time, told herself how lucky she was to work for a boss who knew what he was doing. Although concerned that Leary Realty's market share was beginning to slip, she was aware that the agency had weathered similar downturns before and had bounced back.

She recalled the story that Martin had told her about his introduction to the real estate business when he was only twenty-one years old. Martin had excelled as a baseball pitcher at Derby High School. While attending the University of Connecticut, he was invited to play for a team in the Norwich Industrial League sponsored by Greg Orloff, sole proprietor of Orloff Realty. Orloff immediately took a shine to Martin. His interest rose considerably when Martin pitched a two-hitter in the championship game.

Orloff invited the young man to lunch. The conversation flowed easily; it was as if the two men had been friends for years. Orloff was pleasantly surprised when Martin began asking questions about his agency and about the real estate market in eastern Connecticut. It was obvious that Martin had a strong interest in the subject, but he hadn't considered pursuing it as a career. Orloff offered to teach Martin the fundamentals of the commercial real estate business in return for his commitment to work for his agency for at least one year. Martin accepted the challenge, studied hard, and within six months, he was able to secure a broker's license. Martin quickly earned a reputation within the community as a competent, ethical businessman.

Nine years into their successful working relationship, Orloff was diagnosed as having incurable testicular cancer. The medical professionals gave him only four to six months to live. Martin was crestfallen; the strength of their friendship had proved to be a winner for both men. With heavy hearts the two men reviewed their options. Greg could sell the agency to a third party, and Martin could stay on with the firm as part of the sale. Martin could leave the firm and go off on his own. Martin suggested a third option: Greg and he could structure a financial package that would enable Martin to purchase the business over time, thereby continuing the business without further interruption, and providing a steady source of income for Mrs. Orloff. Greg chose Martin's option. They prepared a ten-year buyout arrangement that included not only the business, but also the Broadway Avenue building.

# 4

A FEW WEEKS AFTER Martin returned from Houston, he accepted Dr. Gerba's invitation to return to Texas to participate in the formation of a startup company tentatively named the Precious Metals Extraction Corporation. Ely wanted Martin to meet with a small group of Texans to discuss the appropriate methods for raising enough capital to build and test a prototype, and to hear a report on the results of recent laboratory tests of the extraction process.

Ely told Martin he'd arrange to have one of his graduate students, José Acuna, meet his flight and provide transportation to the hotel and to the university's chemistry building. Exiting the deplaning ramp, Martin spotted the young man holding a sign that displayed his name. Martin smiled at the gesture; it made him feel important. He'd watched a similar sign routine at LaGuardia in New York many times, and always wanted to be welcomed that way. Martin walked toward the young man with his arm extended, and introduced himself. "Good morning. I'm Martin Leary. Are you José?"

"Yes, sir. I'm happy to meet you, Mr. Leary. Did you check any luggage?" The young fellow was thin, swarthy, and probably not more than 5'6" tall; Martin towered over the young man. Martin thought of an Aztec Indian when he looked at José; high cheekbones, jet-black hair, dark eyes and brown skin.

"Please, José, call me Martin. Yes, I checked one bag."

They began the long walk to baggage claim, moving from side to side to avoid the oncoming masses. Communication was next to impossible because of the constant change of direction, and the noise level. When they finally reached the automated walkway the noise level subsided somewhat and Martin was able to ask, "How's the project coming?"

José's eyes lit up. "Great! We were able to automate the extraction component in a pre-prototype breadboard. We're going to go ahead with the design of a prototype, and may be able to complete construction in a couple of months. The metals separation component could be a problem, though. We can do it manually right now, but we haven't been able to automate it yet. We've just got to find a simpler method." José stopped to take a breath, and said, "Sorry, Martin, that's probably more information than you wanted, but once I get started talking about our project, I can't stop." As they approached the carousel, Martin was pleased to see that his bag was already making its way around and around.

During the ride to the hotel Martin questioned José about his graduate studies and his plans after earning his doctorate. "Dr. Gerba has asked me to stay on in Austin and work with him on the precious metals project. An opportunity like that doesn't come along very often. He said he wouldn't be able to pay me very much, but suggested I accept a part-time teaching position to supplement my income. I accepted his offer." Martin was impressed; José seemed to have a strong career focus.

Martin was giddy with anticipation when he entered Dr. Gerba's Chemistry Department the next morning. This would be his first direct exposure to the precious metals extraction technology. The two men shook hands and Dr. Gerba said, "Martin, we're pleased you could take the time to visit with us. Did José meet you at the gate as planned?"

"He certainly did. He was at the gate flashing a sign with my name on it."

Both men laughed. Martin felt comfortable with Dr. Gerba. He was not arrogant, nor did he flaunt his knowledge, or assume a superior attitude and talk down to him. Ely reached out and lightly touched Martin's shoulder. "Martin, all of us here at the lab appreciate the contributions you've already made. Without you and Roy DeWitt, the project would still be a stalled pipe dream. If we can secure the additional funds you and I talked about the other day, we should be able to complete a prototype within two months, and then begin field-tests a few weeks after that.

"Roy's Hidalgo Disposal is an ideal location to test the prototype. The quality of the brine Roy receives can vary considerably, and we need that. If our technology is to be viable, we'll have to extract metals from a variety of brines." Ely hesitated a moment before continuing. "I hope I'm not overly optimistic, but we could be on the threshold of a significant scientific breakthrough." He straightened, raised his shoulders and declared, "Enough of this blabbering! Let me take you on a tour of the lab, and then we'll have José demonstrate the extraction process."

At the conclusion of the hour-long tour, Ely and Martin joined with Austin securities attorney Dick Hammil, Roy DeWitt, and Ely's associate, Dr. Jim Robinson, in a conference room adjacent to Gerba's office on the third floor of the Chemistry Department. Hammil explained what was needed to form a startup company, and the legalities of soliciting funds from potential investors. Martin recounted his successful meetings with his close friends Bill and Lois Davis, and his conversations with a few of his other friends in Norwich. He enthusiastically reported that he and his wife Shirley decided to match the Davises' commitment of $50,000. With the first $100,000 already in the bank, Martin was confident he could secure another $150,000.

Roy DeWitt, wishing not to be outdone by the Yankee from Connecticut, also committed to a personal investment of $50,000 and said he would also raise another $200,000 from his friends and associates in south Texas. Given those pledges, Ely would have the one-half million needed to move forward with the prototype construction and field tests.

Before Ely closed the meeting, Dick Hammil reminded everyone that potential investors must be issued a prospectus, and be invited to an orientation meeting. He said it was extremely important that each investor be given the opportunity to question Dr. Gerba about the technology. Such a meeting would also give Ely the opportunity to explain the market potential for the fledgling business and establish a solid communications link with investors. Checking respective calendars, it was decided to schedule the investor meeting for the second week in June at Roy DeWitt's disposal facility in Elsa, Texas.

It was obvious from their demeanor as they left Dr. Gerba's conference room that everyone was pleased with the outcome of the meeting. After all, they had just agreed to form a company that could be the driving force behind the development of a proprietary technology with unlimited potential, and provide an endless supply of strategically important metals to industry and to the military.

Ely caught up with Martin as they walked toward the front entrance. "I forgot about tonight's faculty meeting, Martin. I won't be able to join you for dinner. Would it be all right if José serves as your host? I'm sure he can recommend a good restaurant."

"That'd be fine, Ely. I'm sorry you can't join us."

"Ask José to show you the capital and the rest of our sprawling campus on the way back to the hotel." Smiling, Ely added, "Don't let him get you in any trouble." They walked a few additional steps before Ely turned, and faced Martin. "I'm very proud of José, Martin. He's my best graduate student. He's had to overcome some difficult problems. His father was killed in a boating accident when he was a little fellow. His mother did a hell of a job raising him. She had to work full time to make ends meet."

When Martin located José, he was talking with another graduate student in one of the laboratories. Martin leaned into the lab. "When you finish here, let's head back to the hotel. I want to change into something a little more comfortable. Then I'd like you to show me around Austin before we go to dinner."

"Sure. I'd enjoy that, Martin. I can't get enough of Austin myself. It's a beautiful city. Might as well get started now." José excused himself from the other student and joined Martin in the hallway. They took the elevator to the first floor and walked out of the building to the parking lot.

"It looks like you take care of your car, José. Was it new when you bought it?"

"No. It's an eight-year-old Camaro. I bought it from a friend in Corpus. It doesn't look it, but it has 90,000 miles on it. My friend pampered it, so I pamper it too. It's the only thing I own."

After completing a brief tour of the area surrounding the state capital, José suggested, "If you're not in a hurry to go back to the hotel, let's stop for a beer and have something to eat. I know a great place on 6th Avenue. They serve the best selection of local microbrews in Austin."

"I'm all for stopping, José. It's been a long day."

Sitting at a table against the back wall of the *Sixth Avenue Saloon*, José and Martin shared stories of friends and family, evoking reactions at both ends of the emotional spectrum. They were well into their third round when José's expression changed to one of sadness. "I don't mean to be maudlin, Martin, but I was just thinking of my dad. I never had an opportunity to share a beer with him."

"Ely told me that your father died while fishing. How did it happen, José?"

José took a deep breath. "It happened when I was about eight. My dad liked to venture out into Corpus Christi Bay to fish alone. He said fishing helped him relax and enabled him to sort through technical challenges that he faced at work. He was a chemical engineer, Martin. That's probably why I decided to go for a doctorate in chemistry." José took a sip of beer before continuing. "Apparently a sudden layer of fog rolled in, and he became disoriented. An oil tanker split his boat in two. The authorities speculated that my father went under the ship. They never found him." He looked at Martin, and added, "You want to know something, Martin? I don't remember being sad. One minute he was there, and the next minute he wasn't. The thing I remember most was how his death devastated my mother." Both men were quiet for a few moments, absorbed in their own thoughts.

"I was about the same age, about eight, when my father was killed."

Martin related the tragic circumstances that surrounded the death of his father. He and his close friend Bill Davis had secured enough money from collecting and cashing-in empty bottles to buy tickets to a Waterbury Yankee/Bridgeport Zephyr baseball game at Zephyr Field in West Haven. The Zephyrs were hosting Waterbury in a weekend series, and the boys wanted to support a young Yankee rookie, Rick Schuster. Martin explained that Schuster graduated from Derby, Connecticut High School two years before he did, attended college for one year, and then was lucky enough to be drafted by the New York Yankees.

Martin said that he practically ran to Bill's house for an early breakfast, and together they walked downtown to the CR&L bus stop. He remembered that the day was clear and sunny, with low humidity for a change. They were dressed in the attire young people wore in those days: soft-soled shoes, hand-me-down slacks, white socks, leather jackets, and soft brimmed caps. "Before I left the house, my mother discovered that my father had forgotten his lunch box. He'd left it on the kitchen table. She asked me to drop it at the rail yard on our way." Martin explained that wasn't a problem because they could get off the bus one stop before the ballpark, and walk over to the rail yard. Normally, the 9:13 bus would take the boys directly to the ballpark.

The Bridgeport rail yard was located on the main coastal route of the New York, New Haven and Hartford Railroad. The yard was the major switching point for freight cars traveling between New York and Hartford, and New York and Boston, and to a lesser degree, between Bridgeport and Waterbury. When the boys arrived at the yard, it was bustling with activity. Cars were positioned on just about every track waiting to be sorted and shunted where and when they were needed. A traffic controller sat in a three-story tower in the middle of the tracks and controlled the switching activity.

"We were a bit nervous because we knew shouldn't be walking across the tracks. I remember bobbing my head up and down trying to avoid tripping, while at the same time watching for rolling stock. I remember trying to talk to Bill, but the screeching wheels made conversation impossible. When we finally saw my father, he was hanging from the tail end of one group of cars. I stopped when I saw him hollering and motioning excitedly to a person in the tower. His group of cars seemed to moving at an unusually swift pace toward another group on the same track. I remember screaming when I realized his group was not going to stop. The cars collided and my father was thrown headfirst into the first car of the stationary group. We ran across the remaining tracks as fast as we could. We were stopped a few yards away from where my father lay; the railroaders wouldn't let us get any closer. We could see him lying alongside the tracks and that his head was bleeding, but I was unaware of the seriousness of the injury."

Mart hesitated, took a deep breath before continuing. "It seemed to take forever for someone to take charge. Finally, one of the men, probably a yard boss, directed his men to lift my father and carry him to the nearest building. The same man yelled, 'Get those kids out of here, and get someone to take them home.' I presume that the man in the tower called for an ambulance. As we were being escorted off the tracks, we could hear a siren in the distance."

Martin emptied his glass of beer and declared, "That's the end of my story, José. I'm very tired all of a sudden. It was probably a bad idea to end the day talking about the deaths of our respective fathers."

"I understand, Martin. Let's go." After dropping Martin at the hotel, José returned to his apartment and he picked up a voice mail message from Arturo Cisneros. The message said simply, "Meet me at Bustamonte's at 4:00 P.M. tomorrow afternoon."

# 5

JOSÉ WALKED TO THE rear of Bustamonte's promptly at 4:00, and sat down across from Arturo. It was the first time José had visited the restaurant. *Bustamonte's Restaurant* was one of Arturo Cisneros's favorite haunts. The owner, Eddie Bustamonte, knew from secondary sources that Arturo was a drug trafficker and that drug deals were negotiated in his restaurant. In spite of that, he was pleased that Arturo frequented his establishment. As long as Arturo remained discreet, Eddie considered him good for business. The man seemed to be a magnet for his free spending friends.

Bustamonte's was small compared with the competition along 6th Avenue; it could seat only fifty patrons. But, in spite of the limited space, the restaurant was usually filled to near capacity from 11:00 A.M. until 9:00 P.M. on weekdays, and until 1:00 A.M. on Fridays and Saturday nights when Eddie offered his customers a variety of musical entertainment.

"How are you doing, Acuna?"

"I'm okay, Arturo. What did you want to see me about?"

"First, I want you to meet Eddie Bustamonte. He owns this place. We've been friends since high school." Arturo grabbed José by the elbow and practically dragged him to the front. "Eddie, meet José. He'll be coming in here a lot. Make sure you take care of him, okay?" Arturo grinned, "Someday this little shit will probably be my boss."

Returning to the table, Arturo asked, "That guy you told me about, the one that's here from Connecticut, what's his name?"

"Martin Leary, why?"

"My cousin, Luis Caldera, is expanding his operation in Groton, and needs some quality cocaine. I want Leary to take a package back to Connecticut with him."

"You're not serious."

"Acuna, I don't have time to play games. I want your man to take a package back to Connecticut with him. He doesn't have to know what's in it. Tell him he's delivering a box of greeting cards to a friend of yours, or a relative. I don't give a shit. Once the package gets to Connecticut, my cousin Luis will pick it up. Make sure you get me Leary's address."

José straightened his back and declared, "I can't allow Martin Leary to take your package to Connecticut. He could get in a lot of trouble. Can't you just send it by FedEx or UPS?"

Arturo, who could have passed for a reincarnated Caesar Romero the 1930's actor, stood, leaned forward and placed both hands on the table in front of him. He looked down at José. He lowered his voice and sneered, "You dumb shit! I can't send it that way. Some damn dog could sniff it out, and I'd be dead meat. My name and my cousin's name would be on the package. You'd better get this through your thick skull. Like I told you last week, you're working for me now. You don't have a choice. You'll find a way for Leary to take the package, period." He sat down again, and in a less energized voice said, "Luis already paid for the cocaine, so I'm committed, which means you're committed. I don't give a shit how you do it, but get it done by Friday, or your ass is mine."

José was a nervous wreck when he returned to the university. What if Martin refused to take the package on his return trip to Connecticut? Arturo might send someone to bet the crap out of him. José walked through the lab and out into the hallway to confirm that he was alone. He returned to his desk, opened the center drawer, reached to the back and pulled out a plastic bag. He walked to the rest room, locked the door, opened the bag, and removed a syringe, a tourniquet and a small vial of heroin. After applying the tourniquet, he loaded the syringe and proceeded to inject the needle into a vein on the inside portion of his left arm.

As soon as the drug began to have its desired effect, José's confidence soared. He left the stall and stopped in front of the mirror. He glared at his refection. *I won't have to deal with Cisneros when I become a great scientist. They'd never touch someone who is highly respected and visible within the scientific community. Screw the cartel!* However, the confidence that had come so easily a few minutes earlier, seemed to dissipate the longer he looked at his reflection. He leaned over the sink and began to sob. He backed away, looked at his reflection one more time with disgust, and walked back to the lab. He picked up the phone and called Martin's room at the Airport Motel.

The red message light on the telephone was blinking when Martin returned to his room. He called the front desk and was informed that a José Acuna had called at 6:45 and left a message to call him at the lab as soon as he arrived.

"José, it's Martin Leary. The front desk said that you called. Is there a problem?"

"No, no problem, Martin. I didn't mean to alarm you."

José sounded like he'd been drinking. Martin asked, "Are you okay?"

"Everything's fine, Martin. I thought we had a great meeting this afternoon, didn't you?"

"Thanks to you. That was another fine demonstration, young man. I believe the project is on track."

José hesitated, and then asked, "Do you have time for a beer? I could be there in ten minutes."

"Sure. I was going to go across the street for dinner. Why don't you join me?" Martin guessed his young friend had more than beer on his mind.

José and Martin left the hotel lobby, crossed the street, and walked one block to *McWilliams Steak House*. The interior was typical of most older restaurants: it was dark. The lighting was subdued, windows were nowhere to be seen, and red Naugahyde covered the upholstery in the booths. After adjusting to the darkness, José led the way to a corner table. Martin ordered two glasses of a local microbrew, settled back and asked, "What's up?"

Knowing that Martin's knowledge of chemistry was limited at best, José got right to the point. "I have a favor to ask. A cousin of mine works in the engineering department at Electric Boat in Groton. He sent me an email a few days ago asking if I could send him a sample of a new compound developed by a chemist in our department at the university. The compound is supposed to neutralize the toxic characteristics of beryllium. I told my cousin I could send him a sample as soon as I figured a safe way to get it there. Since you're going home to Connecticut tomorrow, could you carry it in your suitcase if I wrap it properly?"

"Are you sure it's safe and will the package fit in my suitcase?"

"Yes, to both questions."

"Okay. I'll pack it before I leave the lab tomorrow morning. I won't have much time to spare. My flight leaves at 11:15 A.M."

"I have an idea. Why don't I pick you up in the morning? We can pack the sample then and leave the suitcase in the car. I can take you to the airport later."

"That's fine. I'll be in the lobby at 8:30. Now tell me what I'm supposed to do with the package when I get home."

"I'll telephone my cousin today. All you have to do is call him when you arrive. He'll arrange to come to your home to pick up the package. My cousin's name is Luis Caldera. Having access to that sample could save him a great deal of time and expense. If he offers a gift, please accept."

José left Martin at the hotel and drove across town to Bustamonte's. It was after 8:00 P.M., but he was confident that Arturo would be stationed at his normal table. José parked by the front door, but didn't get out. He sat in the driver's seat staring into space. Several minutes passed before he leaned forward and placed his hands over his eyes. He mumbled, "If I don't stop this, I'm a dead man. Either the heroin will destroy me, or the cartel will." José slowly regained his composure and mustered enough strength to enter through the front door. With his head high he walked to the back of the restaurant.

"It's all set. Martin Leary agreed to take the package in his suitcase. You can tell your cousin that Martin will call him and give him directions to his house. I told him that Caldera was my cousin."

Arturo smiled. "It sounds like this Leary is a naive bastard." Arturo stood up and shook José's hand. "Well, Acuna, you earned another supply. As soon as Luis calls and tells me he has the stuff, I'll bring the heroin here. I'll leave it with Eddie. I have a meeting in a few minutes, so you'd better leave."

Martin called Luis Caldera from a service station just outside the Norwich city limits. He introduced himself and explained why he was calling.

"My cousin said you'd be calling today, Leary. I need directions to your house."

Martin was taken aback by the man's brashness, but let it slide. He expected that his first impression would change once they had an opportunity to talk face to face. "Take Route 16 north from New London. Turn right on Route 77; it's a rural road that parallels the west bank of the Thames River. I live a few miles north of that intersection. Birch trees hug both sides of the road in front of the house. An old, three-foot high stone wall separates the property from the road, and white picket fences run down both sides of the house, from the road to the riverbank. Be watchful, the house is hidden from the road by a few maple trees."

When Martin and Shirley built their rambling, single-story house in 1980, they were careful not to disturb a half-dozen mature trees in the center of the two-acre parcel. To provide some degree of privacy the house had been sited on the eastside of those trees, midway between the road and the river.

Caldera said he'd drive up to Norwich immediately and that he expected to arrive at Martin's home within the hour.

Shirley answered the doorbell, and without fanfare, Caldera asked for the package that José Acuna had sent with her husband. "Martin told me to expect you. Care to come in for a cup of coffee?"

"No thanks, lady. I'll just take the package and be on my way."

Shirley left the door open and walked to a table in the hallway to retrieve the package. Based on the limited view from the front entrance, Caldera could see that the interior of the house was filled with antiques and projected a lived-in feeling. It appeared to be comfortable; not at all ostentatious.

"Do you wish to speak with Martin? He's out back."

"No thanks, lady. I've really got to go. Give this to your husband." Caldera presented Shirley with a box containing two bottles of wine, abruptly turned and walked toward his car.

Shirley mused, *Hum, if that's an example of José Acuna's relatives, I'm not sure I want to meet the rest.*

# 6

JOSÉ RETURNED TO BUSTAMONTE'S the following evening to pick up the supply of heroin he'd been promised. Eddie Bustamonte was counting the contents of the cash register when José approached. "Hello, Eddie. You remember me? José Acuna?"

"Sure, kid. What can I do for you?"

"Did Arturo leave a package for me?"

"Not with me, kid. He's in the back. Check with him."

José was reluctant to talk with Arturo tonight. He just wanted to pick up his heroin and go home. He dreaded the thought of being given another unpleasant assignment. In spite of his misgivings, he had little choice. He walked to the back of the restaurant. Arturo saw him approach and said, "Surprise, surprise. Sit down and have a drink, Acuna. I have a few minutes to spare. What would you like?"

"Nothing, thanks."

"You do good work, kid. Everything worked as planned. Luis picked up the stuff from your man in Connecticut yesterday. Luis said he gave him a couple of bottles of wine for his trouble."

"That's a relief, Arturo. I came for my stuff, but Eddie doesn't have it."

"Sorry about that. I'm a little short right now. I'll have someone deliver your stuff in a day or so. But, in the meantime, here's a bonus for your trouble." Arturo peeled off a $100 bill and gave it to José. "I may have another assignment for you next week, so stay in town."

José became agitated. "Thanks for the money, Arturo, but I need the heroin more than the money."

Arturo's displeasure became apparent. He didn't like to be challenged. He leaned forward, and said, "I'll deliver the stuff when I'm good and ready. Now get the fuck out of here. I'm meeting some people in a few minutes."

A day went by, then two days, and no word from Arturo. The promised heroin delivery still hadn't arrived. José had mixed emotions about not hearing from Arturo. On the one hand he was anxious about his dwindling supply. But on the other hand he was happy that Arturo wasn't bothering him. He husbanded his remaining heroin by meticulously rationing his injections, and partially offsetting his desire by throwing himself into his work at the lab. When his stash dipped to just a day's supply, however, he called Arturo.

"I was thinking of you, kid. I was wondering if you had located another source, and didn't need me anymore."

"The delivery you promised never arrived, Arturo. What's going on?"

"Sorry, kid, I've been busy. I'll take care of your delivery today. I'll personally deliver it to Eddie." Arturo paused, "I've been thinking about promoting you to the big leagues, kid. You can earn enough stuff to last for months with your next job. I want you to take a few days off from work—sick days, vacation, whatever. I need you to go to Matamoros and pick up some stuff and deliver it to a customer in Corpus Christi."

Concerned, José asked, "Who in Corpus? I have to be careful. My mother's real estate business is in Corpus."

"I know that. The guy's name is Hoskins. He's a slime bag, but he's willing to pay a premium."

José practically shouted into the phone, "Christ, Arturo, that's a mistake! Even I've heard about Hoskins. My friends in Corpus say he can't be trusted. He plays both sides; he sells drugs and then turns around and helps the local narc agents."

"I don't trust Hoskins either, kid, but if we're very careful, it should work. I have a plan. Meet me at 8:00 at Bustamonte's, and I'll go over it with you. Tell you what, I'll deliver your stuff tonight, and buy dinner. How's that?"

"I'll be there, Arturo." José thought, *What choice do I have?*

José was wracked with both self-doubt and guilt during the entire trip to the Mexican border city of Matamoros. Instead of withdrawing from the drug cartel as he'd vowed, he was digging a deeper hole for himself. To make matters worse, he'd betrayed a friend's trust. He'd never deceived another person to the extent that he'd deceived Martin Leary. If Martin's luggage had been searched, the cocaine would certainly have been discovered, and Martin's life would have been ruined.

Although Matamoros was familiar territory to José—he'd visited it many times while he attended high school in Corpus Christi—this visit would be different. He'd be in direct contact with Mexican drug suppliers. He was fearful of being stopped at the border and caught with drugs in his possession on the return trip. Even more troublesome was the thought of making a mistake and incurring the wrath of Arturo.

José knew Matamoros had become a major conduit for drug deliveries to the United States, and had become a very dangerous place. That had not always been the case; following the annexation of south Texas by the United States after the Mexican-American War, the city served as the main port of entry for the exchange of agricultural products between Mexico and the United States. Years later Matamoros developed into an important crafts and house wares emporium that attracted retirees from Canada and the United States wintering in Harlingen and Brownsville. Tragically, that legitimate commerce served as the foundation for illegal drug activities.

José could feel his heart pump as he approached the bridge over the Rio Grande River that connected the cities of Brownsville, Texas, and Matamoros. He was distracted and missed a critical turn. He pulled off the road onto the shoulder to regain his composure. He turned the car around, backtracked and proceeded over the bridge toward the border crossing. Clearing Mexican customs, José drove past a few dilapidated apartment houses and into the main part of the city. He pulled into a parking lot near a busy intersection, and checked the time; he was early for his 2:00 P.M. appointment with Juan Calderon.

He locked the car, located a number on the nearest building, and walked east searching for 655 ½ Calle Olivera. He didn't have far to walk to find number 655; it was only four buildings from the corner, and the number was large. He stood on the sidewalk and inspected the building carefully, but couldn't find 655 ½. A T-shirt and sundry dry goods shop that catered to tourists occupied the ground floor of the building. There were no other entrances. He was puzzled and a little concerned. He checked his watch again; he had fifteen minutes to find the address. José walked around to the side of the building and discovered a narrow thirty-foot long alley to the right of the shop. He was relieved when he discovered the address at the end of the alley was 655 ½.

José approached the entrance and looked through a window in the front door. It was dark; he could distinguish only a small hallway and staircase. To kill time, José retraced his steps, crossed to the opposite side of the street and began to window-shop.

The street was typical of a Mexican border town, jammed with retail outlets selling everything from banners to watches. Merchandise displays took up half of the sidewalk, and Mexican children lingered about selling

Chiclets. José was so nervous, however, he paid almost no attention to his surroundings. He continued to check the time. Instructions from Arturo had been specific: make contact promptly at 2:00, not any sooner, not any later. At five minutes before 2:00 P.M. he re-crossed the street, entered the alley and knocked on the door of 655 ½. After a few excruciating minutes, a short, muscular, swarthy man in his twenties opened the door. He didn't say a word; he just stared.

José said meekly, "Vive aquí el señor Juan Calderon? Permita usted que me presente, José Acuna, para servirle." Without comment, the man turned and ascended the staircase leaving José standing on the front step, staring at an open door, not knowing if he had made contact with Calderon or not. Confused, José decided to remain where he was and hope for the best. Except for an ornate metal stair railing and a small table placed under a mirror, the narrow hallway was bare. He turned around, looked down the alley. If he encountered trouble, there was no escape route.

The man reappeared at the top of the stairs, holding a box in his right hand. As he descended, José noticed that the box was similar in design to a six-pack used to carry wine. But the man was not carrying wine; José recognized the shape and color of Kahlua bottles. The burley fellow lifted the box above his waist and extended his arm, clearly inviting José to take the box. As José accepted the delivery, the man placed a piece of paper on top of the box with his left hand, pushed José away from the door, and closed it. José stood staring at the door with his mouth open.

Realizing that the delivery was complete and he'd been summarily dismissed, José studied the document. It was a purchase receipt for the six bottles of Kahlua from a duty-free shop at the Matamoros Airport. He placed the receipt into his pocket and returned to the main street. With his mind working overtime to understand what had just transpired José began to walk slowly back to the parking lot. *Why would Arturo send me to Matamoros to pick up six bottles of Kahlua when he could have purchased the stuff in any liquor store in Austin? What the hell is going on?*

José placed the box on the floor in front of the passenger seat, pulled the receipt from his pocket, and studied it again. He reached down, retrieved a bottle from the box, and examined it closely. The bottle looked normal. As he was about to replace it in the box, he noticed that the box had a false bottom. He reexamined the bottle and realized it was slightly shorter than normal. "Holy shit! The bottom of the box is filled with cocaine." José could feel his skin tighten, and a cold sweat form under his arms. *If I can see the difference, so can a customs agent.* "Shit," he shouted. He slapped at the steering wheel. "I'm in deep trouble. If I get caught with this stuff, I'll end up in prison for twenty years!" José leaned back, placed his head back on the neck support and closed his eyes. He tried to calm down so he could think through the situation unemotionally. After a few moments, his eyes snapped open and he sat up. Maybe he could reduce the chance of discovery by purchasing additional items from the duty-free shop at the airport. He checked his wallet and found $76 dollars, enough to buy a few items. Yes, he told himself, that made sense. He'd spend his entire $76 at the airport duty-free shops, and then attempt to cross the border.

Cars were lined up twenty deep on the Mexican side of the border waiting for access to enter the U. S. when José approached the border crossing. José selected a line of vehicles on the extreme right and waited, all the while drumming his fingers on the steering wheel. He counted ten inspection stations all painted tan and connected by a single red tile roof. He estimated that there were at least two hundred cars waiting in line to cross.

José turned around for umpteenth time to check the collection of merchandise he'd positioned on the back seat: a bottle of scotch, a sweater, a stuffed teddy bear, and the six-pack of Kahlua. After a fifteen-minute delay, it was José's turn. He moved slowly toward the inspection hut and stopped. A single thought flashed through his mind: *stay relaxed and keep cool.* A large, overweight customs officer moved forward, and José opened the window. The agent bent forward and looked into José's eyes. "Are you a citizen of the United States?"

"Yes, sir."

"May I see some identification? A driver's license or a birth certificate?" José retrieved his wallet from his back pocket, pulled out his driver's license. He willed his hand to remain steady as he handed the card to the guard. The guard's eyes moved back and forth from the license to José's face. "Where's your home, son?"

"Corpus Christi. But I currently live in Austin. I'm a graduate student at the University of Texas."

"Do you have anything to declare, Mr. Acuna?"

"Yes, sir. I purchased some things at the duty-free shop at the airport. They're on the back seat."

"May I see the receipts?"

José reached back and snatched three receipts from the seat, one for the Kahlua, one for the scotch, and one for the sweater and the stuffed animal, and handed them to the officer. The man reviewed the receipts, looked through the window at the items aligned on the back seat, straightened and said, "Thank you, son. Stay to the left as you leave the area. There's a stalled truck in the right lane."

José smiled, "Thank you, Officer. Good afternoon." When José reached a point on the highway where he could no longer see the border station in the rearview mirror, he pulled over and shut down the engine. He closed his eyes, breathed deeply in an attempt to calm down before continuing on to Corpus Christi.

José walked out of Hoskins's apartment with a frown on his face. He hadn't attempted to hide his disdain for the man or his displeasure at being in the same room with him. Hoskins looked like, and smelled like, someone who washed infrequently. He hadn't shaved in days, his hair was disheveled, and his T-shirt had food stains on the front. Hoskins was a walking advertisement for "white trash." The bastard had even ridiculed José's educational achievements. To compound José's discomfort, he was distressed by what he'd just done; his delivery was certain to end up being sold to kids on the streets of Corpus Christi.

José's original plan was to visit with his mother after he made the delivery. But, he was too exhausted and disgusted with himself to talk with anyone; he just wanted out of the city as quickly as possible. He drove a few miles to the outskirts of Corpus, located a service station with a pay phone, and, using the long distance account number provided by the university, he called the chemistry laboratory, and asked for Pat Duncan or Sonja Hyde.

"Pat Duncan, may I help you?"

"Pat, it's José. Are we still on for dinner at the bistro?"

"Yes. We've got a couple of surprises for you. First, Martin Leary is here."

"Really? When did he arrive?"

"He just appeared this morning. He said Dr. Gerba told him that we planned to run an extraction test this morning. He came down to see it. He's a conscientious son of gun."

"Will he be able to join us at the bistro?"

"Yep, he'll be there. Martin said he's looking forward to talking with us without all the interruptions and distractions."

"What's the second surprise, Pat?"

"Our test was successful, but not without a few problems. We'll fill you in tonight."

"I'm about to get on Interstate 35. I should be able to meet you about 7:30. I can't get there any sooner. Are you taking care of Martin's transportation?"

"Not a problem. Take your time. We'll see you around 7:30."

# 7

MARTIN WAS LOOKING FORWARD to witnessing the first test run of the automated extraction component. Dr. Gerba had told him the students were planning to test the component every morning for a week, and Martin flew down to Austin to see one of the tests firsthand. While he was confident that Dr. Gerba's team of graduate students would successfully automate the precious metals extraction process and build an operating prototype system, Martin believed it was incumbent upon him to stay "on top of" developments by visiting Austin frequently. He wanted to be able to provide knowledgeable answers to questions from the investors that he'd solicited.

When he arrived at the lab unannounced, he was surprised to find that José was out of town. It didn't concern him, however. He knew that Pat Duncan and Sonja Hyde were capable of providing him with a thorough review of project developments. The first few attempts to test the component, however, resulted in one disappointment after another. Every time Pat and Sonja ran through the operational sequence, the effort failed. In spite of the failures, Martin kept encouraging them to continue trying.

During a lunch break, Martin suggested, "I'm not sure what the hell I'm talking about, kids, but I thought Dr. Gerba specified an AC charge followed by a DC charge. The charging sequence might be backwards. Let's check your notes when we get back to the lab."

All three crossed their fingers when Pat initiated another sequence. This time, the test succeeded. "Eureka," Sonja yelled. "We did it. It actually worked. I was beginning to have my doubts."

"Maybe that was a fluke. Before you start drinking the champagne, let's see if you can do it again."

"Good idea." Pat poured a gallon of brine into a glass jar suspended above the "spinner," a customized centrifuge, and then zapped the liquid with an AC charge. He opened a spigot to allow the electrically charged brine to flow into the "spinner." When the jar was empty, he zapped the liquid with a DC charge and activated the "spinner." They waited a few tense moments before Pat shut down the system. He opened the top to look inside. He turned and smiled, "It's all there, Mr. Leary. Just like before."

Martin shouted, "Damn good job!" He slapped Pat on the back. "You should be proud. I just wish José had been here to see this. He'll be pleased when we tell him tonight." Martin sat down, looked at Pat and Sonja and said, "Before we quit for the day, please take a few minutes to detail the process one more time. I want to take a few notes. I should be able to explain it the other investors, but I'm not comfortable with it right now."

"You want to handle that, Sonja?"

"Sure. Are you ready, Martin?" Martin nodded. "The AC charge causes the precious metals to crystallize while they're suspended in the brine. When the brine is loaded into the 'spinner,' it's whacked with an AC charge. Now, here's where the process might get a little confusing. There's a small reservoir, loaded with mercury, attached to the inside wall of the 'spinner' chamber. The AC charge drives the crystallized metals out of the brine to the surface of the chamber. While this is happening, the 'spinner' is rotating at over 1000 rpms and drives the mercury to the surface of the chamber where the metals combine with the mercury. That's the process in a nutshell, Mr. Leary." She raised her palms in the air and added, "I don't know what happened this morning. We got everything 'bass ackwards' and nothing was working. Thanks to you, we got it straightened out." She clapped her hands together. "Well done, Mr. Leary."

"I'm not certain I'll be able to repeat what you just told me tomorrow, but, at least it's clearer now. Thanks, Sonja." Martin stood up and stretched. "It's 4:30, and I'm tired. Let's quit."

Pat Duncan dropped Martin at the hotel just after 5:00 and said he'd pick him up around 7:15.

After he talked to Pat Duncan, José called Cisneros to report on his delivery to Hoskins. "Arturo, I delivered the cocaine to Hoskins about 15 minutes ago. I have your money."

"Good job, amigo!" Cisneros had a broad smile on his face. His confidence in José was on the rise; the young man was reliable, intelligent and resourceful, and in Arturo's eyes, had a bright future with the cartel. Arturo was beginning to really like the kid, and had begun to think of him as a protégé. The successful completion of the Hoskins's cocaine delivery would solidify his own reputation as a reliable source within the city of Corpus Christi. That single transaction could be worth many thousands of dollars in future profits. "Come directly to Bustamonte's. You should be there by 8:00. I'll wait for you."

"I can't, Arturo. I have dinner plans."

"That's too bad. Put Hoskins's money in an envelope and leave it with Eddie Bustamonte before you go to dinner. Tell Eddie I'll pick it up about 8:00. I've got another bonus for you, so we'd better meet tomorrow. Call me."

Martin was prompt as usual. He was waiting by the hotel entrance when Pat and Sonja pulled up to the curb. He climbed into the back seat and asked, "Have either of you heard from José?"

Pat answered, "Yes. He called me a while ago. He said he was leaving Corpus Christi and he expected to meet us at the bistro between 7:30 and 8:00. We can have a drink and talk while we wait."

Martin asked hesitantly, "How long have you known José?"

Sonja turned and faced Martin. "Pat and I met José back in September when we entered the graduate program. José was already into his second year working with Dr. Gerba."

Martin smiled, and said, "Please call me Martin. Mr. Leary is so formal. José calls me Martin, if that's any help."

Pat glanced at Martin in the rearview mirror and smiled. He said, "That'd be fine with us, Martin."

"How long have you known each other?"

"Since our junior year." He smiled. "We're roommates now."

"I may be asking the wrong question, but does your relationship go beyond roommates?"

"Yes, sir. We hope to marry after we earn our doctorates."

"I'm happy for you." Martin hesitated before continuing. "Don't answer this if it makes you uncomfortable. Is José sick?"

Pat took his eyes off the road for a few seconds to look at Sonja. There was instant communication. "Go ahead, Sonja. You answer."

"We're concerned about José's health, Martin. We've noticed changes in his appearance; the area around his eyes seems darker, and he appears to be losing weight. There isn't much to lose to begin with." Sonja turned again to face the back seat. "The thing that really disturbs us is his emotional state. Something's wrong. We decided just the other day to talk with him to see if there's something we can do to help."

"I'm concerned too, but I don't know him well enough to make comparisons."

Pat responded, "José respects you, Martin. You might be the best person to talk with him."

"I'll give it some thought, but not tonight. Let's revel in today's success."

Bishops Bistro was a small, intimate restaurant; only ten tables. Each table was covered with a white tablecloth with matching napkins, and a red rose placed in the center. The lighting was muted and the woodwork a dark walnut. Martin felt comfortable immediately. He was reminded of the lounge at the River Inn in Haddam, sans the river view. All but one of the tables was occupied when Sonja, Pat and Martin arrived. Fortunately Pat had called ahead and made a 7:30 reservation.

José arrived at 7:45. He looked exhausted, but said that he felt fine, that he'd been looking forward to the dinner for the last hour. The evening was filled with laughter and fellowship. Although Martin had forty years on the students, he seemed to fit right in. He entertained them with stories about his childhood friends, especially his baseball buddies Billy Davis, "Inky" McCarthy, "Icky" Nixon, "Ears" Anderson, and especially Fred "Holes" Sodlawsky.

All three laughed heartily when Martin explained how Holes got his nickname. "Holes pants were always to short, well above his ankles, and rarely was he without holes in his socks. Every time he walked past one of my friends, he'd point at Fred's heel and yell, 'Holes.' When I think about it now, we were cruel. Since I'm on the subject of my old friend 'Holes,' you might like to hear about our gaming activities while I attended college."

José asked, "Gaming business? You mean gambling? How long did you do that, Martin?"

"For about a year and a half. But, in the end it turned out to be a real downer for me, José." Surprised by this revelation, all three encouraged Martin to continue. He started his story by giving them a geography lesson. "During my freshman year at the University of Bridgeport, I worked in Derby, my home town, and commuted to class. Derby is only about fifteen miles from the city of Bridgeport. One Saturday my friend Bill Davis and I decided to grab a soda at our old hangout, *Toland's Drug Store*. We ran into 'Holes.' We talked about old times, and then he started telling us about his bookmaking activities in and around Bridgeport. He'd joined up with a Bridgeport gaming group right out of high school and was making most of his money from numbers. Since I was broke all the time, I was impressed. The gaming business sounded exciting. Most of all, I saw it as a way to stop the damn commute back and forth from Derby to Bridgeport. The commute was killing me. I joined his gaming organization as an apprentice, and after a few months, I was on my own."

Martin surveyed the faces of his young friends and grinned. "Maybe I shouldn't continue. It might give you some bad ideas." All three laughed.

Pat looked at the faces of his friends, and then said, "We'd like to hear the rest of the story, Martin."

"I give you a little history first. All WWII veterans were given an opportunity to attend college following their discharge through a program called the GI Bill. The Federal government provided each veteran with enough money to attend college if he or she wanted to.

"I built a small, efficient numbers operation based on my belief that the veterans would enthusiastically accept my numbers games. They were mature when compared with high school or prep school kids, and were not unfamiliar with poker and other games of chance. Coupling that gambling experience with a craving for discretionary funds to recreate, I thought veterans represented a fertile market.

"I was deliberate and discrete the first year, and in the process, made a lot of money. During my sophomore year, however, greed and overconfidence became my Achilles heel. Soliciting veterans off campus was one thing, but soliciting on the university campus raised the risk substantially."

Martin said that he naively thought that his gaming activity would be ignored by the university, as well as the police. "But I was sadly mistaken. One of the veteran's wives blew the whistle when her husband lost a chunk of money. She contacted the Dean of Students, who in turn contacted the police. The police interviewed the man, and I was immediately identified as the solicitor.

"Two detectives appeared at my apartment door early one Monday morning. They flashed their badges, announced they were from the Bridgeport Police Department, and asked for me. I'm sure the blood drained from my face." Martin grinned as he recalled the scene. "Excuse my language, Sonja, but I nearly soiled my pants. After I identified myself, I was told they had a warrant for my arrest for operating an illegal gaming operation on the campus of the University of Bridgeport.

"The next day I experienced my 'fifteen minutes of fame.' A headline in my hometown paper read: 'Martin Leary Arrested: Former Derby Athlete Charged With Soliciting Bets.'" Martin's dinner companions sensed a subtle change in his eyes as the memory of that arrest came flooding back into his consciousness. It was obvious it had been a traumatic experience. "I guess I'd have to say that it was the low point of my life." Martin took a sip of his drink, and continued, "I was placed in a small room, not much larger than a closet, surrounded on three sides by waist-high panels of glass so that the officers could see me from anywhere in the room. I sat in that damn room for over an hour." Martin forced a smile. "I recall thinking it was strange that only uniformed men occupied the desks; not a woman in sight. Finally, I was fingerprinted, and led to a holding cell.

"About 9:00 the next morning, I was taken from the cell in handcuffs and moved across the street to the courthouse for arraignment. The judge was quick; he set bail at $1000 and a trial date of June 12. In less than three hours, I was back to in the cell. That same afternoon a guard informed me that someone had made bail and I was free to leave. But I was instructed not to leave town before the trial.

"'Holes' was standing at the entrance to the police station when I left. He said that he'd arranged bail through a bondsman. Looking back, I guess I was lucky not to have been arrested on a Monday. I could have spent an entire weekend in jail if I'd been arrested on a Friday."

Sonja asked, "What happened at the trial? Were you sent to prison?"

"No, I pleaded guilty before a trial. Since it was my first offense, the judge sentenced me to one year of community service, two years probation, and I was barred from the University of Bridgeport campus for five years."

"What an experience. Did having an arrest record cause any problems later on?" Pat asked.

"Not really. I'm self-employed. I've been involved with the same real estate business since I graduated from college."

The conversation segued into how Martin became involved with Dr. Gerba and the precious metals project. He told them the story of his contaminated water well, and his being jolted into activism. "I did a little research and found some disturbing information about fresh water. Accessible fresh water in lakes, rivers, and aquifers accounts for less than one-tenth of one percent of all the Earth's water, and many of those sources are already polluted. We can't afford to contaminate anymore. As my old partner used to say, 'all politics is local,' so I'm trying my best to protect the water table in and around my own city."

Martin was surprised when he looked around and realized that only one other table remained occupied. "Since I'm the senior member of this group, I guess I'd better be the voice of reason. We should pay the bill and get some sleep. Tomorrow will be another busy day."

The following day José agreed to meet Cisneros for lunch at Bustamonte's. When José arrived he was pleased to find that Arturo had finally left the promised supply of heroin with Eddie. He was all smiles when he walked to the back of the restaurant.

"Glad you could join me for lunch, Acuna. Did you pick up your stuff?" José nodded. "That was good work yesterday. The Hoskins's delivery was very profitable for me. Here's the bonus I promised." Arturo peeled off $500 and handed it to José.

Not expecting any payment beyond the guaranteed supply of heroin that had been promised, José gasped, "Thanks, Arturo! I sure can use the money."

"There's a lot more where that came from if you concentrate on the important things, like making money."

José was upbeat when he returned to the chemistry lab; $500 for only a day's work! With that much money in his pocket, and reinforced by the heroin he'd just shot in the men's room, José began to question his negative thoughts about Arturo and the cartel. Could he have been overreacting? Perhaps he had the best of both worlds after all; an easy source of income that required a limited investment of his time; and, a job at the lab, which he loved.

# 8

MARTIN PRESSED THE BUTTON on his automatic door opener, pulled into his garage and parked. He closed the door and strolled down the driveway to the mailbox, checking his rose bushes on the way. He found three pieces of mail: two bills and a letter from Dr. Gerba. Standing by the box, he tore open Dr. Gerba's envelope and read:

> *The Interim Board of Directors of the Precious Metals Extraction Corporation cordially invites you to a meeting to review the company's proprietary technology and development plans. The meeting is scheduled for June 16, 1998, at the Hidalgo Brine Disposal Facility in Elsa, Texas. A catered lunch will be served at the conclusion of the meeting. Directions to Hidalgo Disposal are enclosed.*
>     *Dr. Ely Gerba, Ph.D., Professor of Chemistry, University of Texas at Austin*

Martin called Bill Davis. "Did you receive an invitation from Ely Gerba?"

"Yes. It came in today's mail. Are you planning to attend the meeting?"

"Definitely. Shirley said she'd like to go with me. How about making it a foursome?"

Bill said he'd check with Lois, but was confident she'd jump at the chance to visit Texas. He called back that evening. "We're on board, Mart. Lois hasn't been this enthusiastic about a trip since we flew down to Florida last winter."

With the Davises on board, Martin suggested an itinerary that included visiting a resort on South Padre Island a few days before the scheduled shareholders meeting, and after the meeting, a trip up the coast to Galveston and the Johnson Space Center.

The friends left Hartford the morning of June 13, flew to Houston, caught a shuttle flight to Harlingen, rented a car at the airport, and drove across the causeway to South Padre Island. They checked into the Alexander Hotel and began what all four were calling their midyear vacation; soaking up the sun on the beach in front of the hotel, reading, playing numerous hands of bridge, and dining out.

After breakfast on the morning of the 16th, Martin and Bill left the hotel for the meeting in Elsa. Shirley and Lois joined a scheduled tour of retail establishments in Matamoros, Mexico.

Dr. Gerba's directions had been clear. Bill and Martin had no difficulty locating the large Hidalgo Disposal sign next to the reddish clay entry road. There wasn't a cloud in the sky. Martin had to shield his eyes because of the sun and was forced to gear down to five miles an hour to compensate for the potholes in the roadway. To make matters worse, the potholes were filled with water from a rainstorm that had passed through the region the previous evening. As the car reached the top of an incline the vehicle came face to face with a huge brown-eyed steer standing in the middle of the road. The animal was not about to move; this was its territory. Martin honked the horn, but to no avail. The steer just reared its head back and mooed as loud as the horn.

Bill placed his hands on the dash and laughed. "Look at those eyes, Mart. The animal is challenging us." The steer remained in the middle of the road until Martin raced the engine. The engine spooked the animal and it finally moved out of the way.

Free of the visual obstruction caused by the steer, Martin kept his foot on the brake for a few moments as they focused on the view before them. The scene was dominated by vast stretches of brown grass the color of straw, and lots of sagebrush. They were a few stunted trees, but those were at least a half-mile away. Martin pointed to his left. "Look at the size of those pits, Bill. They must take up over an acre. They look like three big tubs of black ink."

"Look at those tanks, Mart." Martin shifted his attention. Six large oil tanks, painted white with a single blue stripe running from top to bottom ran in a line about two hundred yards away. A large tent had been erected in front of the tanks to protect the guests from the direct rays of the brutal south Texas sun.

Roy DeWitt built Hidalgo Disposal in the late 1980's to satisfy a growing need for more oil field waste disposal sites in south Texas. The plant was located just four miles from the village of Elsa, on 50 plus acres of unincorporated land in Hidalgo County, and only a few miles from Roy's home in Edinburg. Within two years Roy built his business into the largest and most efficient facility of its kind in south Texas.

"I guess we should head for that small trailer straight ahead. I'll bet that's DeWitt's office." Martin parked next to the trailer and both men got out. Dressed casually in short sleeve sport shirts, lightweight slacks, and comfortable shoes, they stood next to the car while Martin looked for a familiar face. Spotting Roy standing near the front of the tent, Martin hurried in that direction, leaving Bill in his dust. Roy saw him approach and reached out to shake his hand. "Martin, good to see you again. Ya'll have a pleasant trip?"

"We arrived a few days ago, Roy. We're staying over on South Padre Island." Smiling he added, "We're roughing it over there, Roy. Sunbathing on the beach can be monotonous. But, we'll survive. Seriously, we brought our wives and we're enjoying a few days' vacation. The ladies are in Matamoros today on a shopping trip arranged by the hotel." Realizing he hadn't introduced Bill, Martin said, "I'm sorry. Meet Bill Davis, Roy. Bill is a PMEC investor, and an old friend from school days."

Shaking hands. "Pleasure to meet you, Bill. Meet Ben Jack Randall. Ben manages this facility for me."

After an exchange of pleasantries, Martin asked why they had had trouble finding an English language station during the drive from South Padre Island. Roy laughed. "It's understandable, when you think about it. Naturalized Mexicans make up over 90% of the population in this region." Roy smiled. "It's a tough area for an Anglo. In fact, many Texans considered this part of Texas as third world and outside the laws of the United States."

Martin commented, "It doesn't look like there are many farms around here."

"You're right, Martin. The land isn't good for growing anything, except cattle. What you see here is typical of the entire region: wild olive trees, grassland, scrub brush, and cattle. South Texas is hot, dry, and desolate, with dust everywhere."

Bill asked Ben Jack if the recent drop in the price of domestic crude oil had affected operations. Ben Jack quipped, "Shit, the brine volume ain't no mor'n it was two years ago. And that new plant just north of Rio Grande City lowered prices again last week. That s'um bitch got to be losin' money. Some of my regular truckers is hauling there now. Hate to lower prices more, but may have to."

While Bill talked with Ben Jack, Martin stood off to the side and watched as the investors milled about the entrance to the tent. There appeared to be a noticeable level of excitement. Ely Gerba tapped him on the shoulder and asked, "Martin, can you join Roy and me for a moment?" Martin followed the two men to a spot about twenty feet from the entrance to the tent.

"Would both of you be willing to help with the presentation this morning?" Roy looked at Martin. Both men nodded.

Martin said, "If you think the investors will get more out it we'd be happy to participate."

"Good. Roy, you go first and explain why we need a facility like this to dispose of oil field brine. Use the boards I prepared. Martin, I'd like you to talk about the importance of platinum group metals. Your independent research should carry a lot of weight. I'll close with a description of the technology. Is that okay with you?"

Martin looked at Roy again. Roy said, "Sounds fine, Ely."

When the attendees were seated, Dr. Gerba rose from behind a long head table and introduced himself. He asked each person to stand and provide a short personal profile. With introductions completed, Roy DeWitt stood and placed a large white board on an easel displaying a schematic layout of the Hidalgo Disposal. "Our brine disposal operation is pretty simple to understand. Trucks haul the brine from producing oil wells and dump it into the first pit. We do our best to make sure that all vestiges of crude oil are removed before we inject the brine into a non-producing formation. Any waste oil that's still mixed in with the brine will gradually move to the top of the pit and remain on the surface until we skim it off. We skim every few days and haul it over to the tanks behind us.

"The three brine pits are connected in series. The brine flows underneath the oil from pit one to pit two, and then on to pit three. From there the brine is pumped into a tank where it's chemically treated, and then pumped into a non-producing oil formation, approximately 2000ft. deep. It may be an oversimplification, but a brine injection well is like a reverse oil well."

Bill Davis raised his hand. "If I understand what you're saying, Roy, brine contains waste oil when it arrives at your plant. But I don't understand why the oil isn't separated from the brine at the oil head?"

"Crude oil production is an imperfect science, Bill. Most oil formations contain brine and oil, but the industry hasn't yet invented a technology to separate the two at the wellhead. During the life of a producing well, the percentage of brine in the formation will rise. When the level gets too high and the price of oil drops, it may become uneconomical to produce the crude. In some older oil producing areas like Ohio and Kentucky, the crude pumped from a stripper well could contain as much as 50% brine."

Roy moved forward for emphasis. "Think about this: brine is nothing more than a waste product." Looking from face to face he said in a confidential tone, "However, Dr. Gerba isn't convinced it's only a waste product. Two years ago he asked me to test the brine to see what was in the stuff, and guess what, the lab found traces of precious metals. We were hesitant about accepting the results at first, so we arranged for another test. To our surprise, the second test confirmed the results of the first. We've been testing off and on for over two years, and in every case, we continue to find precious metals." Roy stopped talking for a few moments to allow his comments to sink in. He noted the attendees were beginning to sit up straight, and that they were becoming more attentive. "Don't ya'll overreact. We haven't found an economical way to remove the metals from the brine, yet. But, it looks like Dr. Gerba may be on the threshold of finding a way."

Roy removed that board and replaced it with a graphic representation of his waste oil treatment. "Those six tanks behind us are part of the other business we operate from this site, the recovery of waste oil. All six tanks are all connected to each other with a complex series of pipe. It's a plumber's nightmare. The waste oil we skim off the top of the brine pits is hauled to this first tank where it's heated, chemically treated, rerouted to tank two, where it's reheated, and treated again. We keep testing the oil until it's clean enough to ship to a refinery. Our goal is to remove 98% of the impurities and harmful minerals before we ship. A bad batch of oil can contaminate a refinery, and it's very expensive to clean a contaminated refinery. If the contamination is traced back to us, we're liable." Roy removed the second board from the easel, and sat down.

Martin stood, and faced his audience. "The primary benefit from our technology is *not* the recovery of gold and silver, but rather, the recovery of platinum group metals, PGM for short. PGM comprises six closely related metals, platinum, palladium, rhodium, ruthenium, iridium, and osmium. Platinum Group Metals have become critical to high technology and defense related industries because of their extraordinary physical and chemical properties. However, nearly all of the world's reserves of PGM are in just three countries, South Africa, Russia, and Canada.

"Allow me highlight a few points. Unlike gold and silver, there are few, if any alternatives to PGM. In certain critical applications that require platinum, one of the other metals in the same group might be used as a substitute except that most of those are even scarcer than platinum. The U.S. doesn't have a domestic source of supply for PGM, and the need for PGM is growing, especially within the high-tech and national defense industries. The elevated prices paid for platinum group metals could make their recovery a very attractive business opportunity.

"There is a new use for platinum that may be more exciting than present uses." Martin paused a moment for emphasis. "I'm sure most of you are aware of NASA's use of fuel cells in the space program. Fuel cells provided power for the Apollo program back in the sixties, and currently provide power for the shuttle. At some point within the next decade or two, fuel cells will provide power for a whole bunch of things, including the automobile, and guess what metal is critical to the structure of the fuel cell? Platinum!" Martin had become so innervated by his own remarks, he'd moved partially down the center aisle that separated the chairs. He stopped, smiled and said, "The important thing to remember is that brine is considered a waste product, and nobody wants this waste product. Roy is even paid to dispose of this waste product! Can you believe that? If we can find a method for extracting the metals economically, think of the potential profits!

"Dr. Gerba believes we can develop a technology to recover PGM. The question is, can we do it economically?" Martin paused and searched the faces of his audience for signs of confusion or doubt. Finding none, he smiled and said, "I'm worn out. Your turn, Ely."

Ely stepped forward. "Thanks, Martin, for that inspiring presentation." He smiled and added, "That was even inspiring for an old curmudgeon like myself." Ely raised his hands in the air. "Let's take a break, people. Ben Jack and his wife have opened their home so we can use the facilities. They have a full bathroom, and a powder room. There's also a rest room in Ben Jack's office trailer. It isn't the best, but it works. See you in 15 minutes."

Bill Davis exited the tent and observed Martin talking with José Acuna just outside the entrance. Martin had his arm around the shoulders of the young man and was smiling. Bill walked toward them and asked, "How about letting me in on the joke?" Establishing eye contact with José, Bill thrust out his hand and announced, "I'm Bill Davis, José. I've been looking forward to meeting you. Martin's told me about your contributions to the development of the extraction technology. You must be pleased with what's happening today." While Bill's words were upbeat and positive, his thoughts were unsettling; he was taken aback by the young man's appearance. José had circles under his eyes, and one eye was bloodshot. Bill thought, *The kid doesn't look right. He's either sick, or he's on something.*

"Martin's talked about you many times, Mr. Davis. I'm glad we've finally met, and thanks for the compliment. You're right, we've accomplished a lot the past couple of months."

Bill smiled. "From the sound of things, I guess we'll be seeing a lot of each other. Maybe we can talk after the meeting. Right now, Mother Nature calls." Bill reached out again to shake José's hand, and excused himself.

Dr. Gerba looked around the tent and noted all the seats were occupied. "Has everyone returned?" The attendees nodded in the affirmative.

Bill Davis leaned over and whispered to Martin, "Is there something wrong with your young friend Acuna? He looks terrible. Is he sick?"

"I don't know what the problem is. He's lost weight since the last time I saw him, and he was frail to begin with. I plan to talk with Ely about José after the meeting." Martin leaned back, and tried to re-engage his attention on Ely's words.

"I'll try to explain in nontechnical terms the essence of our technology. I must ask for your cooperation before I commence, however. Since we intend to apply for a process patent, what you hear today is strictly confidential. That includes descriptions of the technological goals presented in the business plan, and the prospectus. I assume everyone here received a plan and a prospectus, correct?" He noted a general nodding of heads. Ely placed a flow chart of the operation of a proposed prototype on the easel, and turned again to face the group. "What you see here is a simple graphic representation of the proposed prototype. Let's look at the operation in sequence. It may be confusing at first because a lot happens at once, so try to stay with me."

Martin's concentration waned during Ely's description of the extraction process. He drummed his fingers on his notepad and brooded. Bill's question about José's health had evoked unwanted discomfort. Martin realized he'd been evading the issue of José's health for a number of weeks.

Ely looked around the tent. "I see that the caterers need to set up for lunch. I'll close by predicting that within three months, we'll be field-testing a prototype of the extraction component right here at Roy's disposal plant. While José and his team are building the prototype, my colleagues and I will be solving the riddle associated with automating the separation process. Now let's eat. I'll field questions while we enjoy the lunch."

Martin caught up with Ely as the rest of the assemblage milled about outside the tent waiting for the caterers to set up. "Ely, am I correct in assuming you can't build the prototype at the university?"

"Yes. We'll have to find space away from the campus. It wouldn't be prudent for me to wait any longer. It could be embarrassing if the university administration approaches us first. I just haven't had time to look, or even think about it. It's one of the issues I will have to face when I return to Austin."

"I could stay on in Texas for a few days, and help you locate space. Shirley could fly home with the Davises."

"I'd appreciate that, Martin. I could use some help, especially from someone with your background and experience."

Martin looked around to locate José. He didn't want José to overhear the next part of the conversation. "Ely, I'm concerned about José. He looks terrible. Is he sick?"

"Now that you mention it, he does look run down. Maybe I've been working him too hard."

"I don't think it has anything to do with his being overworked. He's beginning to look like one of my former employees who contracted hepatitis from a blood transfusion. The young man was dead in less than a year. He left a wife and two small children." Martin began to fidget, and continued, "I feel like a damn snitch, but I feel it's incumbent upon me to ask. Were you aware that José was in Mexico about a month ago when Pat and Sonja successfully automated the extraction process for the first time?"

Dr. Gerba was startled. "No. I didn't know he'd gone to Mexico. I'm afraid I've been so busy with final exams, I've let a lot of things slip by me. I'll talk with him when I get back to Austin."

# 9

JOSÉ WAS FILLED WITH pride as he left the shareholders meeting and headed back to Austin. Dr. Gerba had singled him out as a key contributor to the development of the precious metals extraction technology. The feeling of euphoria was short lived, however. His mind was beginning to understand that his heroin addiction could derail his goal of earning a Ph.D. in chemistry. *If I don't get off the heroin, someone in the Chemistry Department is bound to find out. I could be kicked out of the program.* Before José realized it, he was speeding along at fifteen miles per hour above the speed limit. He eased up on the accelerator, and looked in the rearview mirror. He sighed. *Thank God! No blinking red lights.* He slapped the steering wheel, and shouted, "Damn it! This has got to stop." He thought of telling Arturo he was through making deliveries. But that was out of the question. He wouldn't be able to remain in Austin if he did that. *I need to talk with someone and try to figure out what to do. But whom?*

José began to list in his mind individuals who might be able to help. When he got to Martin Leary's name, he stopped. *Why not Martin Leary? Martin's a good man. I trust him.* In spite of their age difference, Martin and José had begun to share time together when Martin visited Austin; meals once in a while, evenings at a movie, and especially watching a sporting event on television. Both were rabid baseball fans; José followed the Texas Rangers, and Martin the Boston Red Sox.

Back in his apartment, José retrieved a yellow pad from his briefcase. He sat down at his small dinette table to explore the best way to approach Martin. *I might be able to persuade him to stay in Texas an extra day or two, but talking privately with Martin in or near Austin, could be a problem. Dr. Gerba, or someone else involved with the project, might want to visit with him. No, that won't work. Somehow I've got to take Martin away from the lab, maybe away from Austin.*

José hatched the framework of a plan. Convince Dr. Gerba that Martin Leary deserves more than a handshake for his contributions to the project. Suggest that he, José, escort Martin to the Coast Guard Station at Port Aransas so he can visit with his nephew. Arrange to stay overnight at his mother's home in Corpus, and if time permits, take Martin across the border into Mexico for a day.

"Dr. Gerba, I've been thinking about Martin Leary's contribution to the project. We haven't shown our thanks in a demonstrative way. Roy lives in Texas and can visit with us whenever he wants. Martin on the other hand, must travel 1000 miles, and we expect him to be here every time we hold a meeting. When you think about it, Martin is exhibiting a high degree of trust in our technological theories, and us. His understanding of the details we live with every day is limited." José could tell from the professor's expression that he was responding as he had hoped. "I believe we should show him how much we appreciate this trust, and his considerable contributions."

"Okay. I can't argue with that. Obviously you have something in mind. What do you think we should do?"

"Martin's talked about a nephew stationed at the Coast Guard Station at Port Aransas several times. I know he'd like to visit with him during one of his trips. He's also shown and interest visiting Mexico. Why not talk him into extending his stay in Texas a few days? I could arrange to take him to Port Aransas. It's just north of Corpus. We could stay with my mother and avoid the expense of a hotel. The following day I could take him on a one-day excursion across the border to Matamoros. At least he'd get a taste of Mexico and life in a border town. We would be back in Austin late Monday night. I doubt that the overall cost would exceed $200."

"Sounds good to me, José. The two of you could leave after he helps me find space to build the prototype. I expect him to drive over from Houston tomorrow. I'll run it by him when he calls me today." Ely retreated to his office, pleased that his earlier concerns about his young protégé may have been exaggerated.

"Shirley, Dr. Gerba asked me to delay my return to Connecticut. He wants me to help locate industrial space to build a prototype extraction machine. Ely offered to have José drive me to Port Aransas so I can visit with my nephew. He said that José had volunteered to be my escort. The project will pick up the tab as a way of saying thank you for my contributions. I should be home in four days."

Martin left Shirley and the Davises at Houston's Hobby Airport on a Monday morning and drove west on Interstate 10. He checked into the Airport Motel, dropped his bag in the hotel room, and drove to the university's chemistry building. Martin picked up a visitor's badge from the receptionist at the front entrance and took the elevator to the third floor.

He was welcomed enthusiastically when he walked into the lab. "Martin, welcome back." José rushed toward Martin to shake his hand. "Your timing is excellent! We just figured a way to attach a mercury reservoir on the outer wall of the 'spinner.' We also developed a system to chemically clean and charge the brine while it's in the drum. Our next challenge is to figure out how to plumb the brine tank to the drum, and then to the 'spinner.'"

Martin couldn't mask his enthusiasm. "Fantastic! It seems as though every time I come into this place, I'm greeted with good news."

José added, "Do you remember me talking about building the prototype on a trailer so we could move it from Austin to Elsa? Well, I think we've figured a way to do that too. All we need now is space to build it."

"That's why I've come back. Ely asked me to help find space. I plan to look into what's available at that industrial park near the airport first."

Dr. Gerba waited for Martin to retrieve his briefcase, and then walked with him to the elevator. "Thanks for your help, Martin. The space you found is more than satisfactory."

"I was glad I could help, Ely."

"Are you ready for your trip?"

"I'm looking forward to it. I haven't seen my nephew in a long time, and from what José tells me, visiting Mexico should be a kick."

"I'd love to go with you, but my class schedule this semester just doesn't permit me to take time off." Reaching out to shake Martin's hand, Ely announced, "Well I'm off to the men's room. Don't let that young man lead you astray."

José approached and asked, "Are you ready to go back to the hotel?"

"Yes, and I think I'm ready for a nap. This has been another long day. You people are determined to kill me."

On the short drive to the hotel, José said, "I suggest we leave the hotel about 9:00 tomorrow morning. It's roughly a two-hour trip to Port Aransas. I've made reservations for you at O'Malley's Fish House for 11:45."

"9:00 sounds good. That should give me enough time to make a few calls before we leave. By the way, what's the phone number at your mother's place? I should give the number to my wife in case of an emergency."

*ELSA*

"626 555 1267. Tell your wife we should get there about 4:00. My mother said dinner would be served about 6:00."

# 10

MARTIN PLACED HIS OVERNIGHT bag in the trunk of the José's Camaro. "We both must have had the same thought when we dressed this morning, José: shorts, sneakers and a sport shirt. It's the only way to travel."

"It seems like I live in shorts lately, especially when I'm not working in the lab."

Martin settled back in the passenger seat, and studied the map José had given him. As they approached the on-ramp to I-35, Martin said, "When I called my nephew yesterday to confirm our lunch date, I realized I hadn't talked with him in over 16 years. Michael's my sister's oldest child. He was only about seven or eight when I last visited with his family in Houston."

José said in a subdued and serious tone, "I'm happy for both of you. I'll bet he's looking forward to the visit as much as you are." José took a deep breath and said, "I need to talk with you about something very personal. I need your advice."

Smiling, Martin said, "Really? How can an old guy from Connecticut give advice to a young Texan?"

"I'm not sure, but let's give it a try. I think you know that I'm committed to the project. I love the work and I'm excited about the intellectual challenge and the career opportunities. There are very few people who qualify as precious metals specialists, and I'd like to be added to that list. We'll all be winners if we can demonstrate that it's feasible to extract PGM from a waste product."

José paused and took a deep breath. "Martin, what I am going to tell you will shock you and test your tolerance and patience." He turned momentarily and locked on Martin's eyes. Martin could read the concern in the young man's face. José returned his focus to the road and gripped the steering wheel so hard his knuckles turned white. José took another deep breath and announced, "I'm addicted to heroin!"

Martin's jaw dropped. "You're joking!"

"I wish I were, Martin. I've been addicted for over a year."

Martin was stunned. He didn't know what to say. Finally, he blurted, "Jesus, how the hell do you function? How can you work at the lab? Does Ely know?"

"No. No one knows, or even suspects. I've been able to keep it a secret. If you're willing to listen, I'll start at the beginning."

"Go ahead." Martin slumped in the seat and mumbled, "I guess it'd be an understatement to say you've piqued my interest. I can't imagine what advice I can give you."

"Dr. Gerba had just told me I was being considered for a scholarship to pursue a Master's degree, and then a Ph.D. After that announcement, I guess I wasn't thinking straight; my head must have been in the clouds." José turned and saw that Martin was staring at him with a deep frown on his face. José refocused on the road, and resumed his story. "A trip to Matamoros with my friend Edgar Martinez seemed to open the floodgates. We drove down for a weekend at the end of our junior year. It was right after final exams, so we were pretty loose. We had a great time, probably our best trip together." José stopped talking for a moment, and then continued in a voice close to a whisper, "Edgar introduced me to heroin that weekend. We inhaled it on the drive down, and later at a nightclub called La Panada.

"Pasqual Ortiz, the lead bartender at La Panada, has been a friend of mine since high school. You'll meet him on this trip." José forced a grin, and said, "You're probably wondering what I was doing in a Mexican border town while still in high school. The drinking age in Texas was twenty-one, and waiting until we were twenty-one to drink was unacceptable to my wild friends and me. We wanted to drink beer in a bar like civilized people, not hide out like criminals. After I obtained my driver's license, I'd borrow my mother's car on Friday nights, and my friends and I would head for Matamoros. Locating bars in Matamoros willing to serve kids was not a problem. I'm fluent in Spanish, so I didn't have a problem communicating."

Martin reacted with a chuckle. "That sounds familiar, José. My high school friends and I would do the same thing, except we'd drive from Derby, Connecticut, to Brewster, New York, to drink. The age limit in Connecticut was twenty-one, but in New York it was only eighteen."

"Well, I'm sure Matamoros is a little different from Brewster, N.Y. An individual can buy just about anything in Matamoros: sex, drugs, liquor, it doesn't matter. One is just as easily obtained as the other. The city is filled with establishments that offer customers saloon services on the first floor and bordello services on the second." José stopped for a moment as he thought about what he'd say next. "It took only a few more visits to La Panada, and I was hooked. I didn't have to pay for the heroin. I didn't realize it at the time, but whenever I'd show up at La Panada, Pasqual would supply the stuff himself. My guess is that he was paying for it out of his own pocket. He probably felt sorry for me. He told me not to worry, that he'd run a tab, and that I could pay for the stuff later, after I earned my Ph.D.

"I was just a recreational user until last fall. I'm not sure what happened, but I went from inhaling occasionally, to injecting regularly. I don't know what the hell I was thinking. I guess the size of my tab was becoming a problem for Pasqual, because after a few months, he said he wanted me to talk with a 'friend' of his, to see if the guy could help me earn some easy money. The friend he introduced me to was Arturo Cisneros, the Sonora cartel's Austin drug boss. Pasqual told me Cisneros was in Matamoros on 'business.' I wasn't aware that Cisneros was part of a drug cartel and that the cartel owned La Panada.

"Cisneros said he'd cancel my tab at the club, pay off what I owed Pasqual, and provide heroin when I needed it, if I'd become a courier for him. The bastard was asking me to trade my labor for heroin. But, I couldn't ignore the offer, Martin. I owed over $1500!" José frowned, and squeezed the steering wheel. "It took just one delivery assignment, and I knew I was screwed. I was locked in."

Martin exploded, "Those bastards! They had you by the gonads. That sounds like extortion."

José gritted his teeth and pleaded, "Martin, I have to find a way to escape the organization and the torment of my addiction, or I'm a dead man." Martin noticed José's body deflate.

Martin shook his head from side to side and mumbled, "That son of a bitch controls you through your addiction, it's as simple as that. He knows you can't afford to buy the heroin, so he supplies the stuff in return for your services. If you didn't need the damn heroin, you wouldn't be making deliveries."

"He didn't have to twist my arm, Martin." José lowered his voice and added, "Lately, the deliveries have become more risky, so he's added a cash bonus every time I complete one. I have to admit that I love having cash in my pocket. I know I'm responding to short-term greed, and I'm ashamed." Neither man said a word for a few minutes. José raised his head and declared, "I need your help, Martin."

"How in the world can I help? I don't know anything about drug

## ELSA

addiction. I'm a simple small-town real estate guy. I still can't see where I can help."

"I haven't told you everything, Martin. There's more. God, this is difficult! I feel so guilty."

"Why do you feel guilty? You haven't hurt anyone but yourself." Martin turned and looked at José again and added, "Or have you?"

"This is the tough part, Martin. I used you, and you didn't know it."

"Used me? How?"

"Remember when I asked you to carry a package to a relative in Groton?"

"Yes. Your cousin came to the house to pick it up. Wait a minute..." Martin shouted, "Oh my God. I was carrying drugs?"

"Yes. You delivered cocaine to one of Arturo's relatives in Connecticut."

"Jesus, José. I could have been sent to prison." Martin seethed. "How could you? Damn it! I ought to wring your fucking neck."

"I'm very sorry, Martin. A person tends to do stupid things when on heroin. Fortunately, no one was hurt as a result of my stupidity." The young man hesitated, but finally said, "That's not the end of the story."

Martin looked at José again, and asked, "Have you harmed Dr. Gerba, or anyone else at the lab? Have you hurt the project?"

"No. No one else has been affected." José turned slowly and looked into Martin's eyes. "But I have another problem, another one that affects you directly. Cisneros expects me to smuggle another shipment of cocaine to Groton in your suitcase."

Martin exploded. "That son-of-a-bitch!"

"I want out of this mess." José pleaded, "Please help me."

"You're in so deep, José, so far in, I don't know how I can help." Martin thought for a moment. "I'm afraid to ask, but am I correct in assuming you have some sort of a plan?"

"Yes. I've thought this through very carefully. It will take a series of calculated steps to extricate myself. Will you listen to my plan?"

Martin sighed in resignation. "What choice do I have? You have me cornered in this car 50 miles from nowhere." Martin sighed, "What's your plan?"

"I'll tell Cisneros the truth. I'll tell him that I've been assigned the responsibility to build a prototype, and supervise field tests down in south Texas. Those assignments will take weeks. Finding time, even on weekends, to make deliveries would be impossible."

"Your plan sounds logical. But what about the Groton shipment?"

"I've got to create a diversion. If you're not here, I can't put the cocaine in your bag, right? What if you received a call to return to Connecticut on short notice; some sort of emergency?"

"Okay, I buy part of what you've said so far. Your diversion plan might take you off the hook for the Groton delivery. You might buy time because of your assignment to run prototype tests, but it doesn't correct the overall problem. What happens after you've completed the tests? How will you kick the habit?"

"That's where you come in, Martin. I can't move back to Austin after completing the tests. I must move away, and enter a drug rehab program. I've researched rehab clinics in the northeast, and found a few that look good. Maybe St. Teresa's in Hartford, Connecticut, would accept me. If you'd help, I'd probably have a good shot. I'll bet you could make the arrangements."

Martin reflected on this request. "That might work. One of my high school classmates is a counselor at St. Teresa's. I'll make a few phone calls tomorrow from your mother's home. Take your mother shopping to get her out of the house while I make my calls." Martin paused again. "If Arturo were to find out, Lord knows what he'd do. He might come after you while you're at the clinic. I don't think we should involve anyone else. Your addiction and desire to enter rehab will have to remain our secret."

# 11

JOSÉ PARKED HIS CAR in O'Malley's lot, and as he and Martin exited the vehicle, Martin said, "Let's walk. We have time." As they moved along Baytree Drive in Port Aransas, the distinctive smells and sounds from the docks brought back pleasant reminiscences: Martin of his childhood in Milford, Connecticut, and José of his visits to the docks of Corpus Christi with his dad. A large group of private yachts were moored in the harbor off the left. Martin recognized the sounds of lines slapping on the aluminum masts and water lapping against hulls. They stood for a few moments and watched the bustling activity on a fleet of fishing boats as crews joked with one another while cleaning decks and repairing nets. Martin guessed they were preparing for an early evening departure to return to the Gulf for another night of fishing. He smiled as he remembered watching similar crew scurry about fishing boats in Milford harbor.

Martin looked up and caught sight of a group of gulls screaming at each other while in flight. "Brings back a bunch of pleasant memories, José." Martin looked at his watch. "It's 11:35. We'd better get back to the restaurant."

When Martin entered the lobby of O'Malley's it wasn't difficult to spot his nephew; Michael Patterson was striking in his summer whites. Michael was a skipper of one of the Coast Guard cutters that patrolled the Gulf of Mexico out of Port Aransas. For the past month, however, he'd been on temporary assignment as the station's port officer responsible for land and air operations. He'd suffered a severe concussion from a fall while he and his crew attempted a rescue. A physician diagnosed his condition as "post concussion syndrome," and informed Michael's Station Commander that he should be limited to shore duty for an unspecified period of time.

Michael had arrived early and was seated at a window table with a view of the harbor. But instead of looking out of the window, he was watching the front entrance. He jumped up when he saw his uncle, rushed to meet him. They embraced. As Martin pulled away, he slapped his nephew on his arms and said, "Michael, your mother was right. You're a handsome son of a gun. You look great!"

"Thanks, Uncle Mart. You look pretty good yourself."

Martin introduced Michael to José. "José is a graduate student at the University of Texas at Austin. He generously provided the transportation today."

After the two shook hands, José turned toward Martin and said, "You have a lot to talk about, so I'll take my leave. I'll meet you at the Station's guardhouse at 3:00. I'm off to Corpus. Glad to have met you, Michael."

"Okay, see you at 3:00."

Martin noted his nephew's erect posture as he led the way to the table overlooking the harbor. He was tall for a Leary offspring, probably close to 6'2", and had the facial features of his father, including the blond hair and blue eyes. His tan was pronounced because of the white uniform. After being seated, Martin said, "It has been a long time, Michael. How are you? Are you still having headaches?"

"Only occasionally, thank goodness. It's been rough not being able to resume my duties as a cutter officer. I'll be okay. I have to be patient."

Both ordered the "fish of the day" meals and ate slowly, relishing the scene in front of them, each with his own thoughts. Large power cruisers of various sizes were entering and exiting the harbor through the jetty, and small motorboats seemed to be bustling about going nowhere in particular. Trolling fishermen occupied a few of the smaller boats; holding poles upright so the lines would drift off to the rear of their craft.

"Michael, look off to your left. Four boys are diving off fishing boats, swimming around, climbing a ladder attached to the pier, and doing it all over again. Years ago my good friend Bill Davis and I would do the same thing in Milford harbor."

Martin reopened the subject of Michael's injuries. "Are you willing to talk about the accident? Either your mother didn't want to talk about it, or she didn't know the details."

"It's not a very exciting story, Uncle Mart. We were just doing what the Coast Guard does most of the time: helping pleasure boat people in emergencies. We received a distress call about 2:00 in the afternoon. A twenty-foot powerboat ran out of fuel and was in danger of being swamped.

As we jockeyed for position to throw lifelines, a large wave hit the starboard side of the bow, and threw me headfirst against a bulkhead. When we returned to Corpus, I was taken to a hospital. I guess I was in a coma for a few days."

"A few days? Your mother said you were out for six."

"Yeah, well I'm okay now."

Martin turned away from the harbor scene and looked into the eyes of his nephew. "Michael, I'm troubled about something. You may be able to advise me."

"Sure, I'll try, Uncle Mart."

"I have a business associate who's addicted to heroin. Since my friend is closer to your age than mine, you might be able to help. I don't know much about drugs. From what I've read and heard, once an addict, always and addict. Is that true?"

"Unfortunately, that's what I've heard. A few are able to break away from the dependency. I guess it's like being an alcoholic; with the help of AA, some people can make a commitment to stay sober, and remain sober for the rest of their lives. I guess it depends on attitude."

"Do you think rehab centers are effective?"

"Yes. But I don't believe the success rate is very high."

Martin sat quietly looking out the window. "Thanks, Michael. I think you've right. If my friend has the will, he can shake the dependency."

Michael asked about what his uncle was doing in Texas. Martin summarized his involvement with the Precious Metals Extraction Corporation. "José is a key player. He's decided to stay on at the university and study for a Ph.D. in chemistry after he earns his Master's. He's very bright, Mike."

"Please don't answer this if it makes you uncomfortable. Is José the addict you were talking about earlier?"

Martin was stunned. He raised his eyebrows and asked, "Why would you ask that?"

"I'm not sure. When you introduced him, he looked like he might be anorexic. Then, when you asked for my opinion about addicts and rehab clinics, I put two and two together."

"Very perceptive, young man. Yes, José is the addict, I'm sorry to say. I've decided to help him if I can. I have a friend who manages a rehab clinic in Hartford. I'm hoping he'll accept José."

Michael realized they were the last patrons in the restaurant, and suggested they tour the Station before José returned.

# 12

When José pulled up to the curb in front of the Acuna home on Staples Place, Martin was surprised and impressed by its appearance. José had described the house as an older single level bungalow, but hadn't elaborated. What Martin saw was a freshly painted house, with a columnar porch that ran the width of the building, and highlighted by a red tile roof. Rose bushes bloomed along the walkway to the porch. As Martin opened the car door, he saw the screen door open and a beautiful woman walk out onto the porch. José called out, "Hi, Mom. I didn't expect you'd be standing watch by the window."

"Mind your manners, young man. I was watching for the postman, not you." When he saw both mother and son smile, Martin realized their repartee was in jest.

"Mom, meet Martin Leary, a real unadulterated Connecticut Yankee. Martin, meet my favorite mother, Rebecca Acuna."

Martin ascended the stairs leading up to the porch to shake hands with Rebecca. "Mrs. Acuna, it is a pleasure to meet you." Their eyes locked and both smiled.

"Please call me Rebecca. May I call you Martin?"

"Certainly."

Opening the screen door, Rebecca said, "Please come in, Martin."

José called from the car, "Go ahead inside, Martin. I'll get the bags."

In spite of being in her late forties, Rebecca Acuna was a beautiful woman. Her figure was that of a twenty-five-year-old: slim waist and attractive breasts. Her well-proportioned face featured a pair of dark brown eyes. She wore her slightly graying black hair in the form of a bun. As Rebecca led Martin through the foyer into her living room, his eyes remained focused on her. Martin's temporary fixation with this lovely creature broke when she turned and suggested he sit in a large upholstered recliner at the end of the room.

Martin's initial reaction to the furnishings was "early attic." That first impression was quickly tempered, however, when he recognized the unsoiled neatness of the room. Sunlight poured through a skylight accentuating the reds and blues in the draperies, upholstery and rug. "This is a bright and cheerful room. My spirits have been lifted already."

"Thank you. May I get you a drink before dinner? I have both red and white Texas wine, or something more substantial if you'd rather."

"A glass of that Texas white would be fine, Rebecca."

"I'll only be a moment." She turned and walked toward the kitchen. Again, Martin watched Rebecca's every movement as she left the room, and wondered why this lovely creature was unmarried.

Martin surveyed the furnishings again, this time with a more discerning eye. He surmised that Rebecca had attempted to communicate an Aztec theme through the furniture and accessories, but hadn't quite succeeded. Pure white walls and ceilings accentuated the blues and reds in the draperies. A pair of matching rugs had been placed in the center of the living room, and under the dining room table. The table and chairs were bulky, ornate pieces, probably pine. Martin stood up and walked over to have a closer look at the chairs. It appeared to him that someone had done a poor job of simulating hand carvings.

"I hope you like our Texas wine, Martin," Rebecca said as she reentered the room with two glasses in her hands.

Martin tasted the Chardonnay and commented, "I'm not a connoisseur Rebecca, but this is good."

José came through the front door with two bags and called, "Where do you want me to put Martin's bag, Mom?"

"Martin will stay in the guest room. You can sleep on the sofa bed in my office. I made up both beds yesterday. Do you want a glass of wine?"

"Please. White, if that's okay?"

"That's what we are having." Rebecca walked back into the kitchen and returned with another glass of Chardonnay. She sat in a chair opposite Martin and said, "Tell me about your visit to Port Aransas, Martin. How long had it been since you and your nephew visited?"

Given this invitation to talk, Martin told Rebecca about his nephew, and his nephew's family in Houston. He segued into talking about his wife Shirley and their only son, Adam, and their daughter-in-law, Ruth. "Shirley and I are looking forward to the birth of our first grandchild. Ruth is due in a few months."

"Congratulations, Martin. Girl or a boy?"

"Girl."

When José returned from the rear of the house, Martin and Rebecca were sharing their experiences as Realtors. José sat in a straight back chair to the left of Martin and listened to their spirited conversation. He smiled, *These two really like each other.* He picked up on the conversation as Rebecca was saying, "In my opinion, whatever differences exist result from different histories within the respective regions. Corpus is a fairly new city. Not much was here until after WWI, whereas your part of the country is 300 years old. South Texas, at least the part south of the Nueces River, was part of Mexico until 150 years ago. When you think about it, that's only about six generations back. People from Starr and Hidalgo counties seem to have their own interpretation of what the rest of the country refers to as the 'law of the land.' There's the rest of the United States, and then there's Starr and Hidalgo counties. Did you know that Dr. Gerba asked José to work in that area for a few months? Working in that crazy, lawless part of Texas has me concerned."

"Mother! What're you saying? I'll be fine. The three of us will live in an apartment in McAllen. That's a civilized place."

Ignoring her son, Rebecca continued, "South Texas is a Mexican enclave that hasn't adjusted to, or accepted, the fact that they are part of the United States. Many Texans believe we should give Hidalgo and Starr counties back to Mexico. The residents of those counties are untamed people, Martin. Those counties are major conduits for drugs."

The following morning José asked his mother to go shopping with him to get her out of the house and provide Martin with the privacy he needed to contact Charlie Nixon at St. Teresa's Rehabilitation Center in Hartford.

After Martin described José's addiction and his desire to enter a rehabilitation clinic, Nixon promised he'd investigate the situation to see if José would qualify. "I'll do my utmost to accommodate the young man. If he has the proper attitude and really wants to kick the addiction, he'll succeed. I'm 99% sure it'll be okay, but let me check on a few things here. Call me next week."

"Thanks, Charlie. I knew you'd come through."

As soon as they were underway, Martin said, "I had a difficult time falling asleep last night. But once I did, I slept right through. I guess I needed that. Your mother must have recognized my exhaustion when she thoughtfully suggested we turn in early. I accepted without hesitation. She's a wonderful lady, José."

*ELSA*

"Thank you, Martin. I knew you two would like each other."

"By the way, I had a very positive chat with Charlie Nixon about St. Teresa's. He seemed confident that he could arrange for you to be admitted, but said he needed time to work it out. He asked me to call him next week."

Martin could see a tear form in José's eye and watched as he reached up and wiped it away with his knuckle. "Thanks, Martin."

# 13

MARTIN COULD FEEL THE adrenaline flow through his body as they crossed the bridge that spanned the Rio Grande River, and entered Mexico. Martin was confident that José's familiarity with Matamoros would enable them to maximize their one-day stay. José had said he wanted to show Martin both the best, and the worst of the Mexican border town. Although Martin was in his early sixties, this was only the third time in his life that he had traveled outside the lower forty-eight states. He'd been to Canada on two brief excursions in the early eighties.

    José pulled into a parking lot across from the Mercado Juarez, an enclosed marketplace several blocks long. He suggested they explore the shops along Aveida Obregon, then walk to the Centro Artesanal, a government operated crafts center. During their walk Martin discovered that José possessed a marvelous sense of humor. He kept him in stitches with stories about his previous experiences in Matamoros while in high school and college. Martin delighted in watching José joke with the sales clerks in Spanish, in spite of not understanding a word that was spoken.

    Martin was a typical shopper from the United States, purchasing T-shirts for Adam and Ruth emblazoned with "Matamoros, the 'Heroic City'" in Spanish across the front, and an ornate piece of glassware for Shirley. As the morning shopping spree slowed, Martin's thoughts returned to recollections of his brief visit with José's mother. Martin recalled quips he and Rebecca shared the day before. He marveled about the vagaries of the human spirit—how two people who had not met before, could be instantly compatible.

# ELSA

The two friends walked from the Mercado Juarez to the Hotel Tamaulipas for a late lunch. The hotel featured the best restaurant in the city, and not inconsequentially, served the best margaritas. The margaritas had their desired effect; Martin felt like a rag doll, more relaxed than he had been in years.

"You order lunch for me, José. I'm not in the mood to make any decisions. Besides, I can't read the damn menu."

"Okay." José turned and called to a waiter standing to his left, obviously waiting to take their order. "Mozo?"

"Sí, señor."

"Mozo, quiere usted traer dos comidas principal cordero asado y ensalada de lechuga con tomate. Ensalada traje de la casa. Hay paneciltos y la mantequilla?"

"Sí, señor."

Smiling, Martin asked, "What did you order?"

"This restaurant is famous in these parts for their roast lamb. So, that's what I ordered. I hope you like lamb."

Martin smiled and said, "Fortunately for me, I do."

While they waited for their order to be served, Martin assumed a serious demeanor and probed José's eyes. "We can't allow you to be caught dealing or delivering drugs, José, you'll go to prison." Sighing, Martin continued, "We must get you into a rehab program as soon as possible. The question is, do you have the will to succeed?"

"I believe I do, but I have to be honest, I'm not sure." José muttered, "I know one thing, Martin. I'm scared, really scared. I've got to get away from the heroin and Cisneros. Far away!"

Emboldened by the margaritas, Martin allowed José to guide him to the La Panada, José's old stomping ground. The lead bartender, Pasqual Ortiz, greeted José enthusiastically as he and Martin slid onto bar stools. "José, my friend. No sabes la alegría que tengo de volverte a ver! I haven't seen you for months."

"I've been busy with my graduate studies at the university." Turning to face Martin, José placed his hand on Martin's shoulder and smiled. "Pasqual, this is my friend Martin Leary. Martin is a Connecticut Yankee. In spite of that, he's a good man." José laughed at his own joke.

"Encantado de conocerle, señor. I'm happy to meet you, Martin." Looking from one to the other, Pasqual asked, "What can I serve you?"

José straightened his back, and announced, "Let's have another margarita."

When Pasqual placed a margarita before him, Martin said, "Thank you, Pasqual. I don't know how many more of these I can handle. I'm beginning to feel a little woozy." He forced himself to focus on the image of the shabby interior of the establishment he saw reflected in the large, dirty mirror in front of him. He slowly counted ten tables, four chairs to a table, and two pictures of what appeared to be bullfights on the far wall. He smiled when he realized there were no windows in the place.

His eyes moved back to the tables, and stopped to watch four garishly dressed females with short skirts, sitting at one table near the back. As if on signal, two of the women rose and walked over to the bar and stood behind him, giggling. Martin watched them in the mirror for moment, and then turned around.

Pasqual winked at José as he placed two more margaritas on the bar. "José, I get the feeling that Maria and Teresa would like to meet your friend." Recognizing that as an invitation, both women moved forward. Maria, the younger of the two, leaned against José. Teresa took one hand and gently touched Martin's leg, all the while making eye contact. She smiled as she moved her hand to the inside of his leg and slowly caressed it. Martin responded immediately with an erection. *God, I haven't been aroused like this in a long time,* he thought.

In Spanish, Pasqual said, "Teresa, why don't you show José's friend our lounge area on the second floor?" To José he whispered, "It'll be a gift from me. I'll hold onto his drink." Teresa leaned forward and in broken English whispered in Martin's ear, "Like some fun, mister?"

Teresa took Martin's hand and pulled. Smiling at Pasqual, Martin slid down from the stool and allowed the woman to lead him up the staircase and into a cubicle behind a thick row of hanging beads that served as a door. The small area was only large enough to accommodate a bed and a dresser. It didn't take long for Martin to discover why he was there. Teresa began rubbing her hand against his erect penis, which was now fighting desperately to get out.

At that moment Martin came to his senses. What the hell was he doing in that cubicle with a prostitute? Martin pulled away, apologized to Teresa, walked out of the cubicle and descended the staircase. He sat down on the same stool he'd vacated just a few minutes before, unsure of what to say to Pasqual. He couldn't hide his embarrassment, so he determined the best way to handle the situation was to be honest. When Pasqual returned to his end of the bar, Martin whispered, "I had to refuse the young lady's offer. As we say across the border, I chickened out."

"I understand. Not to worry. I'm sure Teresa was not offended. Look behind you. Teresa's not upset."

Martin looked in the mirror and saw that both women were back sitting at a table just behind him, giggling. The two men remained quiet for a few minutes before Martin asked, "Pasqual, how well do you know José?"

"Very well, señor. José has been coming here for over five years. José is like a son to me."

"He told me a disturbing story on the way down here from Austin."

Before Martin could say another word, Pasqual interrupted, "I know what he told you. He called me a few days ago. He told me that he thought you were the only person who could help him. José's desperate." Pasqual lowered his head, and looked at his hands. "I am a miserable man, señor. I supported his heroin habit." Raising his eyes again, he said, "I can't help him, señor. I'm too close to the owners of this place. They would kill me. Can you help him?"

Martin could readily see the concern and sadness on the man's face. He was deeply affected by the man's pleading eyes. "I'll try my best. I made a phone call this morning. A friend might be able to arrange for José to enter a rehab clinic near Hartford."

Pasqual leaned over the bar, his chest practically touching the surface and whispered, "José has another big problem, señor. He told me that Cisneros expects him to trick you into taking more cocaine to his cousin in Connecticut. If you don't take the cocaine, they may hurt him, señor. I know these men. Rodriguez is a devil."

Martin responded in a whisper, "Rodriguez?"

"He is the boss of Cisneros. He lives in San Antonio." Pasqual straightened and began to wipe the bar, eyes focused on Martin, waiting for a response.

Again in a whisper, Martin said, "I have a wife, a son and a grandchild on the way. I have a business to run, and employees who depend on me. If I were caught, I'd be finished, my family would be hurt and my business would be finished!"

"I understand. But if you don't help him, he's in bad trouble." Pasqual moved down the bar to service another patron.

Martin Leary looked at his reflected image in the mirror behind the bar. Even though the noise level in the club had risen dramatically, Martin heard nothing. He began to question his courage. He knew Pasqual was right. The organization would not allow José to renege on an assignment without some sort of retribution. In order to set an example, the retribution would probably be severe. Martin waited for the bartender to return to his end of the bar. He whispered, "I'll think of something, but I can't take another cocaine shipment to Connecticut in my suitcase. The risk is too high." Martin looked behind him from table to table. He asked, "Where's José? We should head back to Corpus."

Pasqual pointed to a door at the end of the bar. "He is in the men's room, señor."

A few minutes later José emerged with a silly grin on his face and sat on his favorite stool. Martin looked at José's reflection in the mirror. His young friend's eyes seemed to be vacant and lifeless, and it appeared he was having trouble focusing. José responded to Martin's half smile with one of his own, and then lowered his eyes to study the margarita glass that he clutched in both hands. *José must be feeling the effects of the margaritas too,* Martin thought.

Pasqual apparently hadn't noticed José's deteriorating condition. He was busy waiting on two customers sitting at the bar, two stools from Martin, dutifully washing glasses, and wiping the surface of the bar when he had the chance. José turned abruptly and smiled. "Martin, you know what's just two blocks from here? 655 ½ Calle Olivera. Can you believe that? I didn't know there were ½ addresses, did you? That's where I pick up the stuff I deliver for Cisneros."

Pasqual stopped wiping the bar, leaned forward and said quietly, "José, shut up! You talk too much."

"Sorry, Pasqual. I thought Martin would be interested in an address like that."

Pasqual straightened. His eyes locked onto Martin's, and recognized immediately that Martin knew what José was talking about. Pasqual said, "I think it's time for you to take José back to Corpus Christi."

Martin didn't wait for further instructions. He announced, "We're out of here, José. I'll drive." He grabbed his young friend's elbow, and led him to the parking lot.

Neither Martin nor Pasqual noticed Teresa turn and stare in their direction. She'd overheard José's remark. She slowly rose from her chair and walked over to a door that read "Office."

Martin was still seething as he steered the car into one of the many lines waiting to cross the border. Except for the occasional question about directions, neither he nor José had said a word to each other since leaving La Panada. Martin broke the silence as they approached the border station. "Better get your driver's license ready. Look sharp and sit up straight. I don't want any trouble at the border." He turned toward José and scowled, "You talk too much."

José bit his lip and looked straight ahead. "Yes, I know."

"When you sober up, we'll talk."

José was sound asleep when they reached the outskirts of Corpus Christi. Martin's anger had slowly subsided and he was able to concentrate on how best to deal with the dilemma that surrounded his young friend. He realized that he had to solve the cocaine delivery problem first before he could help José enter a rehabilitation clinic. José's suggestion that he fabricate a family emergency and leave Texas immediately seemed to make sense. *José's right. If I'm not in Texas, I can't be expected to be a courier. It wouldn't solve the major problem, but at least it would buy some time. I'd better leave tonight.*

Martin exited U.S. Route 77 and followed the signs to the Corpus Christi airport. He didn't wake José until he was only a few miles from the terminal. He punched José's arm lightly. "Hey you. Wake up." José sat up slowly wiping the sleep from his eyes. He looked around before finally realizing where they were.

"Listen and listen carefully, José. It's 3:00 A.M. I plan to wait in the terminal and catch the first flight to Houston. Call Cisneros around 9:00 and tell him I caught a flight out of Corpus Christi late last night to return to Connecticut to deal with a family emergency. Tell him he'll have to find another way to get the cocaine to his cousin in Groton. Remember what I told you: be firm and resolute." The young man nodded. "By the way, you may have put both of us in grave danger when you mouthed off back there. Hope and pray Pasqual doesn't report your outburst. Now go home and get some sleep." Martin climbed out of the car, grabbed his suitcase from the back seat and was gone.

Martin moved so fast, he didn't hear José say, "I'm sorry."

Teresa pushed open the door to the nightclub manager's office, and without saying a word, sat down in the only side chair. Miguel Zarate watched her closely as she crossed her legs with a provocative flourish, and then crossed her arms. They looked at each other, waiting for the other to speak. Teresa said in Spanish, "I have information you're gonna want, Miguel. But, if I tell you, I want an additional five percent."

"Ha! Must be good stuff if you want five percent more. Let's hear it."

"Not so fast, Miguel. Do we have deal?"

"Teresa, if you was a guy, I'd say you have the balls of a bull. Yeah, you have a deal."

"You know that little shit, Acuna, the one who comes in here to be with Maria and visit with Pasqual? Well the little shit got high and told the gringo he brought with him an important address."

"What address?"

"Where he picks up drugs that he delivers for Cisneros."

Zarate stood up and asked, "Who's the gringo?"

"I don't know. Pasqual may know who he is."

"Is the gringo still here?"

"No, he left with Acuna."

"Shit! Tell Pasqual that I want to see him, now."

Pasqual reluctantly confirmed Teresa's account of what had just happened at the bar. "This is serious. That kid is a loose cannon. I'm gonna have to report this, Pasqual."

"Yes, I know."

Zarate stood up and began to pace. He saw this as a great opportunity to score points with Rodriguez. However, Rodriguez told him not to contact him by phone unless it was an emergency. Rodriguez suspected his secure line had been compromised by the Drug Enforcement Agency. Zarate stopped, and turned toward Teresa. "You still have a passport?"

"Yeah, why?"

"I'm gonna send you on a vacation to San Antonio. You're gonna drive up there and deliver your information personally. One day to get there, one day for you, and one day to return. I pay for the trip. How's that sound?"

"I like it."

"Okay. Get some sleep. I want you to leave first thing in the morning." Turning toward Pasqual, he said, "If you want to continue living, Pasqual, I suggest you keep that kid out of here."

# 14

JOSÉ WAS EXHAUSTED. INSTEAD of going across town to his mother's house in Corpus to sleep, as Martin had advised, he continued on to Austin. He showered, ate a little breakfast and made arrangements to meet Arturo at Bustamonte's for lunch.

He sat down across from Arturo at Arturo's usual table, and with all the will power he could muster, tried not to show that he was nervous. "Leary didn't take the stuff, Arturo. He had a family emergency and had to fly home last night. He left from Corpus."

"You're kidding, right?"

"No. I'm not kidding. He left early this morning."

Arturo sat up straight and hit the table with the palm of his hand. "Son of a bitch! Luis will be pissed. I'd better call him right away."

"I have some more bad news." José took a deep breath and said, "I'm going to be extremely busy for the next three to four months. I've been given the responsibility to build a prototype incorporating our new technology, and then move the prototype to south Texas for tests. The site is near Elsa, a very small town just north of the Mexican border in Hidalgo County. Do you know it?"

"No, and I don't give a shit. You'd better have that assignment canceled, Acuna. I need you here in Austin."

"I'm sorry, I can't do that." Martin had coached José to be strong and not vacillate; he must be prepared to go all the way. "I'll also be in charge of the field tests. That means I'll have to move down to McAllen. I have a lot riding on this assignment, Arturo. The project represents my future."

"Listen, you little fuck. You can't just quit when you feel like it."

José's heart began to pound in his chest, but he forced himself to sit quietly and look directly into Cisneros's eyes. "Another thing, Mr. Big-Shot, where will you get your heroin? We control distribution from the border to Houston. I'll see to it that you won't receive another gram. You can't decide to take a vacation from the organization whenever you want."

Cisneros leaned back in his chair and in a fatherly tone of voice, said, "I have big plans for you, José."

"I'm sorry, Arturo. I appreciate your concern, but my decision is final. The organization will have to find another delivery boy."

"As soon as I report this to my superiors, it's out of my hands. I won't be able to protect you. My boss may decide to cut your balls off."

José's jaw dropped. He was temporarily dazed by Arturo's threat. With his courage faltering, he blurted out, "I'll kick the habit! I won't need your heroin anymore after the field tests."

"Ha! That's a good one. You're hooked, kid, I made sure of that."

"Martin Leary said he'd help me find a good rehab program in another state after the tests are completed." As soon as he spoke, he knew he had made a serious blunder.

"Oh, now I'm beginning to see what's happened here. You little bastard! You talked with your Connecticut friend about me, and about the deliveries. That wasn't smart, Acuna. I'd better have a little talk with—"

"I'm sorry, Arturo. I have to get back to work." José stood up and walked out of the restaurant. Arturo, stunned, couldn't believe the little shit had the balls to walk out on him. He frowned, and then slapped the table. Slowly, a sense of panic replaced the anger. He realized he'd be in deep trouble himself when he reported this defection to Santiago Rodriguez.

Arturo dreaded making the call to Rodriguez; he hated to admit to himself that he was afraid of the man. Rodriguez was an intimidating force. He looked more like a Scandinavian hit man, than a Mexican-American drug lord; he was tall and slender, with light skin and piercing gray eyes. Arturo expected that Rodriguez would rant and rave, and then order him to make sure the kid didn't become a loose canon by using more persuasive methods.

Rodriguez answered the phone with an abrupt, "Yeah." Arturo could visualize him sitting in his lounge chair smoking a cigar. Rodriguez's response to Arturo's report was calm, but firm. "You should've known better than to involve a college boy. I warned you. The kid knows too much about our Matamoros operation, and now I get a report that says he's got a big mouth. Es bastante malo, Cisneros. Your ass is on the line, man. I want this problem taken care of now! You got that? I don't want to hear any more about that kid, ever! Entiende?" Rodriquez gently placed the phone in its cradle. He lit his cigar, raised his chin and blew a smoke ring.

The silence on the other end of the line was deafening. Arturo just sat there, paralyzed, his mouth dry from fear. He continued to hold the telephone long after Rodriguez hung up. Arturo knew his superior had no patience for betrayal, but he hadn't anticipated that Rodriguez would order Acuna's termination. The reality of the order stunned him.

Arturo had been in the Mexican cartel for many years, but had never killed anyone, at least without a legitimate reason and he didn't consider this situation legitimate. He'd come to like Acuna. Arturo had no family of his own, and felt, in his own twisted way, like a father to the young man. Although reluctant to admit it to himself, Arturo was proud of José's academic accomplishments at the university. Arturo liked the kid, but the situation was out of his control now.

Arturo's thoughts slowly made the transition from fear to logic. He removed his hand from the phone, sat back in his chair. Logic told him that José would be on the defensive, and suspicious of any attempt to communicate with him. On the other hand, someone else could make the contact, and fulfill the directive from Rodriguez. Arturo decided that his brother-in-law, Sergio Dominguez, was the one person he could trust, and at the same time possessed the courage to kill. Arturo reached for the phone again, called Sergio and arranged to meet for a drink at Bustamonte's.

Arturo leaned forward, and whispered, "I've got a problem, Sergio. You know that student, Acuna, who's been going to Matamoros for me? He told me this morning that he can't make any more deliveries. He's been assigned new responsibilities with some damn university research project. When I told Rodriguez, he said the kid knows too much, and ordered me to take care of the situation right away.

"After I talked with Rodriguez, the bartender from La Panada called me. He said the little fuck had already talked too much. The kid got drunk and told some shit-head from Connecticut the address where he picks up my stuff." Arturo fidgeted and searched the eyes of his brother-in-law for some sign of understanding, or a show of sympathy for his predicament, but saw none. Sergio was in no hurry to respond to his brother-in-law. He sat quietly with his right hand surrounding a glass of beer. He sensed Arturo was stressed about what Rodriguez ordered him to do, and because of that his brother-in-law might need his services.

"So? What do you want from me?"

"Maybe you can think of a way to shut the kid up."

"Why waste time trying to shut him up? It sounds like he's already a pain in the ass. Get rid of him."

Arturo stared at Sergio. Although he was taken aback by the man's bluntness, he wasn't really surprised by his brother-in-law's response. Sergio had the disposition of an assassin. Arturo knew firsthand that his brother-in-law could be a mean son-of-a-bitch. He had to intervene a few times when Sergio abused his sister. After being dishonorably discharged from the Army, Sergio had signed on with an oil services company and joined the union. He quickly earned the reputation as a reliable, fearless, and ambitious "tough guy." When the Mexican cartel "appointed" Arturo to head up drug operations in Austin, he offered Sergio a job as his "assistant."

"Shit. You're probably right, Sergio. I've got to do something, or my life won't be worth a nickel." He remained quiet for a few moments. "But, I can't kill the kid, Sergio. I like him." He picked up his drink and swished it around while he thought. "How about if I pay you to get rid of him? From what my sister tells me, you can use the money."

Sergio responded with a straight face, "I've never killed a civilian."

Recalling that Sergio served as an explosives expert while in the Army, he asked, "How about you use your bomb making experience? Make a bomb, and mail it. That way, you can do it without facing the kid."

Sergio sipped his beer. "I don't like that idea, Arturo. Mailing a bomb is too risky." Sergio sat quietly while he wrestled with other alternatives. "How much can you pay me?"

"How about $10,000. I can't afford any more right now."

"Here's my deal: $10,000 now, $10,000 in six months, and I decide how I kill the kid. I don't want any interference from you, or anyone else."

Arturo pondered the proposal for few moments. He reached out to shake Sergio's hand and said, "It's a deal, man, but do it quick." Arturo added, "I'm gonna have to do something about that guy from Connecticut. If Acuna gave him the Matamoros address, the son of a bitch could be real trouble. He even told Acuna that he'd help him beat the addiction by getting him into drug rehab program."

"Why don't you call your Connecticut cousin and ask him to have a heart to heart talk with the guy, if you know what I mean?"

Arturo thought for a moment and said, "That's a good idea, Sergio. I'll call Luis tomorrow." Arturo asked a waitress for a piece of paper and pencil and wrote a list of pertinent information about Acuna; phone number, apartment address, and what little information he could remember about the precious metals project.

"Luis, how'd you like the stuff I sent?"

"It's the best, Arturo. I could sell a lot more if you can get it up here. But,

I wouldn't send the stuff UPS again. That's too risky."

"I had no choice, amigo. I'll tell the story sometime. Hey, I have a favor to ask. That gringo, Leary, the guy who delivered the stuff to you a while back, needs to be encouraged to keep his mouth shut." Arturo explained the situation regarding José and Martin, and concluded, "I'd like you to put the fear of God into Leary. It has to be convincing, Luis. I want the guy shitting in his pants, okay? Can you get on it right away?"

"For you, anything, Arturo. I'll drive up to Norwich this afternoon and do a little checking around. When I have a plan, I'll call. Don't worry, I'll take care of it."

With fake business cards in his pocket, Sergio Dominguez, alias Sergio Alverez, commercial Realtor, approached Space #2 of a four bay industrial building near the Austin airport. Sergio was dressed the part: coat and tie, shined shoes, briefcase, horned rimmed glasses, and a wig. The leasing agent had been reluctant to provide Sergio with information about the space Martin rented in the name of the Precious Metals Extraction Corporation, but relented when Dominguez lied and convinced him he represented a well-known Austin business enterprise. Sergio also made sure he intimidated the agent by standing only a few inches away from his face, when he talked with him.

Sergio found an unlocked door next to a large retractable garage door and entered. He observed a young man and woman installing what looked like plastic pipe to a drum at the back end of a large flat bed trailer. A second man was working at a bench with his back to the door. All three heads turned when Sergio said, "Hello."

José Acuna, the one standing by the workbench, turned and asked the uninvited visitor, "This is secure area, sir. I'll have to ask you to leave."

Ignoring José's order, Sergio smiled broadly and walked toward José with his right hand outstretched. Sergio thought, *This must be the kid that Arturo described*. He handed José a business card. "My name is Sergio Alverez. I'm a commercial Realtor in the area. I'm looking for space for a client. Do you know if any of the tenants are vacating their units during the next few months?"

Taken aback by Sergio's brashness and puzzled by his question, José turned to look at his two associates, and shrugged. Both Pat Duncan and Sonja Hyde lifted their shoulders indicating that they too were unaware of any forthcoming vacancies. "I'm sorry, sir, we can't answer for the tenants in the other three bays. We've occupied this space for two months and don't know the other tenants. Our project should be completed by the end of this month and we intend to vacate this bay. Would that help?"

"It certainly would! Where're you moving to, if I might ask?"

"We plan to move the trailer to south Texas and run some tests," José explained.

"I'm from south Texas. Where in south Texas?"

"We'll tow it to a brine disposal plant near Elsa, a small town west of McAllen."

Sergio persisted. "What will the machine do?"

José began to show impatience with the stranger's interrogation. He turned toward his associates, and frowned. He turned back and said, "I'm sorry, sir, that information is proprietary and confidential."

"Who do you work for?"

Sonja Hyde walked over, stood beside José. "We're graduate chemical engineering students studying for our Ph.D.'s."

"I'm impressed. I don't think I've met a chemical engineer before. What did you say the machine would do when you're finished?"

José answered, "I didn't. I'm sorry, sir, the technology is proprietary. We can only tell you the machine is related to recovery of oil field waste."

"You're working with an oil company, is that it?"

"No. This project is privately funded. We're not affiliated with any of the oil companies."

"Sounds interesting." Sergio realized he wouldn't gain any more information, so he changed the subject. "Can you tell me how I can contact the leasing agent for the building? Do you have a phone number?"

José answered, "It's in the filing cabinet." He walked over to the file cabinet, pulled a folder from the top drawer, retrieved a business card and handed it to Sergio. "Please write down the information. That's the only card we have, and I need to call the leasing agent myself within the next few days."

Sergio pulled another of his own cards from his wallet and wrote down the pertinent information about the owner of the building on the back. He handed the agent's card back to José. "Well, I'd best be on my way. Thanks for the information. Good luck." With that Sergio shook hands with all three and left the building with a smug grin on his face.

Before meeting Arturo for lunch at Bustamonte's, Sergio picked up a map from Railroad Commission Headquarters in downtown Austin showing the location of brine disposal plants in south Texas.

"I checked a Railroad Commission map. There's a brine disposal plant near Elsa. It's called Hidalgo Disposal. I know where the place is, Arturo, but I don't know nothing about disposals."

Arturo was silent for a moment. "Who do we know in the oil business?

Maybe we could find out about the disposal plant by making a few phone calls."

"I know a brine hailer named Witnauer in Laredo. I'll bet he knows about the plant."

"Be careful what you say when you talk with this guy, Sergio. We don't want him asking questions later." Cisneros hesitated and added, "I think you'd better drive down to south Texas yourself and nose around."

"Okay. I'll drive over to Laredo on my way, and visit with Ed Witnauer."

Sergio hadn't talked with Ed Witnauer since he stopped working in the oil patch two years before, and hadn't visited the Laredo Trucking "field yard" for over five. Nonetheless, he was confident Ed would remember him. Sergio reflected on what the graduate students had told him about "moving the trailer to a brine disposal plant in Elsa." Based on that one tidbit, he fabricated a story he believed Ed would buy.

Ed was standing next to his wife's desk when Sergio entered. His office was in a run-down trailer he'd converted into an office. The interior hadn't been thoroughly cleaned in years. Documents, manuals and three ring binders were everywhere. Ed was an imposing figure for a man of 47 years; he looked as though he could play professional football any Sunday, without pads. He was as disheveled as his office; dirty shirt and Levi's, and work shoes stained by oil. He was not a handsome man; his mostly bald head seemed to conflict with a full beard that was beginning to show signs of gray.

Sergio reached out and said, "How ya doin', Ed?"

"I can't believe it. It's Sergio Dominguez." Ed shook Sergio's hand. "Are y'all still causing chaos in the oil patch?" Both men laughed.

Reaching out to shake Ed's wife's hand, Sergio said, "Hello, Edna. You're prettier than the last time I saw you." Edna had been a pretty young thing twenty years ago, but now she was an overweight, matronly woman.

"You're a liar, Sergio. But I love the compliment."

Ed asked, "Where've y'all been hiding?"

"I live up in Austin and run a legitimate business. I'm a commercial Realtor."

"Congratulations, Sergio! Now that y'all are finally doing something legit, what brings you to Laredo?"

Sergio pointed toward the yard and said, "It looks like you're still in the brine hauling business, Ed."

"Yeah. But if you have something else in mind, I'd like to hear about it. With the price of crude where it is, it's difficult to make a living."

Sergio explained that he'd been talking to a friend who wanted him to invest in a new chemical technology for separating waste oil from brine.

"It sounds like bullshit, Sergio. I've been hearing that kind of talk for years. But, tell me more."

"All I know is that they plan to run tests at a brine disposal plant in east Texas." Sergio said that he wanted to learn more about brine disposal operations before he made up his mind. "I've heard good things about Hidalgo Disposal. Do you know anything about the place?"

"Yeah. Owned by Roy DeWitt, a guy I've known for over ten years. He's one of the few honest people in south Texas. It's a big operation, Sergio. Roy runs two businesses at the same location: waste oil processing, and brine disposal."

"How often do your trucks dump at Hidalgo Disposal?"

"Every day. Texaco has production just northwest of the plant, and we have a contract to haul their brine. Why'd y'all ask?"

"I'll be in McAllen tomorrow. Could I ride with one of your drivers to look the place over? I don't have a reason to drop in unannounced."

"I have a better idea, Sergio. Edna can call Roy and ask if it's okay for you to visit."

While the two old friends reminisced, Edna made the arrangements for Sergio to visit with DeWitt's site manager, Ben Jack Randall.

Ed asked, "Where are y'all staying?"

"In Rio Grande City. Rosa still lives there most of the time. She doesn't want to move, so I keep a small apartment in Austin."

"Give me your current phone number in case there's a problem and we have to get in touch with you." Sergio gave Ed his listed number in Rio Grande City and his unlisted phone number in Austin.

Sergio slowed to five miles per hour because of the potholes. When he reached the top of the incline, he saw a tanker truck backed up to one of Hidalgo Disposal's brine pits. Brine was pouring out of the rear end of the truck directly into a concrete funnel-like structure, and from there, into a pit. Sergio smiled to himself when he recognized that the truck was one of Ed Witnauer's. *An interesting omen*, he thought. He stopped and studied the two buildings at the end of the dirt drive. It was obvious the smaller building had been a trailer at one time, because the wheels were still attached. Sergio guessed it was probably Ben Jack's office. The second building was a well-maintained mobile home with a fence around a children's play area.

Sergio parked his car in front of the trailer. Before he could exit, Ben Jack Randall appeared in the doorway of the trailer, and descended the steps. "I'll bet y'all are Sergio," he called out. "Old boy Witnauer's wife called yesterday and told me y'all would be comin' this mornin'."

Extending his hand, "Glad to meet you. Ben Jack, Thanks for agreeing to show me around."

"No problem. Want a Dr. Pepper?"

"Yeah, I sure could use one. It's a little dry and dusty."

"Let me give you the ten-cent tour." Ben Jack explained the purpose of the brine pits. "The brine goes from the last pit into that tank over there, and then pumped down to about 2000 feet. Shit, not much to it, Sergio. If there ain't been a lot of brine comin' in, we don't even need to turn on the injection pump. Regular gravity does most of it. I skim the waste oil off the top of the pits, and haul the stuff to them tanks over there." Pointing to a row of tanks off to his right, one of which was much larger than the other five.

The two walked further down the dirt drive toward the tanks. Ben Jack devoted more time explaining the waste oil operation because of the complexity of the plumping, and the need for constant chemical treatment, heating, testing, reheating, and re-testing.

On the way back to the office Sergio said, "Ed told me that you'd be testing a new technology in a few weeks. What's that all about, Ben Jack?"

"Shit, I don't know what the hell they're all doin'. All's I know is Roy's startin' some tests over there." Indicating a cleared area roughly halfway between the waste oil tanks and the pits. "Some college kids are doin' the testing."

Acting surprised, Sergio asked, "Really? How will it be set up, Ben Jack?"

"Don't know that either. I weren't part of it. Mr. DeWitt himself is in charge."

"Did Ed Witnauer tell you why I'm interested in your operation?" Sergio recounted his trumped-up story about possibly investing in a new technology that involved oil field waste. "Ed said you had the best operation in south Texas and suggested I come and see for myself."

Ben Jack smiled at the compliment and said, "I'll tell Mr. DeWitt."

"If it'd be okay with you, I'd like to walk over and take a look at the test site."

"Y'all go ahead. I've got to make a few calls. Stop in the office when you finish lookin' around."

Sergio paced off the distance from the back end of the first pit to the test site: 92 paces, about 270 feet. He quickly scanned the surrounding area for an elevated location that might make a good observation position. Selecting a spot, he mentally estimated the distance from the test site to the spot to be about half the distance of a football field. *I should be able to watch the action with a pair of binoculars,* he thought.

Sergio returned to the office. "Thanks, Ben Jack." He handed Randall a business card. "Let me know if I can help in any way. Take care."

"You too, Sergio." Turning, Ben Jack placed the card in his pocket without looking at it, and ascended the two steps that led into the trailer.

Satisfied that he had a clear mental picture of the physical layout of the disposal plant, Sergio left the Elsa area, and sped north toward Austin. He knew that he had to hurry; a few days earlier he'd observed surreptitiously that José and his two fellow students had completed the prototype and were preparing to move it. Sergio didn't want to leave anything to chance; he felt that if his plan was to work without a glitch, he needed to observe the move from start to finish.

# 15

MARTIN SHOWERED AND DRESSED in a sport shirt, shorts and deck shoes. He decided to skip breakfast and check out of the Harlingen motel before 6:30 A.M. He placed his suitcase and briefcase in the truck of the rental car and began the twenty-mile drive to the Hidalgo Brine Disposal Plant. Martin tuned the car radio to one of the few English language stations in south Texas, Brownsville's KMEX news radio. At the conclusion of the regular early morning newscast, the weatherman gave the forecast for September 27; he expected it to be a hot one. The temperature in south Texas had already reached the mid-seventies, and the forecaster predicted it would climb into the mid-nineties by noon. Martin Leary shook his head. Temperatures should be going down in late September, not up.

Martin stopped at a combination service station/general store to gas up in the small village of Elsa. While waiting for the attendant to complete his "full serve" tasks, Martin scanned the area surrounding the station. Except for a very tall grain elevator across the highway, and a group of rail cars amassed on a siding waiting to be loaded, the balance of the view featured a brown, desert-like terrain as far as the eye could see. It was broken only by the occasional smoke tree and a smattering of scrub brush. Martin shook his head. *Give me Connecticut over this place any day*, he thought.

Ten minutes after leaving the service station Martin found what he was looking for; a large sign that read 'Hidalgo Disposal' in blue letters on a white background. This would be Martin's third visit to the disposal since he invested in the Precious Metals Extraction Corporation the previous spring. Dr. Gerba had arranged the September 27 get-together to give Martin and

Roy an opportunity to witness, and then comment on the students' test regime before formal tests began. The disposal plant provided more than enough space to comfortably accommodate the prototype system that the students had moved from Austin two days earlier.

Martin turned into the gravel road and drove toward Roy's office trailer. Roy was sitting on a lawn chair in front of the trailer. A quick smile creased Martin's face when he recalled that Roy had been sitting in the exact same spot the last time he'd visited. Dressed in his usual attire, Roy wore pressed jeans, boots and a long sleeve shirt. As Martin opened the driver's side window, Roy stood and, with a grin on his tanned and weather-beaten face, said, "Welcome to God's country, Martin. Y'all want a cup of Ben Jack's Texas mud?"

Martin's smile turned into a frown when he opened the car door and encountered the all too familiar smell of crude oil. "Sure, I'll drink a cup of Ben's mud. It'll probably eat a hole in my stomach, but I'll risk it."

Ben Jack poked his head out of the office door. "Don't listen to that ugly old man, Martin. He don't know shit about making coffee." Martin could see that the friendship between Roy and Ben was similar to that of father and son relationship, rather than to employer and employee.

Ben Jack Randall was a unique and interesting character. With an ever-present plug of tobacco in his mouth, and dressed in a stained T-shirt and denim jeans with holes in the knees, he seemed to be the personification of the uneducated and opinionated redneck that Martin had often read about. Martin guessed that Ben was in his mid-twenties, and from the looks of his shoulders and arms, was probably as strong as an ox.

Ben lived with his wife and two preschoolers in a mobile home only a few dozen yards from the disposal pits. On a previous visit to the disposal, Ben told Martin he'd left school when he turned sixteen, and never looked back. Roy had met Ben when the latter worked at a local lumberyard. Roy was impressed with the young man's work ethic. In spite of his limited education, Roy hired Ben on the spot.

Martin sat down on a second lawn chair next to Roy. Roy asked, "Y'all run into much traffic driving in from Harlingen, Martin?"

"No. It's fairly light this time of the morning. The weatherman said it's supposed to reach into the mid-nineties today." He pulled a handkerchief from his pocket, and wiped his face. "This heat is not my cup of tea, Roy. We don't get this kind of weather in Connecticut in September. I'm sweating already."

"Yeah, but it's dry heat, Martin."

"Bull crap. It's hot, no matter how you cut it." The terrain around the disposal plant was bleak: flat, dry and dusty. Martin squinted, and then placed a hand over his eyebrows to shade the glare as he looked into a cloudless, bright blue sky. He lowered his eyes and observed Ben's children playing in the front yard of the mobile home, probably the only patch of green in miles.

Roy said, "Good reason for us to meet with José as soon as he's ready. After that, we can move into the air conditioned trailer and talk."

"When will Ely and José get here?"

"Ely won't arrive until mid-afternoon. He was asked to substitute for a sick faculty member this morning, and it's at least a three and a half-hour drive from Austin. He told me to go ahead without him. I expect José to drive up any time now."

Ben Jack reappeared in the doorway of the trailer holding two mugs in one hand. He descended the stairs and handed one to Martin declaring, "Here's the cup of Texas mud Roy talked about." Sarcastically he added, "Did y'all notice, I don't get no respect around here?"

Holding the coffee mug in his hand, Martin walked the short distance to the test site to observe how the students had set up the equipment. He estimated the trailer that held the prototype was about twenty feet long. A drum of some sort was bolted to the back end, and a water tank was bolted to the front end. Plastic pipe connected the tank to the drum. A centrifuge, that Dr. Gerba called a "spinner," had been placed on a stand a few feet from the trailer. More plastic pipe connected the drum to the centrifuge.

A workbench had been placed in front of the carport, undoubtedly positioned so José could observe the interaction between the centrifuge and the drum while he worked at the bench. Martin noticed a package on a laboratory bench wrapped in brown paper. He moved closer so he could see what it was, and saw that it was addressed to José Acuna, with a University of Texas return address.

Martin returned to the office trailer, and sat down again next to Roy. "We've come a long way, Roy. Watching that prototype operate is going to be exciting as hell. If it performs like José said it will, I don't think we'll have any trouble raising additional capital." Martin leaned back and was about to take another sip of coffee when he noticed a pickup truck reach the top of the rise, and navigate around the potholes as it moved toward the office trailer. "Is that José?"

"Yep. That's the pickup the kids rented." Looking at his watch, Roy said, "They're a little early. Probably want more time to set up the equipment. Those young people are conscientious."

As the pickup pulled up in front of Martin and Roy, Roy called, "Y'all are early, José."

Acuna answered through the open driver's side window. "Yes, sir. But we haven't eaten yet. Sonja and I are going to set up the equipment while Pat goes back into town and picks up breakfast for us. We should be ready in about an hour." Turning toward Martin, he said, "Morning, Martin. It's great that you could join us for the demonstration."

"It was a long way to come, but I wouldn't have missed it."

"Well, I guess we'd better get set up. I'll talk with you later."

As Martin watched the pickup drive off to the test site, he heard the distinctive sound of a diesel engine. "It sounds like we're about to have more company." A tanker truck reached the top of the incline, and moved toward the first pit, only about fifty feet from where Roy and Martin were sitting. As Martin and Roy watched the driver back the truck into position, flush up against the concrete, funnel-like structure and prepare to dump his load of brine, the pickup moved past them going the other way, back toward the Farm Road with Pat Duncan in the driver's seat.

The brine truck driver jumped down from his cab, waved and asked, "Roy, that road's getting worse. When're you gonna fix it?"

"I've got a grader coming over from McAllen tomorrow, Earl. We should have it fixed in a couple of days." The driver nodded, walked to the rear of the truck and opened a large valve. The concrete funnel directed the brine from the trailer into the first brine pit.

Martin smiled as he listened to the flowing brine water. The sound brought back a distant memory from his childhood: water being discharged from a fire hydrant in front of his home in Derby, Connecticut. Martin was about to comment on the long-ago memory of playing in the water when a *horrific explosion* almost threw him from his chair.

Sergio Dominguez watched impassively as the explosion threw Acuna backward, crashing his head into the front bumper of the pickup truck. Sergio was certain he saw an arm land in the grass a few feet from the torso. The force of the blast lifted the shed off its foundation and moved it a few feet, ending up on its side with the young woman still inside. Satisfied the explosive had done the job he was contracted to complete, Sergio yawned, stretched, returned the binoculars to the case, and, to prevent being seen, scurried in a crouched position back toward his vehicle.

Momentarily stunned by the severity of the noise, Martin put his hands over his ears, stood up, and turned toward the test site. He saw dust rising from the ground, and a funnel of smoke billowing up toward the sky. Ben Jack bolted through the front door of the office trailer smashing the door against the wall, jumped over the steps, all the while shouting, "Call 911. Call 911." He and Earl, the truck driver, were halfway to the site of the explosion before Martin and Roy could react.

## ELSA

Ben found Acuna sprawled on the ground in front of the pickup truck, minus his right arm. He checked for a pulse and found that he was still alive, but his heart was working overtime, pumping blood through the shoulder stump directly onto the sandy soil. In a knee jerk like reaction, Ben yelled to Roy to go back to the office and grab the first aid kit. After he said it, he thought, *That ain't gonna help.* There wasn't anything in a first aid kit that could stop bleeding like that.

Earl ripped off his shirt, handed it to Ben, who began to wrap the shoulder. José stopped breathing. Ben Jack quickly began mouth-to-mouth resuscitation. After many exhausting minutes, he asked Martin to check for a pulse. "Nothing," was the response. In spite of that pronouncement, Ben resumed the resuscitation. After a few more exhausting minutes, Martin tapped Ben on the shoulder, and mumbled, "He's gone, Ben."

Martin looked down at the battered body of his young friend; José's right arm lay to the right of his body, and his head was tilted to one side like a rag doll. His face looked as if it had been barbecued. Tears began to roll down Martin's cheeks. Martin felt dizzy and sick to his stomach. He placed his hand over his mouth, moved off to the side, and threw up. When he recovered, he asked excitedly, "Where's Sonja?" The men quickly realized that she must be in the shed. Martin dropped to his knees and looked through the door. Sonja was lying in a heap against the back wall, unconscious. He crawled in next to her and felt for a pulse. Her pulse was strong and she seemed to be breathing without any difficulty. Martin backed out, stood and said, "Sonja's unconscious. I think she's okay, but we probably shouldn't attempt to move her until the paramedics arrive and they can check her over."

Martin returned to stand by José's body. As he stared at his dead friend, all sorts of disjointed images began to flash though his mind. He recalled José's infectious laughter while they were in Matamoros. He vividly recalled the agony on José's face when he admitted that he was addicted to heroin, and his plea for help.

Martin turned around, and asked Roy if he had anything to cover the body. Without comment, Ben walked the short distance to his house, and returned with a blanket and a clean shirt for Earl. Martin said, "Thanks" in a voice that was lifeless.

A paramedic vehicle suddenly shot over the top of the rise, caromed over the potholes, and sped in the direction of the office trailer. Ben Jack ran toward the vehicle waving his arms indicating they should turn and head for the test site. One paramedic worked feverishly to revive José. The second medic dropped to his hands and knees, and crept into the shed. A few minutes later he backed out holding onto Sonja's hand as she slowly crawled forward. "Be careful, she's still groggy." Martin and Ben Jack each grasped an arm, helped Sonja to her feet and then led her to a chair next to the ambulance.

After several minutes Sonja was able to look up, and ask, "What happened?" Martin knelt down in front of her. He explained that something had exploded, and José was dead.

She stared into Martin's eyes, obviously not comprehending what she'd just been told. Her eyes moved away from Martin's, and settled on José's body. She covered her mouth with her hand, and screamed, "Oh my God!"

The paramedics practically lifted her into the vehicle. They placed a pillow under her head and covered her with a blanket. "She may have a concussion, so we're going to take her to the hospital in McAllen where they can examine her more closely." They radioed the appropriate authorities, re-stowed their gear, and drove off with lights flashing.

Ben Jack asked, "What'a we do now?"

Martin knelt down next to José's body. "I'm not leaving José until the medical examiner arrives."

Within minutes, a pickup truck with a "Texas Railroad Commission" sign on the door, raced over the dirt road toward the site of the explosion. Daryl Burkhardt and Joel Albright jumped out. Daryl ordered, "I'm sorry, but I have to ask you to leave the immediate area until we can test the air. Please, leave now, there may be toxic substances floating around."

Martin said, "Before you jump to any conclusions, I suggest you talk with Dr. Ely Gerba in Austin. He can tell you if they were using any harmful chemicals."

"Okay, I'll call him after we test the air. Please leave the area, now!" Martin, Roy, Earl and Ben Jack quickly moved off toward the office. Joel retrieved a gas detection instrument from the truck and tested the quality of the air within the immediate vicinity of the field lab. After a few tense moments, he announced that the readings were normal. Daryl called out to the others that the air was okay, and walked over to where Martin, Roy and Ben Jack were standing.

"Sorry for the abrupt entrance, Roy. We had to check air quality before we did anything else. The air is fine." He nodded toward Ben, and extended his hand toward Martin. "I'm Daryl Burkhardt with the Railroad Commission."

"Martin Leary."

"Roy, can you get me Dr. Gerba's phone number? I'll call him now."

Earl stowed his gear, climbed into his truck cab and started the engine. Roy walked over to the truck and asked him not to say anything about the accident until the Railroad Commission could determine the cause. As Earl drove off, the others stood next to the trailer wondering what to do next.

The medical examiner was the last to arrive. He completed his investigation and photographed the scene from many different angles. Martin inquired about what he intended to do with the body, and was informed that an autopsy was mandatory after an accidental death. The body would remain in the County morgue in McAllen until the post mortem was completed. Acuna's body was delicately bagged, and loaded into a van.

Daryl Burkhardt didn't pull any punches when he talked with Dr. Gerba. When Daryl finished describing what had happened, Gerba's skin tightened, his eyes filled with tears, and his mouth turned dry. He had difficulty speaking.

"Dr. Gerba, did you hear me?"

Gerba mumbled in barely audible voice, "Yes." He sighed. "I can't talk right now. I'll call back." Ely placed the phone in its cradle and slumped in his chair. After a few moments he lifted his slender, but imposing 6'2"-frame, out of the chair and walked over to the window. He stood for a few minutes, but there wasn't any room in his mind to appreciate the view. He placed his hand on his chin and then moved it up to his forehead. He felt for the edge of his receding hairline, thinking, *Middle-age has finally caught up with me.* When Ely's mind began to clear, he moved back to his desk, reached for the phone and dialed the number for Hidalgo Disposal.

Ben Jack Randall answered on the first ring. "Hidalgo Disposal."

"Ben Jack, it's Dr. Gerba. Is Roy still with that fellow from the Railroad Commission?"

"Yes, sir, Dr. Gerba."

"I need to talk with Roy. Please ask him to come to the phone."

Ely heard Ben Jack go to the door of the office, and announce, "Mr. DeWitt, Dr. Gerba's on the phone."

Roy DeWitt responded immediately. He followed Ben into the office and grabbed the phone. "I'm here, Ely."

"Please fill me in on what happened. Then, tell the Railroad Commission investigator I'm ready to talk."

Daryl radioed the Railroad Commission office in Corpus Christi. "Darlene, this is Daryl. Can you patch me through to Inspector Jenkins?"

"Hold on, Daryl. He's here in the office, but he's on the phone."

"I'll hold. It's important." Daryl leaned against the door of his truck. He was dressed in a long sleeve shirt, creased jeans, and boots. As he waited he focused his attention on Roy DeWitt's six waste oil tanks, approximately 100 yards beyond the site of the explosion. The tanks, painted in the owner's special colors, appeared to be undamaged. He shifted his eyes back to his left and watched the arrival of Sergeant Joe Godfrey and Dave Collins from the Sheriff's Department. They parked next to the office trailer, and immediately began talking with Martin, Roy, and Ben Jack. Burkhardt straightened as he heard Jenkins pick up the phone.

"Daryl, was anyone else injured?" asked Chief Inspector Jenkins. Jenkins was in charge of the Southern Region of the RRC, with offices in Corpus Christi.

"Yes. A young girl colleague of Acuna's was knocked unconscious. The paramedics took her to the hospital in McAllen. It sounds like she'll be okay."

"Describe what's happening now, Daryl."

"Joe Godfrey and Dave Collins just arrived and are talking with Roy, Ben Jack and one other gentleman who I hadn't met before. I'm sure Sergeant Godfrey is as puzzled as I am about what the hell happened. We both suspect the explosion resulted from the accidental ignition of a gas. Were you aware that U.T. graduate students were running tests of a new chemical technology?"

"Roy told me a few weeks ago he planned to run some tests to determine the chemical composition of the brine hauled into his plant, but he didn't say anything about testing a new technology."

"Well, it may go beyond that, Travis. I just got off the phone with a chemistry professor at the university up in Austin. His name is Dr. Ely Gerba. He told me the students were preparing to run a test of a chemical process that removes precious metals from brine."

"Are you talking about gold and silver, and regular oil field brine?"

"Yes, sir. That's what he told me. Not only gold and silver, but platinum, palladium, and that whole group."

"Jesus! I've never heard of such a thing. Have you been able to determine the cause of the explosion?"

"No, but when Joel and I got out of the truck, we smelled an odor. Neither of us could make out what it was at first, but after talking with the professor, we think that gas from one of the metals might have ignited accidentally. According to the professor, removing the precious metals is a two-step process. Joel and I think the explosion might have occurred during the second step, when the student was attempting to separate a metal called osmium from the rest of the metals. A spark from the centrifuge could have ignited gas from an acid associated with the osmium."

"Osmium acid can be very poisonous, Daryl. Have you tested for toxins in the air?"

"We did. Joel tested the air and the readings are in the safe range."

"Good. Now let's get back to what you said about precious metals. I'm confused. What did you mean when you told me the students were attempting to separate the metals?"

"I'm confused too, Travis." Daryl repeated what Dr. Gerba had told him about separation process, then said, "When we talked with Roy, he said that he doubted the students could have had enough time to set up and run any tests this morning. He said they'd just arrived. They were at the test site for only about ten to fifteen minutes before it blew. It's a puzzler, Travis."

Concerned that the disposal plant itself might be damaged, Travis asked, "Are Roy's brine disposal and waste oil operations involved?"

"No, sir. The test site is at least 100 yards away, about in the middle, between the two. I can't see any connection."

"Good. When you finish, post a sign, and rope off the area to keep the curious away. Write up your findings in as much detail as you can, and bring your report to me in the morning. Tell Roy to shut down the test facility until further notice. In the meantime, I'm going to have a long talk with that chemistry professor in Austin."

After hanging up, Travis sat for a moment and thought through what Daryl had told him. He'd learned over the years to listen to his hunches, and he was beginning to have one now. He didn't feel comfortable with Daryl's preliminary conclusion that something had ignited a gas. He muttered, "There's more to this than meets the eye."

# 16

FEELING WEAK FROM SORROW and stress, Martin retreated to the office after the policemen left. He dropped down onto the first chair he encountered. A concern for the project began to creep into his consciousness and cause some anxiety. He tried to separate his sorrow over José's death from thoughts about the project, but found that he couldn't. Were the two inextricably connected? Was the explosion the result a chemical imbalance? Was it human error? Or, had something more ominous occurred?

Roy and Ben Jack joined him a few minutes later. The three sat quietly, consumed with their own thoughts. Martin leaned forward resting his elbows on his knees, and commented to no one in particular, "I haven't the slightest idea what caused that explosion." He sat back and pointed toward the test site. "All I know is that something very strange happened over there." He looked at Roy, and asked, "Could it have been the chemistry, Roy?"

"No. I'm confident there wasn't anything in the chemistry that could've caused that."

A few more minutes passed before Martin stood up, and said, "Someone has to tell Mrs. Acuna before she hears about the accident on TV, or reads about it in the newspaper. We can't just call her on the phone." Martin was silent for a few minutes. Then he stood up and declared, "One of us needs to tell her in person. I'll drive up to Corpus and tell her. How long would it take me to get there?"

"It's a two-hour trip, Martin. If you leave now, you should be there about noon. I'm sorry I can't go with you. I've got too much to do here."

"I'm useless here. I think I'll fly home from Corpus."

Martin stopped at a gas station just outside the city limits of Corpus Christi and called the real estate office where Mrs. Acuna worked. It was just after noon, only a few hours after the explosion. She wasn't at the office, so the receptionist suggested that Martin try her home phone. Instead of calling, he drove to 138 Staples Place, parked his car in front of the house, climbed the stairs to the front porch, and knocked.

"Martin Leary! What in the world are you doing here?"

"Hello, Rebecca. May I come in?"

Rebecca studied Martin's face, and noted the concern. She shivered, and a surge of fear ran through her body. "Is there a problem? Is José all right?"

"Rebecca, may I come in, please?"

For a moment Rebecca was paralyzed. Finally, she opened the screen door, and moved to the side to allow Martin to pass into the house, and directed him to the living room. Martin suggested, "Let's sit, Rebecca." Not removing her eyes from his, Rebecca attempted to sit, but bounced off the armrest before she finally settled into the seat. Martin sat in a chair opposite Rebecca. Tears formed in his eyes as he announced, "There was an accident at the test site. José is dead. He was killed instantly as the result of an explosion."

Rebecca Acuna's eyes glazed over. She slumped sideways in the chair and fainted. Pouncing out of his chair, Martin cried out, "Rebecca!" Not sure what to do, he rushed to the kitchen, found a dish towel tucked into the handle of the refrigerator, soaked it in cold water and returned to the living room. He placed the cold cloth on her forehead and stroked Rebecca's hand in an attempt to revive her.

Rebecca finally opened her eyes and looked at him, but without recognition. Realizing she was not yet fully conscious, he hastened to say, "Rebecca, it's Martin Leary. Can I get you a glass of water?"

"Oh! Martin. I'm sorry. I must have fainted." Remembering she had just been told her only son died, she lowered her head into her hands and wept.

Martin knelt, continuing to hold her hand, and pleaded, "Is there someone I can contact? A relative, a neighbor?"

Mumbling into her hands, Rebecca whispered, "Sylvia, next door."

"Which house, Rebecca?" Without another word, Rebecca pointed to her left. Martin quickly exited the house and sought the assistance of Sylvia Moscoso.

Rebecca attempted to lift herself out of the chair. Halfway out, she weakened and fell back, her head bouncing off the chair back. Surprised by her lack of strength, she looked at her hands, and then stared straight ahead.

Her vision, blurred by tears, slowly began to focus on the piano in the corner of the room. Her mind was momentarily flooded by the memory of José seated at the piano, laboriously practicing his lessons. Rebecca smiled and whispered, "Be patient, son. You'll get it next time." Her smile disappeared when she realized she would never see her son sit at the piano again, and began to weep uncontrollably.

Before Martin could complete his account on what had happened next door, Sylvia Moscoso dropped everything, hurried out of the house and ran across the front lawn to care for her friend. Like a top-sergeant, she assumed control of the situation immediately, ordering Rebecca to her bedroom, and telephoning the family's doctor. The latter agreed to call the local pharmacy, prescribe a sedative and arrange for its immediate delivery.

After delivering the crushing message of death to his young friend's mother, Martin felt helpless and discombobulated. He could only pace back and forth in the living room while Sylvia moved from one room to another, caring for Rebecca. Interrupting one of Sylvia's trips from the bedroom to the kitchen, Martin said, "Mrs. Moscoso, it appears you have command of the situation. Is there anything I can do for you before I leave?"

"No, thank you, Mr. Leary. I'll stay here with Rebecca for a few days. I know who to call if I need help."

"Does Rebecca have any family in Corpus?"

"No. There was just the two of them, José and his mother. She'll miss him terribly. Rebecca's been a widow for over sixteen years. The only relatives are cousins of her late husband, and they live in Monterrey, Mexico. She hasn't communicated with them for over ten years."

"When Rebecca feels better, tell her that I'll arrange for someone to collect José's things from his apartment, and ship them." He paused and said, "I'm glad you're here to take over, Mrs. Moscoso." They both moved toward the front door, and again tears blurred Martin's vision. "Please tell Rebecca again how sorry we all are about her son. José was my friend."

Martin returned the rental car to the Corpus Christi Airport. He had to pay an extra charge because he'd rented the car in Harlingen, but he didn't care; he just wanted to go home. Martin bought a ticket on a Southwest flight leaving for Houston in two hours, and then called Bill Davis from a pay phone.

Bill was sitting at his desk preparing for an upcoming executive committee meeting at Standard Insurance of Hartford when his secretary announced Martin Leary was on the phone. Bill picked up, and in a lighthearted voice asked, "How'd the demonstration go?"

Martin didn't respond to the question. Instead, he announced, "There was an explosion, and José Acuna was killed."

## ELSA

Bill slumped in his office chair. "Come on, Mart, don't kid around."

"I'm not, Bill. José is dead!"

"Shit!" The two friends were speechless for a few moments. Martin broke the silence. "I just left José's mother. I had to tell her that her only son was killed. That was the toughest thing I ever did. She was devastated." Martin paused to regain his composure. "We were sitting outside the trailer waiting for José to set up for the demonstration when something exploded. I thought my eardrums had burst." Martin described the scene of the accident and the condition of the body. "It was awful. I'm sure I'll have nightmares."

Martin adopted a different tone of voice. "We need to talk about the project. I'm concerned. I'm flying back to Connecticut this afternoon. Can we meet at the River Inn for dinner and talk about it?" Martin could hear Bill check with his secretary.

"I could meet you at the inn about 7:00."

"I'll make it. Please ask your secretary to call Shirley. I don't want to go through the details of the explosion again. Tell her I should be home before eleven, and not to worry. I'll call her when I arrive in Hartford to let her know how I'm doing."

Bill hesitated, took a deep breath, and said, "I'm sorry if I appear to be an unfeeling bastard, Mart, but my insurance background forces me to ask a tough question. Is the project adequately insured?"

Martin said he thought it was, but maybe it'd be a good idea to check. "Why don't you call the agent who wrote the policy? You'll ask the right questions. Hold on a minute. I've got the agent's number in my briefcase."

In spite of not having eaten all day, the thought of airport food was not very appealing to Martin. He browsed in the gift shop and selected a current issue of a news magazine. He walked slowly to the boarding area as if in a trance, and found a vacant seat. He tried to read, but found that he couldn't concentrate. Thinking a little exercise might help him settle down, he began to pace from one end of the terminal to the other. He even considered walking outside, but it was too damned hot. He gave up on the exercise idea, and just sat and brooded. The aching sorrow about José's death was slowly being pushed aside by anxiety.

The business opportunity he'd been counting on might have just slipped away. Was he too old for another chance to "grab the brass ring"? Probably! He attempted to think of ways to salvage the project, but couldn't. He knew that additional funds would be needed to continue development, but reasoned that no one in their right mind would risk investing capital in a venture with a tainted track record. More to the point, what was the likelihood he'd recover his own investment of $50,000? *Not very high*, he thought. He muttered to no one in particular, "Shit!"

Martin began to wring his hands. He stood up and renewed his pacing, then stopped abruptly. What about the status of the investments of friends and business associates he'd solicited? Would Shirley and he be personally liable for any losses? Could the investors claim he was fiducially negligent, and sue? How should he protect myself? Martin decided he'd better visit with attorney Tom Hardin first thing in the morning. Tom was familiar with the precious metals extraction project because Martin had asked him to review and comment on the original business plan eight months earlier. His suggestions had been well received by Dr. Gerba, and he was asked to assist with the preparation of an investment prospectus. Tom had been cash poor at the time, or he would have invested along with the other individuals Martin solicited.

The River Inn, located in Haddam, was approximately halfway between Martin's home in Norwich and Bill's home in Farmington. The main dining room, perched above the east bank of the flowing waters of the Connecticut River, provided patrons with a wonderful view of the river, and, during certain times of the year, spectacular sunsets. As he drove into the parking lot, Bill could see that a red hue was beginning to steal into the sky, and hoped that this would be one of those sunsets.

The maître d' greeted Bill when he entered the lobby. "Good evening, Mr. Davis. It's good to see you again." William Stone Davis was still a handsome man at age 61. Although he'd lost most of his hair and put on a little weight, he could still turn a few female heads. "Will Mr. Leary be joining you for dinner?"

"Yes, Ed. I expect him in about ten minutes."

"May I show you to your table, or would you prefer to wait in the lobby?"

"I think I'd rather sit at the table and watch the sunset. It's developing into a beauty."

Fifteen minutes later Ed ushered Martin to the table and provided both men with menus. After exchanging pleasantries, Martin tried to relax and enjoy the pink and red sunset unfold before his eyes. But, it had been a long and stressful day. He turned away from the view, and looked at his friend. "Normally, I'd never tire of that view, but I can't appreciate it tonight. I'm sad and tense all at once. I feel like I could snap any moment."

Bill kept his eyes riveted on Martin as he listened to an expanded account of the Elsa tragedy. Bill interrupted only when he needed clarification of a crucial point. Martin was exhausted when he finished. He looked at his watch and said, "I'm sorry. I didn't mean to ramble so long. I guess I needed to talk." Martin reached for a cup of coffee a waitress had silently placed before him, and asked, "What did the insurance guy say when you called him?"

"Gibson assured me that the project is adequately covered. He said the policy Gerba negotiated covers accidents like the Elsa calamity. Unless the courts find that someone was criminally negligent, we're adequately covered." Bill paused, drank a sip from his of coffee cup, and continued. "Gibson asked a question I couldn't answer. Do we have an independent appraisal of Gerba's chemistry? If we don't, he suggested we contract for one right away."

As Martin pondered that question, he nervously drummed his fingers on the table. "I'm not aware of any independent appraisals. I doubt that anyone even thought about an appraisal."

"If we don't have an appraisal, Gibson believes we should take defensive measures to protect ourselves."

"Isn't that like closing the barn door after the horse left?" Martin asked.

"Maybe yes, maybe no," Bill responded. "It might be smart to have our own arm's length appraisal of the chemistry as well as the test regime, so that we can develop a defensive posture, if needed. If some aspect of the field test design is found to be faulty, or the technology is inherently risky in the opinion of the Railroad Commission, the Sheriff's Department, or an attorney retained by the young man's family, we could be declared liable for his death. An appraisal may also determine if we should continue development, or lick our wounds and walk."

Martin considered Bill's assessment of the situation, frowned and said, "I'll call Roy DeWitt tomorrow and ask his opinion. I should call him anyway, and get an update on what the Railroad Commission intends to do. Investigators were still at the site when I left. The RRC may decide to shut down the project until they know exactly what happened."

The two friends talked until after 8:30 P.M. Bill looked at his friend and said, "You must be exhausted, my friend. Go home and get a good night's sleep. I'll call you before lunch tomorrow."

# 17

LUIS CALDERA MEANDERED PAST Martin's office building a few times before crossing the street to study the old mansion from a different angle. There was only one sign by the front entrance, so he concluded that Leary's business was probably the sole occupant of the building. He sat on a concrete wall across the street and patiently watched the comings and goings for over an hour. As he watched, he hatched a plan. But, to make it work, he'd have to know the exact location of Leary's office inside the building.

Luis called Leary Realty from a pay phone, and was told by Claire Wilson that Martin Leary would not be in the office today, but he was expected back in the morning. Knowing he wouldn't encounter Leary, Luis entered the front door, and confidently sauntered up to Claire's desk. He introduced himself as Luis Sanchez, a Realtor from Groton.

"I'm sorry you missed Martin, Mr. Sanchez. I'm sure if you call tomorrow you'll be able to arrange a convenient time to meet with him."

"Thank you, Miss Wilson." Luis turned toward the front door, and acting as if he remembered something, turned around and said, "Say, one of my associates told me about the history of this marvelous building. He suggested that I ask to see Mr. Leary's office. Since he's not here, could I take a peak?"

"Certainly, Mr. Sanchez. Mr. Leary is very proud of his office." While the two stood by the office door exchanging small talk, Luis was evaluating the quality of the alarm system, especially the wired connections to the windows. Satisfied he could break in without being detected, he turned his attention to the décor of the office. The room was large for an office, approximately twenty foot square. An elaborate fireplace featuring an ornate dark mahogany mantel extended from the door to far right wall. A large grandfather clock dominated the wall to the left of the entrance door. Claire explained that the furnishings were primarily antiques acquired by Martin's wife over the past few years. Luis's eyes were drawn to Martin's elaborate desk facing the fireplace. "That's quite a desk. I haven't seen one that large before. My friend was correct; it's definitely a unique office. Well, I'll let you get back to work. Thank you for allowing me to see the office."

The following morning, Martin entered the building through the back entrance, and was greeted warmly by Claire. "Welcome back, Martin. We were very sorry to hear about the death of your young friend. It must have been a traumatic experience. Are you okay? Is there anything we can do?"

"Thanks, Claire. There isn't anything anyone can do, except maybe pray for José's mother. She's the one that will suffer the most. I may be a little preoccupied for a few days, but have patience. It's good to be home. Any important phone calls?"

"You had a few. The messages are in your box. Oh, and a Mr. Sanchez stopped by yesterday to see you."

"Who stopped by?"

"A Mr. Sanchez, a Realtor from Groton. I assumed you knew him."

"Nope. Never heard of the guy. Well I guess I'd better get to work." Martin moved toward his office, opened the door, took two additional steps and cried out, "My God!" A six-inch dagger protruded from the center of his mahogany desk like a beacon. His face turned ashen. He stumbled and nearly fell.

Claire jumped up, and in five strides was standing by his side. "The window's open, is that... Oh my God." She moved to the desk and said, "There's a note under the knife!" Martin joined her by the desk and he read the note aloud.

> *This shows I can get to you whenever and wherever I want. Mind your own business when you're in Texas, and keep your mouth shut about Acuna's heroin problem and the deliveries. If I find out you talked with anyone, you'll hear from me. It'd be a shame to see this beautiful building go up in smoke.*

Claire and Martin looked at each other. Claire broke the silence. "Call the police, Martin."

"No. I don't want to involve the police yet. I need time to think this through." He took a handkerchief out of his pocket, carefully removed the dagger and placed it and the note in a desk drawer. "I know you don't agree with me, Claire, but I don't want you to say anything to anyone about this.

This is to remain our secret, until I tell you otherwise."

Martin suggested Claire find a blotter to put over the hole, and go back to work as if nothing had happened. He closed the office door when she left, and began to pace back and forth considering his options. He concluded that he didn't have many. The best he could do right now was to think of something else, so he picked up the phone and called Roy DeWitt.

While Martin waited for Roy to come to the phone, he visualized the man moving his ballooning body from one chair to another to take the call. Middle age was not doing Roy any favors; he had a considerable paunch, probably from too much beer, and a balding head. The ever-present cowboy boots and starched jeans made Roy look like an overweight Texas stereotype.

"When did y'all get back to Connecticut, Martin?"

"About 6:00 yesterday afternoon." Martin sighed and asked, "Is there anything I can do?"

"No, I don't believe so, but thanks for asking. There isn't much more that anyone can do. I don't know about you, but I'm still numb."

"I'm a walking zombie, Roy. I didn't get much sleep last night. I even bumped into my bedroom door this morning." His lip began to quiver. "José was such an exceptional young man. I'll miss him." Both men remained silent for a few moments, lost in their own thoughts.

Roy broke the silence. "Investigators from the Railroad Commission didn't stay long after y'all left yesterday. I expect things will be quiet this morning, thank God."

"Do the investigators have any theories?" Martin asked.

Roy responded that the cause of the explosion was still in doubt. However, the RRC suspected that the accidental ignition of osmium gas might have been the culprit. "I'm beginning to believe the RRC theory that there must have been some sort of gas leak. Shit, I just don't know." He said that he had talked with Ely last night, and Ely was incredulous.

Martin summarized the conversation he'd had with Bill Davis, and about the question of whether there'd been an outside appraisal of the chemistry. Roy said he was unaware of any appraisals, and asked, "Y'all are not suggesting José died because of some flaw in the chemistry, are you?"

"Yes, that's exactly what we're suggesting. We're concerned that the Railroad Commission, the Sheriff's Department, or an aggressive attorney retained by Rebecca Acuna, may uncover some flaw in the chemistry and claim it caused the explosion, and José's death. We could be charged with criminal negligence if it's proven we should've known about the problem. I know this may sound paranoid, but our insurance doesn't cover us if we are found to be criminally negligent. You're an expert when it comes to brine and oil field waste, but you're not a chemist. Were you present at any of the lab tests, or analyses?"

"No."

Martin moved forward in his chair and placed his elbows on the desk. "Even if you had been present, would you have been qualified to evaluate Gerba's work? I know I wouldn't. When Ely told me about his extraction technology last January, I never thought to question the chemistry. I wasn't qualified. Just like you, I was impressed with the business opportunity. But, I only saw dollar signs." Martin paused, and sat back in his chair. "I'm beginning to believe you and I may have screwed up. We should've arranged for an arm's length appraisal of the chemistry, before we solicited investors."

"Y'all are overreacting. Ely's chemistry is solid. An appraisal would have been a waste of money."

"Okay, you may be right. But let's look at it another way. We came to the table with credibility. We served as the information conduit between Ely and the investors." Martin explained that the investors relied on their recommendations regarding project goals and business potential, and on their knowledge and understanding of the technology. "If one of the investors gets suspicious, or pissed, and then retains a chemist who finds a problem that we should have known about, we could be in deep trouble."

"I'm not worried about having misrepresented the technology, and I have a problem paying for an appraisal now. It's too damn late in the day. Besides, we can't make it appear we don't trust Ely."

"I trust Ely. But people make misstates, Roy, even chemistry professors. I plan to make discreet inquiries on my own to see if I can find a qualified and well-respected chemist to evaluate the technology. Please don't say anything to Ely about my concerns. I'm coming back down to Texas again as soon as I can break away. I want to talk with both of you together."

Martin left his building and walked the short distance to Tom Hardin's office. Tom ushered Martin into a conference room, and closed the door. "Okay, Mart, start from the beginning, and don't leave anything out."

Martin described in detail the situation at the disposal plant before, during and after the explosion. Tom watched the tears well up in Martin's eyes as he relived the heartache and sorrow. Martin finally was able to set aside the subject of José's death, and address his concern for the project. "Roy just told me that the Railroad Commission may shut us down until they can determine what caused the explosion. If that happens, I don't know when, or if, we'd be able to restart. Based on what I heard this morning, I'm pessimistic. My main concern now is my personal liability. Can the investors I solicited come back and claim I'm personally responsible for their losses if the project goes in the tank?"

"From what you've told me, I'd say no. But, I can't give you a firm answer today. I'll have to reread the prospectus, talk with my associates, and research securities law. In the meantime, don't worry. We'll work it out."

# 18

DICK HAMMIL, ATTORNEY FOR the Precious Metals Extraction Corporation, was a discouraged man when he initiated a scheduled telephone conference. When all the parties were connected—Ely Gerba, Roy DeWitt, Martin Leary and Jim Robinson—Dick bluntly announced, "Everything's come to a screeching halt, gentlemen. The Railroad Commission just issued a 'cease and desist' order. They are demanding that PMEC discontinue further tests of the new technology until the Commission completes a thorough investigation of the accident, and an evaluation of the chemistry. They even socked us with a $5,000 fine."

Martin practically shouted, "A $5,000 fine? What the hell for?"

Ely answered, "For conducting chemical tests at an oil field waste disposal site without a permit. I paid the damn $5,000 fine, but Dick plans to appeal."

After a prolonged discussion of options, the participants concluded that only one option made sense; vigorously appeal the ruling. The appeal would maintain that brine, when employed as a raw material in the precious metals extraction application, should not be classified as a waste product. Since the RRC had no jurisdiction over raw materials other than oil, the cease and desist order was invalid, and the $5,000 fine was, therefore, unjustified.

Ely said, "Looking at the bright side, the situation's not as bad as I originally thought. The direct financial loss is actually less than I expected. Except for a few minor repairs, the prototype survived unscathed. If it weren't for that damned $5,000 fine, the financial loss would have been fairly modest, considering what happened. My main concern now is that the RRC may want us to unveil the fundamentals of the technology. I'm reluctant to do that."

Martin asked, "Where's the prototype now?"

Roy answered, "I moved it off the site the day after the explosion. It'll remain locked up in my garage until we determine what to do next."

Martin asked, "When will you file the appeal, Dick? And when do you think the RRC will schedule a hearing to consider the appeal?"

"I'll file the appeal tomorrow. I'm sorry to have had to report bad news, but that's the way it is. I guess that does it for now. I'll be back in touch as soon as I hear something."

Ely placed the phone in its cradle, turned his desk chair toward the window and stood up. His mind was centered on the possibility the Railroad Commission would ask him to reveal the confidential elements of the technology. He mumbled to himself, "What will happen if I refuse?"

"Ely, got a minute?" Ely spun around and saw John Bower, the President of the University of Texas at Austin, standing by the door.

"John! What a pleasant surprise. Please come in."

"I don't think you'll feel that way when I'm finished, Ely. I just left an emergency meeting of the board of trustees. Press reports of the tragedy in south Texas have connected the university with your precious metals project. The trustees are hopping mad. They see it as a potential scandal that could involve the university.

"When I approved your request a few months ago to establish a business incubator to pursue commercialization of the technology, I never envisaged it could lead to the death of one of our best and brightest doctoral students. The board has instructed me to inform you that unless you can prove, unequivocally, that the technology was not responsible for the death of that young man, you can expect a strong reprimand.

"We've known each other a long time, Ely. You've been a credit to this university. But, this new development is a serious matter. It's conceivable you could lose tenure, and be terminated."

Ely could feel his heart pound in his chest, while beads of sweat began to form on his forehead. This ultimatum was certainly not expected. He responded defensively. "José Acuna's death has caused me much pain, John. He was a young man with great potential. It would be a terrible irony if he were killed as a result of a flaw in the technology he helped develop. Please understand, there isn't any firm evidence our technology caused the explosion. Chief Inspector Jenkins of the Railroad Commission has cooled to the original theory that the explosion was caused by the accidental ignition of osmium gas. But, in spite of Jenkins's opinion, we still don't know what did cause the explosion. I hope and pray it was not our technology."

"For your sake, and for the reputation of this institution, I'll pray with you, Ely. Keep me posted." With that President Bower turned on his heels and walked out down the hallway.

Daryl Burkhardt worked most of the evening to complete his report. He left his home in Falfurrious early the following morning and drove to the district offices of the Railroad Commission in Corpus Christi to deliver his report to Chief Inspector Jenkins.

"Thanks for expediting the report, Daryl."

"I gave it my best shot, Travis, but I'm beginning to question my own findings. I'll be interested to hear your opinion after you read it."

"Why don't you come back here around noon. I should be finished by then. We can have lunch together and talk about it."

Travis held Daryl's report in both hands long after he finished reading it. He kept staring at it until his vision began to blur. His mind, however, was clearly focused on what the report said, or rather, on what it didn't say. He didn't agree with Daryl's conclusion that the ignition of osmium gas was the cause of the explosion. While he couldn't ignore the fact that Daryl had smelled gas when he arrived at the site of the explosion, a small field lab couldn't produce the amount of gas needed to support an explosion of that magnitude. Even if osmium gas had escaped somehow, Travis believed the gas would've dissipated rapidly. To support this reasoning, Travis could point to Daryl's measurements of air quality within fifteen minutes of the explosion; not a trace of gas. Everything appeared to be in the normal range.

One other item in the report distressed him even more: the centrifuge and the field lab were separated by more than four feet. How could a spark from the centrifuge ignite a gas four feet away? There had to be a large concentration of gas for that to happen, and because the operation was outside, that possibility was unlikely.

Travis walked down the hall to confer with the district's staff attorney, Judy Thompson. "Got a minute, Judy? I need your advice."

"Certainly, Travis. For you, I have plenty of time. I was just reviewing a landowner complaint. It can wait."

"I'm sure you've heard about the explosion down in Hidalgo County."

"Yes. I saw the distraught mother being interviewed on TV this morning. I cried, Travis. What a tragedy! Why do you ask?"

"I sent my two best men to investigate, and they concluded it was an accident, an explosion of osmium gas. But after reviewing their report, I don't feel comfortable with that finding. I sense foul play, Judy. I think we should make a formal request for local law enforcement to reopen the investigation. What do you think?"

"Damn, that's heavy stuff, Travis. Can you trust the law enforcement people down there? They don't have the best reputation for ethical behavior."

"I know, Judy, but I trust Tony Zedillo, the Sheriff of Hidalgo County. He's a good man. Given the political constraints he faces in that county, he tries his best and does a decent job." Travis smiled, and added, "Unless the explosion was perpetrated by some county official, I trust he will tell me straight."

"Why do you suspect foul play, Travis? Are you suggesting the college student was murdered?"

Jenkins hesitated, "I can't answer that yet. I don't know anything about the student. It's hard to explain, Judy. It's mostly a gut feeling I have. If you saw the report and had visited the facility as often as I have, and knew where the owner of the disposal had placed the field lab, you might question the findings too."

"If you don't think the explosion was an accident, then I strongly advise you to contact the sheriff. If he concurs with your suspicions, let me know, and I'll notify the Attorney General's office."

Returning to his office, Travis thumbed through his business card file, and located the card for Hidalgo County Sheriff Antonio "Tony" Zedillo. Sheriff Zedillo was a second generation Mexican-American; born and raised, and still resided in Starr County. His mother and father were short, small boned, and somewhat chunky. Both had jet-black hair and a dark complexion. Tony inherited all of those physical characteristics, but with one pronounced difference; Tony Zedillo was as strong as an ox.

"Tony, Travis Jenkins from the Railroad Commission."

"Hello, Travis. Haven't talked with you for a long time. I remember you telling me at the last statewide safety meeting that your wife was about to undergo surgery. Is she okay?"

"Thanks for asking, Tony. Emily has fully recovered from the surgery. She's back running the house, and giving me a hard time." Jenkins hesitated, and then assumed a serious tone. "Tony, I'm calling because I need your help."

"That sounds serious. What's the problem?"

"Did you have one of your men investigate that explosion at the brine disposal facility in Elsa yesterday?"

"I guess you could say we made an appearance. Based on a conversation Joe Godfrey had with your man Burkhardt, we accepted his determination that it was an accident. Why? Is there a problem?"

"I'm not sure, but I think so. I just finished reading Daryl's report, and I don't feel comfortable with the findings. I have a very bad feeling about this one, Tony. I don't think it was an accident. Could you send someone back for a second look? It might be a good idea to send an arson specialist if you can. If you think he could help, I'll ask Daryl to meet your people."

"Can you be more specific about your suspicions?"

"I don't think it was the gas that exploded, Tony. And if wasn't the gas, then what was it? I'm beginning to think that the explosion was caused by something that was brought to the site from the outside."

"Damn! I guess we should have been more thorough. I'll call back and let you know if we'll need Daryl."

"Your intuition was correct, Travis. That was no accident. The kid was murdered."

"Shit! I was hoping I was wrong. How'd they do it, Tony?"

"George Olson pinpointed the cause right away. The profile of the explosion directed him to one spot, a workbench. George believes somebody may have placed a packaged bomb on the bench, and that the student was killed when he attempted to open it. Fragments of brown paper were found near the bench. Get this, Travis, Joe Godfrey thinks that some son-of-bitch stayed around and watched the kid get blown up. Can you believe that?"

"What makes him think that someone watched?"

"Joe searched the area surrounding the test site and found a spot to the south where someone had kneeled recently, or sat in the high grass. That's our only indication at this point, but Joe's going back to the site within the hour to conduct a more thorough investigation of that spot, as well as the area around the test site."

Tony said that he'd assigned Joe Godfrey to lead the investigation, and asked if Travis could assign Daryl Burkhardt to work with Joe for a few weeks. "We'll want to interview everyone that came in contact with the kid over the last few months. Since Daryl knows everyone in the disposal business, his contacts can save us a lot of time." Jenkins agreed and said he'd process the paper that day.

"Don't tell anyone about what we found, Travis. Joe and I think we'll be more successful with our investigation if the public continues to believe it was an accident. If the media contacts you, refer them to me, okay? I'll call the medical examiner and alert him to our findings."

Jenkins mused, "I know it may sound strange, but I'm kind of glad it wasn't the osmium gas that exploded."

Tony Zedillo descended the stairs from the second floor to the basement of the County Courthouse building and entered the office of the Hidalgo County Medical Examiner, Dr. Peter Arnet. He repeated the report he'd given Travis Jenkins, and requested that Dr. Arnett look for traces of an explosive during the autopsy. "There's another important development you should be aware of, Dr. Pete. I received a phone call from the Corpus Christi Police Chief this morning. Apparently his department received an anonymous phone call claiming that Acuna was a drug addict and a courier for a Mexican drug cartel. If you find signs of drugs in his system, please call me or Joe Godfrey immediately." When Tony returned to his office, he motioned for Joe Godfrey to join him in his office.

Sergeant Joseph Godfrey was completing his fifth year working with the Hidalgo Sheriff's Department when José Acuna was murdered. At 6'2", 210 lbs., Joe was by far the largest man in the department. Even though he'd played every major sport while in high school and loved football, Joe realized early on that he'd be a mediocre athlete if he were able to earn a football scholarship at a major college. Joe talked it over with his dad, a veteran policeman within the Houston Police Department, and instead of expending a lot of energy going after a football scholarship, he decided to forget football and apply for entry into the criminal justice program at the University of Houston.

It didn't take long for Joe to realize that he had an aptitude for law enforcement. During his senior year he even toyed with the idea of earning a law degree and becoming a prosecutor. However, when Sheriff Zedillo from rural Hidalgo County in south Texas came to the campus on a recruiting trip, Joe decided to postpone a law career for a while and tackle the challenge of working in a small, rural Sheriff's Department handling homicide investigations.

"We may have a problem, Joe." Tony dropped down heavily in his chair. "As soon as the media finds out that Acuna's death was a homicide, and that he was a graduate student at the university, the entire bureaucracy in Austin will be on us like a cheap suit. I'd better call the Austin Chief today to ask for his cooperation. We're gonna have to work fast to solve this case. I want you to interview everyone who's had contact with the kid over the past six months. I don't give a shit if they are college professors, or college administrators; it doesn't matter. Just take it easy on the mother for now. Travis Jenkins has agreed to assign Daryl Burkhardt to work with you for a while.

"Go back out to the disposal and check out more of the high ground around the facility, and then comb the area around the test site. We need to know how the bastard built the bomb and what materials he or she used." Tony looked at his hands and added, "Based on what you found on the hill near the site, whoever did this must be a sick bastard. See if you can arrange for a state forensics specialist to come down to McAllen to help us. He may be able to find something that will enable us to make a DNA match.

"I know it may sound like a reach, but I want you to give special attention to a possible drug connection. The Corpus Christi police received an anonymous phone call earlier today. The caller's claim that Acuna was involved with drugs, sounds a little far fetched to me, but let's check it out. We'll get help from the FBI and DEA if we need it.

"By the way, tell George he did a hell of a job determining that the explosion was caused by a packaged bomb. Ask him to prepare a report, and send copies to Travis Jenkins, and me. Make one more copy for the District Attorney. I'll deliver it personally. No other copies for now." Standing, he said, "This has got to be a first-class, professional investigation, Joe."

One of the more distasteful responsibilities of a homicide detective was to observe the autopsy of a victim. Most detectives hated that part of their job and Joe Godfrey was no exception. Seeing bodies cut open and organs and brains removed was repugnant. Joe showered, dressed and left his apartment before 6:00 A.M. He wanted to arrive at the morgue in the basement of the County Courthouse building before 6:30 A.M.

"Oscar, got any coffee?" Oscar Tatis served as Dr. Arnett's assistant.

"Yep. There's a fresh pot next to the file cabinet. You here for the postmortem?"

"Unfortunately, yes."

"Seems to be a lot of interest in this one. I usually do the accident victims, but late yesterday afternoon, Dr. Arnett decided to do it himself. Any truth to the rumor that the kid was murdered?"

"No comment, Oscar."

Dr. Arnett set a tape recorder on a small slide-out appendage at the end of the table, attached a microphone to his lab coat, and commenced his dictation. He started by identifying the victim, and described the circumstances surrounding the death. After a few minutes, Arnett turned toward Joe. "The young man's arms and face are peppered with what may be tiny specks of a plastic explosive. I'll bet my next months salary that we'll find that the killer used a commercial grade explosive, the kind that's used in the military and in business. The stuff was probably stolen."

Another few minutes passed. "Here's something else of interest, Joe. He was a heavy user of a drug, probably heroin. His arms are like pincushions."

When Arnett got around to opening up Acuna's chest, he said, "Look at this, Joe. The drug was beginning to have a debilitating effect on his heart. His veins were starting to collapse. At the rate he was going, he was on his way to a plot in the ground."

Joe was exhausted; autopsies had that effect on him. He dragged himself up the stairs to the second floor, and knocked on the door to Tony Zedillo's office.

"Come on in."

"Dr. Arnett completed the postmortem a few minutes ago. He found clear indications that Acuna was more than a casual user of heroin, Tony."

Tony sat up straight in his chair. "Well, now we're getting somewhere. Those findings raise the obvious question. Where was the kid getting his supply?"

"Not only that, but where was he getting the money to buy the stuff?" Joe dropped down into a side chair. "The autopsy supports our theory that Acuna was in the process of opening a package when it exploded. Dr. Arnett found traces of what appear to be a plastic explosive, and tiny fragments of brown paper imbedded in his arms, hands and face."

Tony Zedillo sat motionless. He couldn't get the question of how Acuna paid for the drugs out of his mind. He was beginning to believe the answer to that question might lead him to the killer. Joe continued, "Dr. Arnett's findings are in line with the evidence we collected yesterday. We found fragments of wrapping paper on the ground near the bench. The kind of paper somebody would use to wrap a package if he planned to mail it. Even though most of the paper was burned or in very small pieces, we found one piece with writing on it. We could make out two words that could be part of a return address—University and Austin, along with a portion of a zip code. It looks like the killer tried to make it look like the package was mailed, but it wasn't. We checked with the manager of the disposal plant, his wife, and his two part-time employees. None of them received a package in the mail for Acuna. We also checked with the postal worker who makes the rural deliveries in the area, and the guy's supervisor. Nothing! The killer was smart, Tony. The son-of-a-bitch knew that Acuna wouldn't ignore a package with a University of Texas return address, especially if he thought the package was sent from someone in the Chemistry Department. He'd sure as hell open it."

After spending most of the afternoon searching for evidence at the site of the explosion, Joe noticed that Sheriff Zedillo's office door was open when he returned to the County Courthouse building. He knocked on the doorframe. "Got a minute?"

"Sure. Come on in."

"We searched the trampled area just south of the plant again. No question about it, somebody spent time there recently. We found two fingernail clippings in the grass and a fingernail clipper. We might be able to recover DNA from the clippings. He or she would have had a clear view of the test site from that location. We think the killer waited to see the kid get blown apart.

"We were able to get casts of one shoe print. The shoe print doesn't match the shoes of any of the disposal plant personnel, Dr. Gerba, or the college students. I sent everything that we collected to state forensics in Austin for analysis. What I can't figure, Tony, is a motive. Why would anyone want to execute a young college student? I can't come up with a scenario that makes any sense. If we can figure out how the kid paid for his heroin, we may find our motive. That phone call the Corpus police got from an anonymous caller may be the key."

Tony thought about that for a few moments, and then said, "I want you to go talk with the Corpus Police Chief. Maybe he or his people will have some idea about who made that call."

Joe said, "That call may tie in with another piece of information we discovered. It looks like the kid was in and out of Mexico numerous times the last few months. We figure he was crossing the border at Matamoros or Reynoso, probably Matamoros. His credit card charges show that he purchased gas near the border on four occasions. All the charges occurred while he was living in Austin, before he was assigned to supervise the tests in Elsa. Why would he be going to Mexico?"

"Who do we know over there that can be trusted and would be willing to check around for us?"

"Paco Benitez comes to mind. He is one of the best, and I've heard that he can be trusted."

"Contact him. Better yet, go over there yourself. Explain the situation. See if he can find out if the Acuna was getting his heroin in Mexico. Maybe he had a girlfriend, or maybe he was gay."

"I'll go over to Matamoros tomorrow. Then I'll go up to Corpus."

As Joe stood to leave, Tony added, "One more assignment, Joe. I want you to drive up to Austin as soon as you finish in Corpus. Contact the Austin Police Chief and the Austin DA. I talked with both of them this morning and they're expecting you. I want you to brief them, and then ask for a warrant to search Acuna's apartment. I'm specifically interested in an address book, a journal, or notes the kid may have left. We need to see his telephone records. They'll probably insist that an Austin P.D. guy accompany you, but that's okay. We're gonna need their help and cooperation, anyway. We need another warrant to search the student's apartment here in McAllen to see if Acuna left anything meaningful. Call Daryl Burkhardt and ask him to make arrangements to start interviewing all the truckers that haul brine into Hidalgo Disposal. I want to see if anyone noticed anything peculiar while they were unloading." Tony laughed and said, "You're gonna feel like a one arm paper hanger before this is over, Joe." Rising from his chair, Zedillo said, "I don't know how long we can keep a lid on this. When the press finds out that it wasn't an accident and that the kid was murdered, we're gonna be in deep shit."

# 19

IT WAS CLOSE TO midnight when Sergio, flashlight in hand, climbed the back staircase and entered a screened-in porch connected to the Cisneros kitchen. Except for a single light fixture above the kitchen table, the house was dark. Arturo rose slowly, walked to the door, opened it, and stepped aside to allow Sergio to enter. Arturo had conveniently arranged to be in Dallas the day Acuna was executed, and hadn't heard the full account of the "accident."

"What's the latest?"

Sergio pulled up a chair and sat. "Oscar Tatis told me Dr. Arnett plans to conduct the autopsy himself."

"Who the hell are Dr. Arnett and Oscar Tatis?"

"Dr. Arnett is the county medical examiner and Oscar is his assistant. Oscar and I went to high school together in Rio Grande City. He still lives there, just a few streets away from my house. I called him late this afternoon. He told me Dr. Arnett met with his staff at 4:00 and made the announcement. Oscar said he asked Dr. Arnett why he, Oscar, was not performing the autopsy. The answer he got was that the kid's death might be a homicide."

Sergio stood up and began to pace. He threw up his hands and said, "Man, how the fuck did they determine that? I was very careful. I know I didn't leave anything behind. The package must have been blown to bits not bigger than sand."

"Son of a bitch! I can't believe this. We've got to find out how much they know. You'd better get your ass down there and talk with that friend of yours. If you leave now, you should be there when the County offices open. Sleep will have to take a back seat, man. Stay there until you find out what the County DA knows and what he intends to do, and then call me. Be very careful about what you say."

There wasn't anything special about the Hidalgo County Courthouse building in McAllen; it was basically a big box, with four floors, each of which accounted for twenty-five percent of the office space. The County used an additional 8000 square feet in the basement for a morgue, the medical examiner's office, and for the storage of records. A walled-in recreation yard for jail inmates was attached to the left rear portion of the building.

Sergio pulled into the parking lot at 7:20 A.M. The office hours printed on the front door of the building indicated Sergio would have to wait an hour before he could talk with Oscar. He decided to grab a cup of coffee, and a breakfast roll at a coffee shop across the street. He purchased a local newspaper from a vending machine and wasn't surprised that the lead story on page one was about the accident at the Hidalgo Disposal. Sergio decided the newspaper story might provide a good basis for questions about the explosion if he could arrange a meeting with someone in the DA's office.

Thinking Oscar might arrive early because of the autopsy, Sergio re-crossed the street and walked to the rear of the building. He located steps to a basement door, and found it unlocked. Oscar had indeed arrived early. He was seated at his desk enjoying his second cup of coffee, reading the same newspaper article about the Elsa accident. Surprised when he saw Sergio approach, Oscar exclaimed, "Sergio! What the hell are you doing here? How'd you get in here, by the way?"

"The backdoor was open, Oscar. I decided late yesterday that I had to come down and look into some land records for a client of mine. I drove most of the night. Do you have any coffee?"

Oscar handed Sergio a mug of black coffee. "Will you be around for lunch?"

"Probably not. I don't think I'll be finished reviewing the land transactions until mid-afternoon, at the earliest." Pointing to the newspaper on Oscar's desk, Sergio said, "I see that you were reading about the accident in Elsa. Is the medical examiner going forward with the autopsy this morning?"

"He started at 7:00."

"Help me understand something, Oscar. If the kid's death was an accident, what's he looking for?"

Assuming the attitude of someone who's in the know, Oscar answered, "That kid's death wasn't any accident, Sergio. The sheriff thinks it was a homicide, and there could be a drug connection. He said he might call in the DEA."

*What'd I do wrong?* Sergio tried not to show his concern, but he began to feel his confidence ebb, and knew that if he remained with Oscar, he'd say something he'd be sorry for later. "I'd better start my research, Oscar. Thanks for the coffee. Where will I find Records?"

"At the end of the hall. Meet me back here about 11:45. I'll take you to my favorite restaurant."

Instead of turning right towards Records, Sergio left the building the same way he came in, and walked to his car. He placed his arms on the roof and looked at the ground. *If the Feds find out where the kid was getting his supply, Arturo may talk. If he talks, I'm dead meat. What do I do now? If the DEA gets Arturo to talk, he'll finger me. If they talk with Ed Witnauer or Ben Jack Randall, those guys will put me at the disposal plant just before the explosion. I may have to eliminate all three.*

Sergio decided he'd better stay around McAllen until he was able to get a report on the autopsy. He'd drive over to visit with his wife Rosa in Rio Grand City to kill time, and then return in time for lunch.

Sergio couldn't remember much about the drive back to Austin. His normally confident demeanor had been replaced by one of fright and confusion. Negative thoughts raced through his head. He subconsciously increased the pressure on the accelerator, and before realizing it, he was speeding along at seventy miles per hour in a fifty-five mile per hour zone. He looked in the mirror and saw what no driver ever wants to see, a patrol car directly behind him with its lights flashing. He slammed his hand on the steering wheel, and shouted, "Shit!" He started to pull over, but the patrol car raced past him at a high speed in pursuit of someone, or something else.

Sergio began to tremble. He found a section of the highway with a wide enough shoulder, pulled over and stopped. He got out of the car, and walked along the shoulder for a few moments in an attempt to relieve the tension. His frown turned into a smile when he envisaged building more C-4 plastic explosives to eliminate Randall and Witnauer. *Those dumb asses! They won't think twice about opening packages they get in the mail.* A more challenging problem was the elimination of Cisneros. *I can't just mail him a package, and I can't just walk up and whack him.*

After a few more minutes, he slapped his hands together and shouted, "That's it!" *I know I have at least one timing mechanism stored in my closet. I can put a bomb under his car while he's in Bustamonte's.* Sergio laughed. *The C-4 will blow the bastard to bits. But, I'd better collect my money first before I cross the border and get lost.*

## ELSA

There was a handwritten note taped to the front door of Sergio's apartment when he reached Austin. It read simply, "Get your ass over to Bustamonte's."

Before Sergio had time to sit down, Arturo said, "Hoskins called me today with some disturbing news. Some asshole telephoned the Corpus Christie police and told them that Acuna was not only an addict, and but that he was a courier for me. Did you know about that?"

"Oscar told me about that call. He said it was the main reason the medical examiner performed the autopsy. Like I told you yesterday, everybody down there is talking homicide. Oscar said the sheriff's thinking about bringing in the DEA."

Arturo pounded the table with his fist. "Shit! We don't need the DEA nosing around. I've got enough trouble maintaining deliveries. Doing away with the kid created a problem for me. I've made three runs to Matamoros myself during the last two weeks. The border guards will start to get suspicious if they see me crossing all the time. You'll have to make the next run, Sergio." Sergio was tempted to complain, but thought the better of it when he realized the trips might offer him an opportunity to split, if the need arose.

"When's the next run?"

"Day after tomorrow. I'll give you the specifics later."

## 20

PACO BENITEZ BEGAN HIS inquiries within one hour of Joe Godfrey's departure from the Matamoros Police Station. Paco had had numerous responsibilities during his twenty years at the Matamoros P.D., but homicide investigations were his favorite. The veteran Mexican detective knew everyone in town, good and bad, and many feared him. Paco was a big man for a Mexican; over six feet, muscular arms and legs and broad shoulders. His short, jet-black, curly hair and goatee were beginning to show speckles of gray. His stomach was beginning to show signs of a beer-induced paunch. Constant exposure to the sun had produced a leathery skin, which made him look older than his 52 years.

Paco believed the best source for information about visiting gringos was the local saloon circuit, especially the bartenders that worked the nightclubs.

It was late in the afternoon when Paco dropped in at the La Panada to visit Pasqual Ortiz. He'd already visited eight clubs, and fatigue was beginning to settle on him. When Pasqual saw Paco walk up to the bar, he sighed and lamented in Spanish, "Shit, a good day just turned bad."

The unfriendly greeting didn't deter Paco. "How's business, Pasqual?"

"You didn't come in here to get a business report, Paco. What do you want?"

"You're not very sociable today, amigo."

"I've a lot of work to do to get ready for tonight, man. Please don't waste my time. What do you want?"

"Okay, I'll be quick. I need information." Paco pulled a photograph of Acuna from his shirt pocket. "Do you remember seeing this man in your club?"

"Sure. That's José Acuna. I've known José for years. He's one of my favorite customers. He was here with a friend only a few weeks ago. Why'd you ask?"

Paco slowly returned the photo to his shirt pocket, then removed a small notepad from the back pocket of his trousers. He waited a moment, and took a deep breath. "He was killed a few days ago." Paco kept his eyes riveted on Pasqual.

Pasqual dropped the glass he'd been holding, and it shattered. Paco noted the startled look on the bartender's face and realized the news of Acuna's death was a complete surprise. He watched as Pasqual glanced down, but then quickly raised his head again. The man was obviously stunned. He appeared to be trying to absorb the meaning of what he'd just been told. His mouth was open and he seemed to be having difficulty breathing.

Finally, Pasqual closed his mouth, regained some of his composure and muttered, "José was the best. How'd it happen?"

Joe Godfrey had asked Paco to continue to refer to Acuna's death as an accident. "He was killed accidentally over near McAllen when some chemicals he was working on, exploded. Who was the friend, Pasqual?"

Pasqual wasn't listening. "I'm sorry, what?"

"Come back to earth, man. Who was the friend that was with the kid? Do you remember his name?"

Pasqual said he didn't remember much about the man, except that he was a good listener. "José's friend was especially amused when José told him about the night he fell for Maria. He thought he could save Maria from a life of prostitution, and even promised to marry her after he earned his Ph.D." Pasqual smiled when he recalled that story. "José was so naïve." When the bartender stopped talking, and began to wash glasses, Paco noticed a few tears in his eyes.

"What's the friend's name?"

"I can't remember the man's last name, but his first name was Martin something. It was a short gringo last name. He was a little taller than me, and a lot older than José. I'm pretty sure he was from up north."

"What do you mean 'up north'? That's a big area. Where up north?"

"I don't remember. José called him a Yankee, I remember that."

"Okay. Tell me about the kid. Since you knew him by name, he must've come in here often." Pasqual hesitated and fidgeted. It was obvious he wasn't sure what to tell Paco. Paco leaned forward and whispered, "If there was something funny going on with the kid, you better tell me now."

Ignoring the remark, Pasqual said, "José started coming here about six years ago. At first, he came with high school friends. Later, he'd come alone. He and Maria would go upstairs for a while, or he'd just sit on that stool you're sitting on and talk with me. If that stool was occupied," pointing while he made his point, "he'd wait until it was free, and then move over. We'd talk while I mixed drinks. Damn, he was a great kid!"

Paco asked, "What'd you talk about?"

"Just about everything. He was a smart kid, very interested in the environment, especially things like contaminated air, like the shit that's going on down in Mexico City. He was a graduate student up in Austin. He was working on something to do with oil field waste."

Paco studied the eyes of the bartender and wondered why the kid would come to Matamoros all the time? Glancing at the sullen, bleached blonde prostitute, Paco thought, *I can't believe he was attached to that Maria over there. There must have been some other reason.*

"How'd he pay for his drinks and food while he was here?"

The bartender became noticeably uncomfortable and agitated. Paco suspected that the bartender was hiding something. "I'm becoming impatient, man. You're not telling me everything. Are you afraid of something, or someone?" As he asked this, Paco remembered where he was. *Ah! The La Panada! That's it. The cartel controls this place.* He leaned forward again and asked, "Was the kid a user?"

Before Pasqual responded, his shoulders sagged. He mumbled, "He was a heroin user."

"Tell me about it, Pasqual. Where'd he get the stuff? From you?"

"Jesus no, Paco!" He hesitated a moment before continuing. "The kid fell for Maria about a year ago, and kept coming back to be with her even though he knew she was a prostitute. He was just an occasional sniffer, until she talked him into injecting. The kid was hooked right away."

"You're avoiding my question, man. Where'd the kid get the stuff? From Maria? I doubt that!"

Pasqual practically spat out his reply; "I don't know, and if I did, I wouldn't tell you."

"Okay, let's leave that for now. Where did the kid get the money to buy the stuff?" He turned his head toward the girl seated at a table to the left of the bar, "And her? How'd he pay for her?"

The bartender's facial expression changed. He leaned forward, and in a half whisper said, "If I keep talking to you my life won't be worth shit. I'm already in trouble because I talked with the kid."

Assuming the same conspiratorial tone; "I'll find out about the kid one way or another. Maybe you'd rather come down to the station and continue our little talk."

"No, I can't get involved! If my boss finds out I've told you about the kid and Maria, God have mercy on me. I've already told you too much."

"Where'd the kid got his money? Did he have a rich father? Did he have a job?"

"I'll answer that, but you didn't hear it from me. This will end it, Paco. No more questions!" He sighed and said, "José worked as a drug courier for Arturo Cisneros, an organization man up in Austin. I got him the job." With that, Pasqual walked from behind the bar into a side office and closed the door.

Paco thought, *I think you're already up to your ass in trouble, man. I'll be back. Next time you won't walk away from me so easily.* He looked into the mirror. As soon as he made eye contact with the prostitutes, one of them gave him the finger.

"Sorry it took so long, Joe, but I think I hit pay dirt at a nightclub called La Panada. The lead bartender confirmed that Acuna was a heroin user. He nearly shit his pants when I started asking questions about how the kid paid for the stuff." Paco summarized his conversation with the bartender, emphasizing the admission that Acuna was a courier for Arturo Cisneros, a drug dealer in Austin. "I don't know the man personally, but I do know he's supposed to be someone important in the organization. I could make some noise down here, but it may not be a good idea. People I know and trust might get hurt. Maybe you or the Austin P.D. can identify this guy. By the way, we believe the Sonora drug organization owns La Panada. It sounds like Acuna was mostly a loner. Started coming to La Panada with high school friends a few years ago. However, he did fall for one of La Panada's prostitutes, and he'd come to be with her. He'd spend the rest of the time sitting at the end of the bar talking with the bartender. They were pretty tight. The bartender was really shook-up when I told him the kid was dead. He tried to hide it, but I noticed tears in his eyes. One more point of interest, Joe. The last time the kid was here, just a few weeks ago, he was with an older man, a Martin something. The bartender couldn't remember his last name, but he said the fellow was a gringo from the northeast. That's all I could get from him."

"Good work, Paco. I owe you big time. I'll pursue your Austin lead, and let you know what we find out."

# 21

JOE GODFREY'S CONFIDENCE WAS on the upswing when he arrived at Dr. Gerba's office on the third floor of the chemistry building. Six days had passed since the death of Acuna, and the investigation appeared to be going in the right direction. "Dr. Gerba, thank you for agreeing to meet with me today. Meet Detective Jack Kelly from the Austin Police Department." Kelly and Gerba shook hands. "Your assistant indicated you canceled a tutoring session. We're sorry if we've inconvenienced you."

"Please don't concern yourself with that, Sergeant. Whenever someone wants to talk about José, I'll adjust my schedule. What can I do for you?"

"We've been informed that Acuna was a graduate student of yours, and was working on a school-sponsored project."

"You're partially correct, Sergeant. José was a doctoral candidate here at the university. However, the project he was working on is not school sponsored. It's a project funded by a startup firm called the Precious Metals Extraction Corporation. I'm board chairman." Dr. Gerba hesitated, "He was more than one of my students. He was a colleague, and a business associate."

"I see. I wasn't aware of that. Tell us about the project, Doctor."

Godfrey and Kelly sat spellbound as Dr. Gerba described in general terms the objectives of precious metals project, the essence of the business opportunity, and the exemplary effort performed by Acuna and his prototype team.

When he concluded his remarks, Kelly exclaimed, "That's a Texas size opportunity, Doctor. Y'all should make a ton of money. How many people know about the project?"

"I'd say approximately 25. Unfortunately, Detective, the entire project may be in jeopardy. It may have died with José. You're talking to a very discouraged man."

"I'm sorry to hear that. Do you have a list of those involved?"

"Certainly. I have a list here in my desk drawer."

"May we have a copy? We'll keep the list strictly confidential. We'll share it with only two people, my superior at the Hidalgo County Sheriff's Department and the officer in charge of the Austin Homicide Bureau."

Dr. Gerba retrieved a file folder containing the list of people who signed non-disclosure agreements, and ran a copy. When Dr. Gerba handed the list of PMEC investors to Joe, it took him less than a minute to match the investor name, Martin Leary, with the information Paco Benitez provided only a few days earlier. Joe resumed his questioning. "Was Acuna in good health at the time of his death?"

"Yes. He was an outstanding tennis player, number two on the varsity team when he was an undergraduate. However, I did notice a slight deterioration in his health of late. I may've been working him too hard."

Kelly forced a smile. "Was he a night owl, a party boy maybe? Not enough sleep?"

"No. He was a very responsible young man." Then, looking at his hands and lowering his voice, he muttered, "No, there must have been some other reason his health seemed to deteriorate."

Joe asked, "Did Acuna use drugs?"

Ely Gerba's raised his head, and looked at the policeman. He frowned, and the sides of his mouth drooped. "I wondered about that, Sergeant."

"What can you tell us about Martin Leary?"

"Martin's a commercial property Realtor from Connecticut, and apparently a good one. He's one of our original founders. Raised a lot of the startup capital to fund the project."

Joe turned toward Jack. "Have we missed anything?"

"I can't think of anything."

"Thank you for meeting with us, Doctor, and for the list."

When the detectives returned to Kelly's car, Joe said that he recognized Martin Leary's name immediately. "Leary may be the gray-haired man who was with Acuna in Mexico just before he died. I'd better find out what sort of person he is. Does he have an arrest record? Is he a user? I guess the best place to start is the Norwich, Connecticut Police Department. I'll call when we get back to headquarters."

"Norwich Police Department. May I help you?"

"Good afternoon. My name is Sergeant Joe Godfrey. I'm with the Hidalgo

County Sheriff's Department in McAllen, Texas. May I speak with your Chief please?"

"Chief Pierson has someone in his office. Should I interrupt him, sir?"

"I'm calling long distance, and the call is important. Please ask him."

After a brief delay, Godfrey heard a pleasant, but businesslike voice; "Chief Pierson here."

"Good afternoon, Chief. Sorry to have interrupted your meeting."

"That's not a problem, Sergeant. We were just winding up anyway. What can we do for you?"

Joe explained the reason for the call. "The young man who was killed was working on a privately funded research project. One of your citizens, a Martin Leary, is one of the investors. Apparently, Leary was also a friend of the deceased."

"Martin Leary, the Realtor?"

"Yes, sir. I'd like to meet with Mr. Leary. He may be able to help us understand why the young man died."

"How did the young man die, Sergeant?"

"He was killed as a result of a suspicious explosion at an oil field waste disposal facility in a small community here in south Texas."

"Am I correct in assuming suspicious is a key word here?"

"Yes, sir. Would you be willing to make arrangements for me to meet with Leary if I fly up to Connecticut?"

"Certainly, Sergeant. When?"

"How about the day after tomorrow?"

"Hold on a moment, Sergeant, while I check with my secretary." Pierson came back on line a moment later, and said, "We set aside Wednesday morning, October 8th. Can you be here by 10:00 A.M.?"

"I believe I can, Chief. One more item before I let you go. Do you know if Martin Leary has a criminal record, or has been involved in any suspicious undertakings the last few years?"

Pierson responded, "I've known Martin Leary for thirty years. I predict he is as clean as a whistle, but we'll check anyway. Why don't you and I meet alone first. I'll invite Martin Leary to join me for lunch. He may get a little edgy when you show up, but he'll get over it. Having lunch in a familiar restaurant should be a more relaxing atmosphere for him. You could continue your interview after lunch if you thought it was necessary."

"Fine, Chief. I look forward to meeting you."

Reconnecting with his secretary, Pierson requested, "Janet, call Martin Leary and ask him to join me for lunch at 11:30 at Charlie's. Make it sound like it'll be just to two of us."

Chief Pierson sat back in his chair and reviewed the telephone conversation he'd just had with Godfrey. He leaned forward and punched an intercom button on his telephone instrument. "Shelby, please come into my office." Jean Shelby, a young woman in her mid-twenties entered with pad in hand. "Shelby, I want you to drop everything you're doing and search the new state criminal records system for information on Martin Leary."

## 22

AS THE JET CLIMBED to its cruising altitude of 32,000 ft., Joe Godfrey looked out the window at broad expanse of Houston's Intercontinental Airport. *I know more about northern Mexico than I do about my own country,* he thought. He smiled. *I must be what people call a country bumpkin.* He recalled the time that he and two college classmates had driven to the Ozark Mountain region of Arkansas to "study" during spring break. A second out-of-state trip had been a little more adventurous. While in junior high school, Joe's father took his family north to meet with his brother's family for a week's vacation at a resort in the Pocono Mountains in Pennsylvania.

Joe remembered being a little anxious when he arrived at the resort to meet his Connecticut cousins for the first time. His anxiety quickly dissipated, however, when he was introduced to Virginia; she was not one of those "pain in the ass" girls he knew at school. Just the opposite; Ginny was warm, friendly and pretty. His cousin Alice was okay, but it was Ginny who sparked Joe's first interest in girls. Joe, Ginny and Alice had a marvelous time that week, swimming, sailing, canoeing, and generally enjoying each other's company.

Ginny and Joe corresponded occasionally during their high school and college years. It wasn't until they both acquired computers, and learned to use email that the communication blossomed. Joe emailed Ginny a few days before his scheduled his flight to Connecticut. She replied immediately and invited him to come a day early and stay with her in her new condo in Granby, only a few miles from the Hartford airport. Joe accepted the invitation immediately. It would be like a reunion of sorts for the two of them. Ginny had divorced three years earlier, but decided to retain her former husband's name, Newberg.

Joe was sleepy. In order to catch a scheduled 10:30 A.M. flight from Houston to Hartford/Springfield, Joe had to take the first flight out of Harlingen at 6:00 A.M. He pushed back the seat to the maximum recline setting, closed his eyes and visualized the colors of the fall foliage in New England that he'd seen in photographs numerous times, and promptly fell asleep.

Ginny was waiting for him at the gate when Joe deplaned. Since Ginny came directly from her office in the administration building, she was wearing her normal executive attire: brown pants, brown loafers, a fluffy white blouse adorned with a colorful tie, loosely hung around her neck. They hugged and held onto each other longer than either had expected. When they finally separated, Joe looked down and commented, "You're more beautiful in person, Gin. The pictures you sent me didn't capture the real you."

"Why, Joe Godfrey, you flatter me. And you," reaching to squeeze his arm, "you're bigger than I imagined. When we hugged, my head was below your chin."

Joe was dressed like a true Texan: starched and creased blue jeans, boots, and a patterned western style shirt. While they walked to baggage claim, Ginny regaled Joe with small talk about family, stories about her job as manager of facilities at the Hartford airport, and especially about the tobacco farms in the area. Having grown up in the Granby area surrounded by tobacco fields, she was able to explain the reason for the white netting that Joe had seen as the plane approached the airport. Joe thought the netting looked like snow from the air.

"Our local farms produce a special kind of leaf that is used for cigar wrappers, and the netting provides the shade the tobacco needs to mature." Ginny stopped abruptly and placed her hands on her hips and said, "I've talked enough, Joe Godfrey. Now it's your turn to tell me about why you're here."

"I'm scheduled to meet with the Chief of Police in Norwich tomorrow. I'm investigating a homicide."

Ginny gasped. "My goodness! I didn't realize your trip had anything to do with a murder. Are you free to talk about the investigation, Joe?"

"Yes and no, Gin. I can only tell you that a young, brilliant doctoral candidate was killed recently in a small south Texas town for no apparent reason. Initially, we thought the death was the result of an accidental explosion. Now, we believe his death was premeditated. The young man was in his mid-twenties; an only child. His mother lives in Corpus Christi." He summarized his suspicions about a drug connection, why they no longer considered Acuna's death accidental, and then explained why he was traveling to Norwich. "During the development phase of the technology the young man befriended one of the investors, Martin Leary, a Realtor from Norwich."

"I know Martin Leary. He owns Leary Realty, one the best commercial Realtors in eastern Connecticut. As manager of facilities at the airport I've gotten to know most of the top commercial Realtors in the state. Martin Leary and I have attended numerous real estate conferences and seminars together over the years. How is Martin Leary involved?"

"Apparently Leary and the victim were close. They took a trip to Mexico together a few weeks before the explosion. We want to find out if Leary can help us understand what the boy was doing in Mexico just before his death. I'll fill you in on the details after we get to your condo. I've reserved a rental car. Let's pick it up after I get my bag. Where's your car, Gin?"

"The employee parking area. If you take me over there, you can follow me to Granby."

Ginny's townhouse was the end unit on the right side of a four-unit brick building, one of five buildings that comprised a development in a secluded, rural setting in Granby. Before Bradley Field became an international airport serving northern Connecticut and southwestern Massachusetts, Granby was a sleepy little village noted only for its primary agricultural crop, shade grown tobacco. Tobacco fields surrounded Ginny's townhouse on three sides. A large shed used to dry the tobacco leaves was only a short distance from her townhouse and on the same side of the road.

As they walked from the parking lot Ginny asked, "Are you hungry?"

"Famished. The snack served on the plane was not enough for a child."

Entering the front door Ginny said, "Let's have some lunch. I'll make turkey sandwiches if you'll open a bottle of Chardonnay."

The entrance to the townhouse opened into Ginny's living room. The dining room and the kitchen were located to the left of the entrance, and the living room to the right. A staircase to the second level faced the front entrance at the end of the living room. A small powder room, located under the staircase, completed the lower level.

"It's such a nice day let's have lunch on the patio. Would you pick out two place mats and matching napkins from the top drawer of the hutch while I change into something a little more comfortable?"

After lunch they remained at the patio table savoring their third glass of wine. The light conversation had continued unabated for some time before Joe asked, "How long will it take me to drive to Norwich?"

"It shouldn't take you more than two hours. I've driven to the beaches near New London many times. I'll pull a map of downtown Norwich off the Internet, and show you the best way to get to your destination."

Ginny returned to the subject of the murder investigation. "Are you hopeful Martin Leary will provide valuable information?"

"Yes. I want to find out how the friendship between Leary and Acuna developed, and most of all, what Leary can tell me about the young man's lifestyle that might point to a motive." Joe sighed, and took a sip from his wine glass. "I really want to catch the bastard that killed the kid, Gin. Unfortunately, I don't have a lot to go on. The case has me puzzled. I still can't figure a motive." Joe paused again, then said, "Would it be okay if we changed the subject?"

"Certainly. Tell me about south Texas."

"If you look at a map of Texas, you'll see that the town I live in, McAllen, is very close to the Mexican border. South Texas is very different from New England. The people, culture and geography are essentially Mexican. It pays to be bi-lingual."

Ginny asked, "How long have you been with the Sheriff's Department?"

"Five years. I like what I do. Being a detective, especially a homicide detective, keeps you mentally and physically alert." Joe took another sip from his wine glass. "Are you sure I won't inconvenience to you by staying over? I could stay in a motel or hotel."

"Nonsense! My invitation still stands." Smiling, Ginny stood, picked up her dish and glass and moved toward the sink. "You're too much fun to have around, Joe Godfrey. I won't let you out of the house until tomorrow morning."

"Okay, I'll stay if you promise to wake me. I'm a heavy sleeper, Gin. I'm afraid I wouldn't hear an alarm clock. Remember, my physical clock is two hours behind yours. It's only 4:30 in Texas right now. What time do you think I should leave to make my 10:00 A.M. meeting?"

"Since you're unfamiliar with the roads and especially the streets in Norwich, I suggest you leave no later than 7:00. Where is your appointment in Norwich?"

"At the central Police Headquarters. Chief Pierson told me it's a new building, only a few years old."

"I don't know where that is, but I'm sure the Norwich map will show us. Grab your bag from the car while I put the dishes in the dish washer."

Shutting off the alarm at 6:00 A.M., Ginny rose, walked into the guest room, reached down and gently touched Joe's shoulder. "Joe, it's time to get up. Joe, wake up."

Turning slowly onto his back and stretching, Joe grunted, "Thanks, Ginny.

I was out like a light. May I take a shower first?"

"Certainly. I'll fix a pot of coffee and some breakfast while you're showering. Do you have a preference?"

Joe sat up and rubbed his eyes. "Just a piece of toast and some fruit." He emerged from the shower fifteen minutes later, shaved and refreshed. Smelling the aroma of coffee emanating from the kitchen, he called to Ginny as he descended the staircase, "I'll take mine black, Gin."

"Coming right up!" She handed him a cup as he walked into the kitchen.

Ginny looked him over, from head to foot. "You look so handsome, so fresh and clean, you put me to shame."

"I can't put you to shame, Gin. Even in your robe and without makeup, you look great."

"You'd better eat your breakfast and get on the road."

As Joe walked to his car, Ginny called, "Say hello to Martin for me, and make sure you tell him you're my cousin."

It took Joe a little longer to reach Norwich than he'd anticipated. After one wrong turn and a stop for directions, he found the police station without any further difficulty, and arrived before 10:00. Joe introduced himself to the receptionist. "Chief Pierson is expecting you, Sergeant. Unfortunately, he'll be tied up for a few more minutes. Can I get you a cup of coffee?"

"Yes, thank you, black, please." Joe stood by a large bay window. The station was situated on a hill overlooking the confluence of the Yantic and Shetucket Rivers, which in turn formed the Thames River. *What a magnificent view! It must be hard to concentrate*, he thought. After a few minutes, Joe turned and surveyed the lobby area. The building design was more contemporary than any police station he had ever visited; the design seemed to maximize natural light from outside through the extensive use of glass windows, and two large skylights.

"Chief Pierson's ready, Sergeant." Janet Simpson escorted Joe into the office and announced, "Chief, Sergeant Godfrey."

"Thank you, Janet." Standing and extending his hand across his desk, Chief Pierson said, "Welcome, Sergeant. Please have a seat. Would you like another cup of coffee?"

"Yes, please." Joe was taken aback by the man's size. Pierson's telephone voice had been low in pitch, and resonant, so Joe assumed the man would be large. Instead, Chief Pierson was a small, blond man, probably under 5'7". Although in his late forties or early fifties, Chief Pierson had a youthful appearance; Joe smiled inwardly as he pictured Pierson being carded if he asked for a drink in a bar. "Thank you for meeting with me this morning, Chief."

"My pleasure, Sergeant. You've come a long way so let's find out how we can help."

Joe told the Chief what he knew about the precious metals extraction project, and the critical contribution Acuna made to the project before his untimely death. Reviewing notes taken during his meeting with Dr. Gerba, Joe explained his understanding of Martin Leary's role as a founding investor in the business. "I was introduced to Mr. Leary at the disposal site right after the explosion. Since we all thought the explosion had been an accident, I didn't think to ask him why he was there. When I looked for him later, he was gone. I expect that he'll recognize me when we meet again."

Chief Pierson mused, more to himself than to Godfrey, "How in the world did a Realtor from Norwich get involved in a business in Texas?"

"Good question, Chief. That's one of the things I'd like to find out. At first we thought the cause of Acuna's death was an explosion of osmium gas. Further investigation, however, disclosed a more sinister cause: a packaged bomb. We haven't rescinded the accident story, and don't intend to, until we know more about what happened, and who may have been involved." He summarized the evidence collected at the crime scene.

Joe shifted in his chair, took a sip of coffee, and crossed his legs. "The autopsy showed significant levels of heroin in the boy's body. We also discovered that he visited Matamoros, Mexico, frequently, a proven hub for drug traffic into the United States. We think Acuna traveled to Mexico to buy heroin. Apparently, Martin Leary befriended the young man. They spent a lot of time together when Leary visited Austin. Leary accompanied Acuna on a brief trip to Mexico a few days before the young man was killed. Since Leary was one of the last people to see Acuna alive, you can see why we want to talk to him. We need more information about Mr. Leary's relationship with Acuna. We also need to know more about Leary himself, without alerting him that he might be on the list of suspects."

Chief Pierson leaned back in his chair, and didn't say a word for a few moments. Godfrey took another sip of his coffee, and asked, "Were you able to check into Mr. Leary's background?"

Pierson leaned forward and punched the intercom button on his phone. "Janet, please ask Shelby to join Sergeant Godfrey and me, and ask her to bring the results of her research. She'll know what I'm referring to."

"Well, Shelby, what'd you find out about Martin Leary? Is he clean?"

Looking from one face, then to the other, Shelby spoke. "I was surprised to learn that Mr. Leary has a criminal record."

Godfrey and Pierson looked at one another. Pierson said, "Continue, Shelby."

"He was arrested in 1953 in Bridgeport. He was 21 and a student at the

University of Bridgeport. Apparently he ran a numbers business and was soliciting on and off campus. The judge didn't give him any jail time because it was his first offense. Instead, he put Leary on probation. A more serious situation occurred later. Mr. Leary was implicated in a college basketball point shaving scandal in New York. He was interrogated at some length, but never charged. His former partner in the Bridgeport numbers business," looking at her notes to get the name correct, "a Fred Sodlawsky of Derby, was charged and convicted along with two St. Joseph College basketball players. That's about it, sir."

"Good job, Shelby." Turning to Sergeant Godfrey the Chief said, "Not serious, Sergeant, but it shows he is capable of mischief. What're your thoughts?"

"I agree, Chief. I'm relieved he's not involved with drugs. That was my main concern. What I need now is for Leary to give me a complete accounting of his time with Acuna, especially the trip to Mexico, and everything he knows about Acuna's drug addiction. I think the informal luncheon meeting you've planned will work. He'll feel more comfortable with you there."

*Seafood Charlie's* was a favorite of the downtown business community; prices were reasonable, and the food was excellent. The restaurant was located on the second floor of the Pavilion, the main building at the Norwich Marina. Floor to ceiling windows dominated the entire east side of the restaurant and overlooked a large boathouse, maintenance yard and dozens of boat slips.

The hostess escorted Chief Pierson and Godfrey from the lobby to a window table. Martin, already seated, watched the two men approach. He thought he recognized the second man, but couldn't remember where they'd met. "Martin, it's good to see you again. Do you remember Sergeant Joe Godfrey from the Hidalgo County Sheriff's Department?"

Martin's skin tightened. He wondered, *What the hell is a Texas policeman doing in Norwich?* Both men shook hands and Martin said unenthusiastically, "Nice to see you again, Sergeant."

Chief Pierson, directing his comments to Godfrey, said, "Joe, sometimes life seems like a blur. Both Martin and I work downtown, less than a mile separates our offices, and yet we never see each other." Turning back to Leary, he smiled and continued, "It seems like Leary Realty signs are all over town. You're hard to ignore, Martin."

Small talk dominated the conversation for the first few minutes. Then, Chief Pierson, assuming a more serious tone, made sure Martin understood where Sergeant Godfrey was from, and whom he represented. "Sergeant

# ELSA

Godfrey wants to do everything he can to prevent another explosion like the one that killed your young friend. Please tell us how that friendship evolved." Martin noticed that Godfrey removed a small note tablet from an inside pocket of his jacket, and proceeded to record salient facts while he talked. Chief Pierson leaned back and was content to listen.

"José and I seemed to click right away. He was a brilliant young man, one of those rare individuals who possess a balance between intelligence and sensitivity. I was very fond of him." Martin looked down at his hands and sat quietly for a few seconds. He raised his eyes toward Joe Godfrey and said, "I was pleased when Dr. Gerba assigned him the responsibilities to manage the construction of the prototype system, and the field tests."

Godfrey leaned forward and looked into Martin's eyes. He asked bluntly, "Was Acuna into drugs, Mr. Leary?" Godfrey noticed Martin flinch. Martin turned away for a moment. He sighed, unconsciously wiped his eyes, and reestablished eye contact with the sergeant.

"Yes, José was a heroin addict."

Before Godfrey could follow with another question, Chief Pierson asked, "Can you tell us how you know this, Martin?"

Martin turned and looked at Pierson. "Walter, I learned about José's addiction while the two of us were driving from Austin to Port Aransas to visit my nephew. I soon discovered the trip was a subterfuge; José really wanted to talk with me alone, without fear of being overheard, or interrupted." Martin recounted José's shocking revelations that he was not only a heroin user, but also a drug courier for the Mexican cartel.

It was after 1:30 P.M. when Martin finished talking. Pierson noticed they were the only patrons left in the restaurant; a waitress had already submitted a bill, and was hovering nearby waiting to clear the table. He said, "We should leave and allow the staff to clean up." Standing, Pierson added, "I'll take care of lunch."

Walking down the stairs to the first floor of the Pavilion, Chief Pierson asked, "Could you stop by the station on the way back to your office? I'm sure Sergeant Godfrey has a few more questions."

Martin was apprehensive as he and Sergeant Godfrey were ushered into Chief Pierson's conference room. The two men sat facing each other on opposite sides of the conference table. Joe was the first to break the short silence. "Mr. Leary, can I trust you with highly confidential information?"

"Certainly, Sergeant. Please go ahead."

"I'm not sure I'm doing the right thing. On the other hand, what I'm about to tell you may trigger additional recollections that may be helpful to us. I believe your friend Acuna was murdered."

The blood retreated from Martin's face, his eyes practically popped out of his head, and his jaw dropped. Martin was genuinely frightened. He was reacting more to the image of a six-inch dagger protruding from the center of his desk, and the content of the threatening note under the dagger, rather than the news that José had been murdered. The image of the dagger pushed everything else aside. Martin had naively thought that the dagger threat would go away if he heeded the note's command, and kept quiet. He'd even promised his secretary that he'd report the incident to the police, but he never did. The revelation that Acuna had been was murdered added fuel to his already high level of anxiety.

Martin stared at Sergeant Godfrey, who sat patiently waiting for a response. Recovering slightly, Martin leaned forward and asked, "My God, Sergeant, why do you think José was murdered?"

"Because of the drug connection, Mr. Leary. Your information about Acuna being a courier for the Mexican drug mob reinforced my belief that he was murdered. We suspect the young man was executed because he knew too much about the cartel's Mexican operation. You told us that you advised him to disengage from the mob as quickly as possible and seek treatment for his addiction, isn't that right?"

"Are you suggesting my advice had something to do with his death?"

"No, Mr. Leary. You probably gave him sound advice, from your perspective. However, Acuna was dealing with ruthless individuals. Killing means nothing to these people. Please think back to your conversations with Acuna. Can you supply us with any names or anything else that might be significant?"

Martin frowned, not knowing how much he should tell the detective. Would he be implicated in Acuna's drug activities if he told Godfrey the name of Acuna's contact in Austin? Should he say anything about the dagger and the threatening note? For his own safety and the safety of his family, Martin concluded that he'd better be straightforward with the detective, at least up to a point. "Would the name Cisneros mean anything, Sergeant?"

"That name sounds very familiar. I think he may be the drug boss in Austin. Do you know in what context Acuna mentioned his name?"

"José told me his drug supply came from Cisneros. It was compensation for his courier services. I tried to discourage him from telling me the man's name, but he told me anyway. I guess I really didn't want to know."

"Let's talk about your trip to Mexico with Acuna. Where'd you go?"

"Matamoros. He said it'd be more interesting because he knew the town and had a friend at one of the nightspots."

"We believe Acuna's Mexican drug connection was in Matamoros. Where'd you go while you were in Matamoros? Who'd you meet?"

"We arrived late in the morning, spent just one afternoon and one evening in the city." Martin paused, and after a moment of refection continued, "We lunched and dined at a hotel. I'm not sure of the pronunciation, something like Tamaulipas. We shopped in various locations. That evening, José took me to a nightclub called La Panada. Apparently he'd been there many times before. He seemed to know many of the employees, but he introduced me to only one person, a bartender. I remember being befuddled that José knew a bartender so well. They seemed to be friends; at least they greeted each other that way. Does that help?"

"I think so. Did Acuna pick up a package while the two of you were in Matamoros?"

Martin flinched, and after a slight hesitation, answered, "If he did, I didn't see it. Unless José had something in his pocket that I couldn't see, he didn't carry anything out to the car. A package couldn't have been left in the car either, because the car was locked while we were in the nightclub. I remember, because I locked it myself." Martin studied Godfrey's face, and thought, *He suspects I know more than I'm telling.*

Joe Godfrey placed his hands together on the conference table, and said, "I need to ask you about a few personal matters, Mr. Leary. Because this is a murder investigation, we have to check the background of everyone that was in contact with Acuna before he died. I think you can understand that." Godfrey reached for his cup of coffee and slowly took a sip. He looked into Martin's eyes. "Chief Pierson checked to see if you had a criminal record. Apparently you do. You were arrested in 1953 for soliciting bets on numbers while a student at the University of Bridgeport."

Martin was startled. "Why is my arrest back in '53 important? Are you suggesting that I may have been involved with José's death? Damn it, Sergeant, where's this conversation going? Should I contact a lawyer?"

"It won't do either of us any good if you become defensive, Mr. Leary. I'm only attempting to determine a motive for Acuna's death. Your record would have been very important had you been arrested for using or possessing drugs. You might have been his source of supply, for all we know. Your revelation that Acuna was a courier for the cartel, however, puts a whole new spin on things. That's very important information."

Martin's anger subsided. "I suspect that José used heroin while we were in Matamoros, Sergeant. I saw it his eyes. I'm not sure how to describe it, except to say his eyes were different; they appeared to be glassy. He started to mumble about some address in the city. Apparently he thought the address was funny. It was half of some number. As soon as the bartender heard him mention it, he told me to get José out of there and take him back to Corpus Christi."

"Do you remember the street address, Mr. Leary?"

"No. It went in one ear and out the other."

Godfrey looked at his watch, stood and abruptly announced, "Mr. Leary, I must get back to Hartford to catch a flight to Houston. You've been a huge help, and I thank you. If you think of that address or anything else that might assist us with our investigation please call me."

As he handed Martin a business card, and started to leave the room, Martin exclaimed, "There's something else you should know, Sergeant. I've been threatened. I may be the next victim."

Godfrey turned back. "You've been what?"

"I've been threatened. Somebody left a note under a dagger stuck into the top of my desk. It warned me not to talk about José's drug addiction. The note threatened that they'd burn down my office building if I continued to talk about him. I'm concerned for my family, Sergeant."

Joe Godfrey mumbled, "Damn! Did you keep the dagger and the note?"

"Yes, they're in a drawer in my desk."

"Do you know who left the note?"

"Not exactly. But I have a pretty good idea. Cisneros has a cousin who lives in Groton. It's on the coast just south of here. The guy's name is Luis Caldera. I suspect he's the one that left the note."

"Did you touch the dagger when you pulled it from the desk?"

"No. I tried to be careful. I used my handkerchief."

Godfrey began to pace. "Can you get the dagger and the note and bring them back here? If we can uncover a fingerprint, Chief Pierson may want to pick up Caldera right away. If we can't, he may want to put a tail on the guy, to see where that might lead."

While the note and the dagger were being analyzed for prints, the three men discussed the next move. Martin asked, "Walter, if you can't get a print, maybe you could get a sample of Caldera's handwriting. Positively linking him to this note would be enough to pick him up, wouldn't it?"

"I'm not sure if a handwriting match would be sufficient, but, it's an excellent thought, Martin. I'll check with our District Attorney." Walter vacillated, and then asked Martin if he'd mind leaving the office for a moment while he discussed a confidential point with Sergeant Godfrey.

"I don't mind, Walter. I could use a trip to the rest room anyway."

Walter turned, and looked at Joe. "Sergeant, this development may give you an opportunity to flush out your killer; think about using Martin as bait." After Pierson explained his plan, Joe said it might be worth trying, but that it would be a long shot. Martin would have to clearly understand the extent of the risk.

When Martin returned, Walter said, "Martin, if you'd agree to become more visible, you could play an important role in Sergeant Godfrey's investigation and avenge your friend's death." Pierson patiently explained his plan.

When he'd finished, Martin said, "I don't know, Walter. It sounds very dangerous. If I become more visible, wouldn't Shirley be a target? And what about Adam and Ruth?"

"I'll see that Shirley isn't harmed. I'll assign people to tail each of you whenever you're out of the house, and watch the house whenever you're home. Adam lives in the downtown section of Putnam near the police station, doesn't he?" Martin nodded. "I'll ask the Putnam Police Chief to patrol the area around his house. It shouldn't be a problem for them to watch his house twenty-four hours a day."

Martin stood and paced back and forth in front of Chief Pierson's desk. "It was a frightening experience to find that dagger stuck in my desk. I think the damn thing left a hole in my courage, as well as my desk."

"We understand, Martin. These are dangerous people."

"If I do what you're proposing, you should ask the Groton police to put a twenty-four-hour watch on Caldera. If he makes a move toward Norwich, your department should be all over him like a cheap suit." Martin stopped pacing. He punched his right hand into his left, and said, "You're right, Walter, if I can help catch the bastard that killed José, and left the damn note stuck to my desk, I'd feel as though I'd accomplished something worthwhile. Let's do it."

Walter smiled. "It would strengthen the story if we could say that you'd agree to return to Texas to assist with the investigation."

Joe leaned forward. "I agree. It wouldn't be a waste of your time, Martin. Sheriff Zedillo and I would welcome you. We could use another mind to help solve this case."

Martin said he'd have to hold off on a commitment until he talked with Shirley, and arranged for one of his senior agents to cover for him at two important meetings he'd scheduled for the coming week. Martin said he could probably leave for Texas within a day or two.

Walter added, "I'll contact the Groton police today. Don't worry about Shirley or Adam. I'll make sure that everyone's protected until an arrest is made. I'll give everyone my home phone number. Your family can call me any time, day or night." Chief Pierson stood and said, "Well. I guess we're all in agreement. I'll make the appointment for first thing in the morning. Let's meet here at 8:00 A.M. We can ride together."

Joe called Tony Zedillo to obtain his approval to move forward with Chief Pierson's plan. "We're meeting first thing tomorrow morning. Chief Pierson seems pretty confident he can convince the fellow to go along with his plan."

"Go for it, Joe, but be careful not to compromise our investigation, or the integrity of this office."

"I'll call you with a report right after the meeting, regardless of what the man decides to do. I'll head back to Hartford after the meeting. I may be able to catch a flight to Houston tomorrow afternoon. If I can't, I'll spend the night at my cousin's and fly out the following morning. I want to visit with Jack Kelly on my way back to McAllen and find out what his department knows about Cisneros."

Chief Pierson beseeched his old fishing buddy, Stewart Whitney, publisher of the *Norwich Daily News*, to modify his schedule and meet with Martin Leary, Joe Godfrey and himself first thing in the morning. Having been a reporter early on in his news career, Whitney found it intriguing that Walter was reluctant to reveal why he'd asked for the meeting. He arrived at his office one half-hour earlier than usual.

On the short drive to the newspaper offices, Joe suggested that he and Martin let Walter do the talking, unless the publisher questioned them directly.

It took Chief Pierson only ten minutes to present his plan. He emphasized that the story he was proposing would be the truth, albeit a somewhat embellished and exaggerated truth, but still would be the truth about Martin's involvement in Acuna's murder investigation. Pierson suggested that the newspaper's cooperation could be interpreted as a public service.

In return for running the story, Chief Pierson and Sergeant Godfrey promised Mr. Whitney that the *Daily News* would be the first news organization to receive communiqués regarding the murder investigation issued either by the Hidalgo County Sheriff's Department, or the Norwich Police Department.

Pierson's strategy worked; Stewart Whitney agreed to run the story on the front page of the morning edition of the *Norwich Daily News*.

>
> LOCAL BUSINESSMAN AIDS MURDER INVESTIGATION
>
> *A local Realtor, Martin Leary, has agreed to assist a Texas law enforcement agency to find the killer, or killers of a young University of Texas graduate student. In an exclusive interview with the Daily News, Sheriff Zedillo of Hidalgo County, Texas, said he was pleased that Leary, a business associate and friend of the deceased, had agreed to help. "Enlisting the services of a civilian to assist in a murder investigation might seem unusual," he added, "but this killing is an unusual case."*
>
> *He admitted that his department had not determined a motive for the killing, but added, "We're confident Martin Leary's insight into*

the habits of the deceased, and his knowledge of the technology the student was working on, will speed up the investigation.

When contacted by the Daily News, Leary said, "Before his death, José Acuna was not only a friend, but a key member of our development team at the Precious Metals Extraction Corporation. I will do whatever I can to help find the cowardly person, or persons, responsible for his murder."

Many of the television and radio stations in eastern Connecticut picked up the *Daily News* story, and reported it during scheduled broadcasts. Luis Caldera heard the report on his car radio while driving home from the delicatessen/booking establishment he owned. He called Cisneros from his car phone. Cisneros exploded, "That dumb son-of-a-bitch. I guess he didn't believe me." He asked, "Does Leary have any children?"

"Yeah, I think he has a son; a teacher in Putnam."

"How far away is Putnam?"

"It's about forty miles north of here."

"Okay, here's the deal. We don't go after the wife. She'll be protected. We'll go after the son. Go up to this Putnam town and nose around. Call me tomorrow night."

Martin was physically exhausted after Joe Godfrey left. It had been a stressful couple of days, and he'd had a restless night; he hadn't told Shirley yet about what he'd agreed to do. He removed the morning newspaper from the roadside box on his way to work. It wasn't unusual for him to take the paper, since Shirley didn't get around to reading it until after dinner anyway.

He mumbled an unenthusiastic greeting when he arrived, and immediately retired to his office, closing the door behind him. Claire had placed a large blotter over the hole in his desk. But, in spite of her effort, Martin couldn't shake the image of the dagger protruding from the center of his desk, or the threatening note attached to it.

He stared at the newspaper headline. He was beginning to have second thoughts about his impetuous agreement to serve as bait to flush out José's killer. But, regardless of his misgivings, it was too late. His biggest concern now, was what to say to Shirley. Martin stood up, grabbed his jacket, and announced to a surprised Claire, "I'm going out for a walk. A walk will help me think straight. I should be back in an hour or so."

Martin reached the end of Broadway before he realized that he couldn't postpone telling Shirley any longer. He had to go home now. *Either she'll be supportive of my decision to serve as bait, or she'll be upset. I pray it'll be the former.* He returned to the office and announced, "Claire, I'm going home. I won't be back until after lunch."

Shirley was standing by the kitchen counter when Martin walked in from the garage. She noted the serious expression on his face. "What brings you home in the middle of the morning? Are you okay?"

"We need to talk."

"Okay, let's sit right here at the kitchen table so I can keep track of the sauce. I don't want it to boil over." When Martin completed his summary of his meetings with Sergeant Godfrey and Chief Pierson, he closed by showing her the story on the front page of today's newspaper. Shirley's mouth dropped open as she read the story. When she had finished, her eyes locked on his and she exploded with anger. "Damn you, Martin Leary! You've exposed this family to physical harm: you, me, Adam, Ruth, the baby. Those drug people have killed once. They'll kill again." She lowered her head into her hands and began to sob.

"Please listen, Shirley. They've got to be stopped. Walter Pierson promised that he'd provide around-the-clock protection for you. And, he promised the Putnam police will protect the kids."

"I don't care what Walter Pierson says. I'm frightened." Shirley stood and announced, "I'm going to my room."

Martin felt a tightening of his skin and beads of sweat form on his forehead. He'd never before witnessed an outburst like that from his wife. He stared at the wall. When he was finally able to roust himself, he walked over to the stove and shut off the burner.

Shirley didn't say another word to him the rest of the day, or that evening. Not even a good night. She'd even turned her back to him in bed.

Martin looked at the clock: 5:00 A.M. *Damn! Another restless night.* He swung his legs off the bed and onto the floor, and ran his fingers through his hair. He sat on the edge of the bed for a moment and looked down at the floor. He decided to prepare a pot of coffee, and read for a while. He shuffled to the kitchen wearing a pajama bottom and T-shirt and flicked on the light switch next to the sink. The sudden glare caused him to shield his eyes. Adjusting to the light, he removed his hands from his eyes, straightened and looked into the darkened window. His reflection was not the Martin Leary he was used to seeing. His features were distorted by a frown and wrinkled brow. His silver gray hair was disheveled and a red tint encircled his pupils, a clear indication of sleep deprivation. He again studied his reflection and mumbled audibly, "You dumb shit," and reached for the coffeepot. He'd never felt so alone.

Shirley left the house before breakfast without saying goodbye. He suspected she'd gone to her office early to escape the possibility of a confrontation. Martin finished packing and placed his suitcase by the front door. He had an hour to kill before he'd have to leave for the airport to catch the midmorning flight to Houston, so he turned on the TV. After a few minutes he realized he wasn't watching, or listening, so he shut it off. He sat motionless in the chair staring at the darkened TV screen. He stood up and began to walk from one room to another. At 6:00 A.M. he decided to call his son Adam.

"You're up early, Dad. I talked with Mom last night. Are you still in the doghouse?"

"I'm afraid so. Your mother is really pissed."

"Mom said that you'd agreed to go back to Texas. If it's any consolation, I support and admire what you've agreed to do. She'll come around."

"I appreciate that, Adam. It makes the situation less stressful when you know someone is on your side. I'm convinced I'm doing the right thing. I'll be leaving in a few minutes. I left a note on the kitchen counter, but she's so mad, she may tear it up. Please call her later and tell her how sorry I am that we've had this difference of opinion." Changing the subject, Martin asked, "How's the new training route working out?"

"It's much better, and probably a lot safer. The roads have wider shoulders. I guess the roads were built to accommodate slow-moving farm equipment. I've been able to shave fifteen seconds off my time for ten miles."

"Good. I'm glad it's working out. I have to leave for the airport. Please hug Ruth for me. I love you."

"I love you too, Dad. Have a safe trip. I promise that I'll call Mom around dinnertime."

"Bill, I'm taking a morning flight back to Texas. Could you meet me at the Heritage on Farmington Avenue for an early lunch?"

Bill checked with his secretary, and said, "I can meet you at 11:30. Why are you going back to Texas?"

"Can my answer wait until lunch? I've got a lot to tell you."

During his drive to Hartford, Martin brooded about some of his recent decisions. The worst example was his believing José's "cock and bull" story about a beryllium sample that needed to be delivered to his cousin in Groton. What a naive fool he'd been to buy into that story!

Then, there was his decision to invest in Dr. Gerba's precious metals extraction technology. He'd risked most of his and Shirley's savings on the venture. However, when challenged, he had difficulty describing the technology's fundamentals because he didn't really understand them. When Shirley asked him for details, he'd become evasive and defensive. Martin reluctantly admitted to himself that, without a chemical engineering background, he probably never would understand the technology.

Martin was also beginning to worry about the viability of the investment itself, and the quality of his due diligence. He reluctantly had to admit that his enthusiastic salesmanship had been based on a gut feeling, and his blind faith in Gerba, rather than on actual scientific knowledge. If Dr. Gerba's extraction process proved unsuccessful and his friend's investments turned out to be worthless, he'd be the person responsible.

He forced himself to dispel these negative thoughts, and concentrate on the positive things in his life. What could be more positive than his marriage over the past thirty-six years? Martin smiled. Shirley. What a lady! Shirley's decision to stop coloring her hair had been a good one. Her gray hair actually complimented her facial features. She still weighed in at 110 pounds, and was a fountain of energy. Even when provoked, like she'd been the previous day, she was pretty. He regretted that he'd left home without a proper goodbye. His smile returned when he thought about the pending birth of his first grandchild in less than two months.

Martin could see that Bill was agitated even before he sat down. "What's going on down in Texas, Mart? Why are you going back?"

"The explosion that killed José wasn't any accident, Bill. The explosion was a drug related assassination. A pre-packaged bomb was placed on the workbench to kill Acuna when he attempted to open it."

"My God, Mart!"

Martin lowered his voice. "José was a heroin addict. The police think he served a drug cartel as a courier."

Bill leaned against the back of his chair. "I can't believe what I'm hearing. Why the hell did Gerba delegate so much responsibility to an addict?" Bill asked irritably. "I'm beginning to wonder about Gerba's judgment, and about the project. It seems like we're snake bit."

"Calm down, Bill. José hid his addiction from Gerba and his fellow students. He didn't hurt us." In spite of his own discouragement, Martin attempted to mollify Bill's obvious consternation and explained that Acuna had been a reliable and productive assistant to Gerba.

Bill pursed his lips, and asked, "What's going to happen to the damn project?"

"Ely told me not to worry about the project. The prototype was not damaged during the explosion. It's stored in a safe place until we need it again. The confidentiality of the technology wasn't compromised either; all of the important documents were retrieved from the sheriff. Our financial losses are limited to the $5000 fine imposed by the Railroad Commission, and that should be returned when the Commission rules in favor of our appeal. Gerba will reactivate the field tests as soon as we get a green light to continue."

"Well, in spite of Gerba's upbeat assessment, I'm concerned. Tell me, why are you going back to Texas?"

Bill's jaw dropped open when Martin described how he found a dagger and a note stuck to the top of his desk. "My God, Mart. It's a wonder you didn't have a heart attack. It sounds like a scene from a movie."

Martin opened his briefcase, pulled out a copy of the Norwich newspaper and placed it in front of Bill. Bill leaned forward and read the article. With a disbelieving look on his face, said, "This is unbelievable! Why would they ask you to help with a murder investigation? You don't know shit about police work."

"Because I'm fairly certain I know who left the note. Both Chief Pierson and Sergeant Godfrey suggested I serve as bait to flush him out in the open. It was my call, Bill. I feel like I should do something to help apprehend the people that killed José. His death was so unnecessary." Martin replaced the newspaper in his briefcase, and added, "The sheriff intends to deputize me when I get down there. Godfrey said that I might work with the Hidalgo County DA to help document the activities of the Sonora drug cartel, especially that bastard Cisneros."

"I know helping catch Acuna's killer is important to you, Mart, but be careful." Bill studied his friend's eyes. "I'm sorry if I sound negative, but I don't like the idea of you getting involved in a murder investigation. Your family needs you."

Martin explained Chief Pierson's commitment to protect Shirley, and to arrange for the Putnam police to protect Adam and Ruth.

"Speaking of family, how's Adam's training coming along? Is he still planning to enter the Boston Marathon?"

"Adam submitted an entry application a few weeks ago, so I guess he's serious. He runs at least ten miles each day, sometimes more, depending on his teaching commitments. He said his time dropped by fifteen seconds when he started running the new route." Martin looked at his watch and said, "I'd better get going, Bill. I don't want to miss my flight. Thanks for meeting with me."

# 23

JOE GODFREY PLACED THE magazine on a table, stood and shook hands with Jack Kelly. "Good to see you again, Jack."

"I hope I didn't keep you waiting too long."

"Not a problem. You have some great periodicals in your lobby. How's your love life, Jack?"

Kelly actually blushed. "Joe, if I told you, you'd be jealous and envious, so I won't reveal my secrets." Both chuckled as Godfrey placed his hand on Kelly's shoulder. Kelly was a handsome young man, with Irish blue eyes and an infectious grin. Joe was comfortable working with him. Jack was willing to undertake the smallest of assignments, and do them well. A recent graduate of the criminal justice program at Texas Tech, young Kelly represented the future of law enforcement—bright, computer literate, verbally articulate and, most of all, committed. Kelly exhibited self-confidence, but without arrogance.

"Let's go into the conference room at the end of the hall. Would you like a cup of coffee before we get started?"

"Sounds good to me. I take it black."

Kelly led Joe into a small, windowless conference room with Spartan furnishings: a metal table, four vinyl-covered chairs, a blackboard, and a small telephone table. Joe thought, *This room would frighten the shit out of a suspect if he or she were interrogated in here. They'd think they were in prison already.*

Joe asked if he'd had time to check out the names in the address book that he found in a small drawer next to the phone in Acuna's apartment. Kelly said that most of the names were Acuna's classmates at the university, friends from Corpus Christi, or family. One name, however, had set off an alarm in Kelly's mind. "I believe we may have hit pay dirt. One of the names was an A. Cisneros. It turned out to be Arturo Cisneros, a local Mexican cartel drug trafficker. My supervisor told me the DEA has been trying to nail this guy for months, but hasn't built a strong enough case to get an indictment." Jack referred to his notes. "Prior to his death, Acuna made eleven calls to Cisneros during a three-month period. Then, two weeks before he died, the calls stopped. I suspect the communication ceased because of some disagreement."

"That fits. During my visit to Connecticut, Martin Leary admitted that Acuna was addicted to heroin, and identified Cisneros as his heroin source. If the kid tried to disengage from the mob, he'd be up to his ass in trouble. I can't imagine that Cisneros would allow him to just walk away."

"I agree, but how can we prove it?"

"The investigation needs a direct link to Cisneros; either a credible witness to testify that Cisneros ordered Acuna's death, or the discovery of irrefutable evidence at the scene of the murder implicating Cisneros. Packaging enough circumstantial evidence to convict the guy will be difficult. What do we know about Cisneros and his Austin operation?"

"Our people believe Cisneros is responsible for all drug traffic in the Austin metropolitan area. His brother-in-law, Sergio Dominguez, serves as his lieutenant. Cisneros takes his orders from a man named Santiago Rodriguez in San Antonio, and our people suspect Rodriguez is in charge of the entire south Texas drug operation. By the way, I learned yesterday that the DEA has been after Rodriguez too, but hasn't been able to pin anything on him either."

"What do we know about this Dominguez? Could he be a suspect?"

"Could be, Joe. From what I've been told he's an enforcer type, a real punk. He does the dirty work for Cisneros. Dominguez definitely should be listed as a suspect."

"Our friend Cisneros has long tentacles." Joe conveyed the story of the threatening note pinned to the middle of Martin Leary's desk at the end of a dagger. "Martin Leary believes a Connecticut relative of Cisneros left the note. When the Norwich Police Chief heard that, he offered a radical plan to snarl the bastard. He convinced Martin Leary to serve as bait to flush the guy out in the open. He agreed without much hesitation." Joe showed Kelly the story about Martin Leary on the front page of the previous day's issue of the *Norwich Daily News*. "It's a risky plan, but Leary is one committed fellow, Jack. He's convinced that if the kid had lived, he would have been a brilliant scientist. To make the newspaper story more convincing, Chief Pierson persuaded Leary to return to McAllen to help with the investigation. Leary knew Acuna better than anyone, except the kid's mother."

Joe stopped talking, stood up and began to pace. After a few minutes, he stopped and looked at Kelly. "The more I think about the kid's death, the madder I get. This investigation gets more complex by the day. We may find that Acuna's death is just the tip of an iceberg. But, we can't afford to get distracted by the damn drug connection. We've got a big enough job finding the kid's killer." Joe sat back down. "Let's piece together what we know."

Two hours later, Joe leaned back in his chair and tried to make sense out of the notes they'd written on the blackboard. "I see three holes in our case. First, whoever placed the packaged explosive on the lab bench must have known about the field tests and about the location of the test equipment. That troubles me. The project's existence was supposedly confidential, right? That's what Dr. Gerba told us, anyway. We should make a list of everyone who might have known about the project and conduct thorough interviews to see if they might have inadvertently told someone else about the tests. I think we should talk with the two surviving graduate students as soon as possible. Do we know where they live?"

Kelly reviewed his notes and answered, "Patrick Duncan, a twenty-three-year-old from Dallas, and Sonja Hyde, a foreign student from Germany. They live together in an apartment near the university campus. I have an address and a phone number."

"Can you meet with them tomorrow?" Kelly nodded. "The second thing that bothers me is the lack of evidence at the scene. We've got to go back out to Hidalgo Disposal in the morning, and go over the entire area again. Whoever placed the explosive must have left something behind." Godfrey began to pace again. "I'm beginning to think that DNA may be a key factor in solving this case, but we haven't received a report from the state forensics lab about the fingernail clippings. I'll have to check on that when I get back to McAllen. Do you have a forensics specialist that could drive down to McAllen for a few days and help me reexamine the site of the explosion?"

"That sounds like a good idea. I'll ask about that today."

"I'm glad Martin Leary's coming to McAllen. I have a gut feeling that he knows more than he's telling. He may be more open now that he's officially part of the investigation." Godfrey looked at his watch. "I'd better head back to McAllen and talk with Sheriff Zedillo. Call me."

Sheriff Zedillo listened intently as Joe briefed him on his trip to Connecticut, and on his analysis of the evidence. "Kelly will interview the two graduate students who were with Acuna at the test site, and then go back and talk with Dr. Gerba again." Joe paused, "Daryl Burkhardt plans to begin interviewing the truck drivers that haul brine and waste oil into DeWitt's plant as soon as we get a list of brine truck drivers. That's a huge job, Tony. Maybe you could assign Dave Collins to help Daryl."

"Okay, I'll arrange that. When do you plan to go back to the disposal and talk with Randall?"

"This afternoon. Daryl said he'd go with me. He wants to pick up the list from Randall ASAP."

"Good! By the way, the cast of the footprint we found in the brush just above the disposal, indicates the person who used the site as an observation spot, was a male of medium height, with a shoe size of nine and one half inches."

"I'm meeting Martin Leary in Harlingen mid-afternoon tomorrow. I'm going to take him back to the disposal plant. He may remember something important while he's there. By the way, Jack Kelly is checking to see if one of Austin P.D.'s forensics specialists can come down to help."

Ben Jack heard the car approach, and exited his office trailer to greet the visitor. "Morning, Ben Jack. Remember me, Joe Godfrey with the Hidalgo County Sheriff's Department? Good to see you again. How's it going?"

"I'm okay, Sergeant. What can I do for y'all?"

Turning to Daryl Burkhardt, Joe said, "I think you know Daryl, Ben. Daryl will be working with the Sheriff's Department until we determine the cause of the recent explosion. Do you have time to answer a few questions?"

"I got time, Sergeant. Don't get much company out here. Mr. DeWitt ain't here though, he's in Harlingen."

"We'll talk with Mr. DeWitt later. Can you supply us with—?" Ben Jack interrupted Godfrey before he could continue.

"That explosion was a bad'un, weren't it? Shit, I got nightmares about it." Gesturing with his right arm, he added, "When I found him, his arm was two feet this side of hisself."

Attempting to regain control, Joe said, "Yeah, it was a tragic accident. We were hoping you could provide us with a list of the truckers that dump here, and phone numbers if you have them."

"That's easy, Sergeant. If y'all wait a minute, I'll get it." Ben Jack turned, climbed two steps, opened the screen door and asked Sue Ann to find the list of truckers that dumped brine at the disposal. Backpedaling he said, "Sue Ann's getting the list for you. Was it the gas that exploded?"

Daryl said, "That's one of the questions we're trying to answer. Any strangers visit the plant during the past few months?"

"Only new fella I seen around was the real estate dude Mrs. Witnauer sent over."

Daryl asked, "Oh? Do you remember his name?"

"No, sir, but he left a card. I kept it. Don't know why, I'll never call the cowboy."

Energized by Ben's response, Joe asked, "Could you find the card for us?"

Ben Jack reentered the trailer and returned with the card and the list. He handed both to Joe. Joe looked puzzled when he read the name on the business card. "Sergio Alverez, Commercial Realtor, Austin, Texas. What's a real estate broker from Austin doing in Hidalgo County?"

Joe then reviewed the list of truckers, and asked Daryl, "Who's this Laredo Trucking? They have more drivers coming in here than anyone else."

"That's Ed Witnauer's company. He uses Hidalgo Disposal to dump brine from a few Texaco wells over in Starr County. I know Ed. He's a good man. Been in the business a long time. We've never had a problem with him."

Looking at the list, Burkhardt said, "I know all of the truckers on this list personally. I can set up appointments for Collins and myself to start interviews tomorrow."

"Go for it, Daryl." Joe handed Ben Jack his business card. "Thanks for your help, Ben Jack. When do you expect Mr. DeWitt will return from Harlingen?"

"Not sure. Could be late today or in the mornin'."

"If I don't catch him today, ask him to call me. If you think of anything else, call my voice mail, or my pager number, and I'll get back to you right away. We're going over to the site of the accident and look around some more."

Joe and Daryl spent the next hour searching for additional clues at the site of the explosion, and at the trampled area just to the south.

Joe saw Roy DeWitt's car return and walked back to the office trailer to talk with him. He sat on a straight back chair in front of Roy DeWitt's desk. "We're trying to close out our investigation of the explosion, Mr. DeWitt. I know we've interviewed you already, but there are still a bunch of loose ends. Can I ask you a few more questions?"

Roy leaned back in his swivel chair. "Fire away, Sergeant."

"Dr. Gerba told me that only company insiders knew about the field tests, was that your understanding?"

"Yes, sir." Roy recited the names of everyone who'd had access to information about the tests, and then added, "Of course, trying to keep information like that secret within a university chemistry department is probably not very realistic. I would imagine rumors were flying."

"You're probably correct. We intend to interview some of the department people later this week. Please think back, Mr. DeWitt. Did you inadvertently mention the testing program to anyone here in the Elsa area—a local businessman while having coffee, another disposal operator, trucker, or anyone you may have talked with?"

"No, Sergeant." DeWitt hesitated. "Wait a minute. I did receive a telephone call from Mrs. Witnauer. She asked if it'd be okay for a real estate friend of Ed's to tour the plant. I said sure, just contact Ben Jack and arrange a time. I don't remember the specifics of the conversation, but she did mention tests. I hadn't thought about it until now, but the Witnauers must have known about the testing before she called. It didn't seem to matter at the time." More to himself than to Godfrey, "I wonder how the Witnauers knew about the tests?"

"Do you remember the name of Witnauer's real estate friend, Mr. DeWitt?"

"No, sir, but I do recall it was Latino. Ben Jack may remember his name."

"Ben Jack gave me a business card. The name on the card is Sergio Alverez, does that connect?"

"I believe that was the first name, Sergeant, but I'm not certain about the last name."

"Ben Jack told me Witnauer owns a trucking company in Laredo. Is that right?"

"That's correct. Ed owns a fleet of brine haulers. He has been in the brine business for a few years. His trucks started dumping at Hidalgo Disposal after I hired Randall. Witnauer is a good man, Sergeant."

"Would I create a problem for you if I went up to Laredo and talked with him?"

"I can't see where that'd be a problem. Hold on a minute while I get his address and phone number."

## 24

M‍ARTIN SPOTTED JOE GODFREY standing at the gate when he deplaned. Seeing someone he knew neutralized the anxiety he'd been experiencing before the plane landed. "It's good to see a familiar face, Joe. Thanks for meeting me."

"Tony and I are glad you were able to come down to help out, Martin. Did you check a bag?"

"Just one."

"Let's go grab your bag. I need to go back out to Hidalgo Disposal for about an hour to look for a specific piece of evidence, and then drive up to Laredo. Do you mind coming along? The visit may trigger something in your memory that could help with the investigation."

"It'll be stressful to go back to the disposal plant, but let's go."

"We should be back at headquarters before five. Tony suggested we go out to dinner together, and discuss what he and the DA want you to do while you're here. By the way, we've made a reservation for you at the Holiday Inn."

Martin was surprised when Joe drove past the entrance to Hidalgo Disposal. When he asked why, Joe said that he wanted to search for tire tracks outside the entrance. "We think the killer may have hidden his vehicle out here, and walked in."

Joe parked on the shoulder, and turned on his flashers. "We're looking for tracks that run perpendicular to the road. Pay special attention to the ground under trees. You take the right side of the road, and I'll take the left. Yell if you see anything suspicious."

Martin felt inadequate for the task. But, by moving slowly, and not allowing his mind to wander, he thought that he could compensate for the inexperience. He wasn't able to find anything out of the ordinary on the south side of the disposal's entrance. But, when he reached the end of the area Joe wanted searched on the north side, Martin found a tree with branches that could very well have served as cover for a vehicle. He bent down so he could see the ground more clearly. He stood up, and called out excitedly, "Joe, I think I may have found something. Come over and take a look."

Pointing at the ground, Martin said, "See that? Are those tire marks under the grass?"

Joe got down on his hands and knees and studied the spot carefully. "Yes, sir, I think this is where the bastard parked." Joe stood up, and added, "When the forensics guy gets here tomorrow, we'll show him this spot. I'll bet he can get a tire tread cast. Good work, Martin. Let's mark this spot with orange tape, and head up to Laredo."

Ed Witnauer was standing next to his wife's desk and talking on the phone when Joe and Martin entered the run-down offices of Laredo Trucking.

Ed Witnauer hung up, and asked, "May I help you?"

"Mr. Witnauer, I'm Sergeant Joe Godfrey with the Hidalgo County Sheriff's Department. This gentleman is Martin Leary. Roy DeWitt gave me your address. You may have information that could help us find the cause of the recent explosion at Hidalgo Disposal. Do you have time to answer a few questions?"

"Me? I can't imagine how I can help." He slowly placed his 5'11"-frame on the corner of the desk, and removed his glasses.

"Roy said your wife called him a few weeks ago, and asked if a friend of yours could visit his disposal."

Witnauer frowned when he realized the policeman was talking about Sergio Dominguez. "Let's go into my office."

"Did your friend talk with you within the past month or two about testing a new technology at Hidalgo?"

"Not exactly. The friend you're referring to is Sergio Dominguez." Joe's eyebrows rose. He remembered what Jack Kelly had said about Arturo Cisneros having a brother-in-law by the name of Dominguez, who worked for him as an enforcer. "Dominguez and I worked together at an oil services company a few years ago, before I started this trucking business. Sergio said he was interested in investing in a new technology that involved the recovery of waste oil. He told me the company that developed the technology planned to test it at a brine disposal plant over in east Texas. He said he wanted to learn more about how brine disposal plants operate, and asked me to make arrangements for him to visit Hidalgo Disposal." Ed took a sip from a coffee mug. "Would either of you like a cup of coffee?"

Joe said, "No, thank you." Martin shook his head.

"I told Sergio to be careful. The technology sounded like bullshit to me. But, I went ahead and made arrangements for him to visit Hidalgo Disposal. Then, my wife reads in the Laredo paper about an explosion over there. The story said the explosion was caused by osmium gas. I can't figure that one, Sergeant. Osmium gas at a disposal plant? It makes no sense to me, but I'm not a chemist."

Martin said, "Mr. Witnauer, you did say the man's name was Dominguez, not Alverez?"

"I don't know any Alverez, Mr. Leary." Smiling, he added, "By the way, call me Ed, and I'll call you Joe and Martin."

Joe said, "Tell us about this Dominguez fellow, Ed."

"I've known Sergio Dominguez for about eight years. The guy has a checkered background. From what I've heard, he seems to get involved in shady deals with shady people. Why are you interested in him?"

"We're attempting to determine if anyone might have, intentionally or unintentionally, brought something to the test site that caused the explosion. By the way, Daryl Burkhardt would like your permission to interview your drivers."

"Daryl Burkhardt? He's working for the Sheriff's Department now?"

"No. He's on temporary assignment until we determine what happened."

"I don't have a problem with Daryl interviewing my drivers. He can contact my wife and she can set things up."

"Let's get back to Dominguez, tell me about his shady deals."

"Sergio doesn't talk much about his deals. My information comes secondhand, from the comments of mutual friends." Witnauer laughed, "Sergio's so damned unpredictable. When he called a few weeks ago, the first time I'd heard from him in months by the way, he said he was a commercial Realtor in Austin."

Witnauer didn't notice Joe's posture straighten, his jaw drop, and his eyelids lift. Ed just continued talking, "Knowing Sergio, his claiming to be a Realtor is probably a bunch of bull. Maybe a drug gopher for the Mexican cartel, but not a Realtor."

Martin asked, "Why do you say that, Ed?"

"He grew up in Rio Grande City, and still has a home there. Sergio told me his wife lives in the house, but he stays up in Austin most of the time. I think he rents an apartment. I don't understand that kind of relationship. Anyway, drugs flow through Rio Grande City like a river." Ed leaned forward and said, "I met his brother-in-law, Arturo something-or-other a few years back. What a piece of work that guy is! He looked like someone who'd put a hole through his mother without a second thought."

"What else can you tell us about Dominguez?"

"I don't know an awful lot. He had a good job with the same oil field services company that I worked for, Texas Tool. That's how we met him. During the week we'd go out after work, and have a few pops together. Sergio was fun to be around. I still don't understand why he left the firm."

"What sort of job did he have at Texas Tool?"

"Good job, Sergeant. When he was in the Army, he was trained as an explosives specialist. He worked on a team that planned and carried out down-hole shots. Tricky business. You really have to know what you're doing."

"What sort of explosives did Dominguez use?"

"Mostly plastic stuff. Different strengths. The depth of the well, and the down-hole temperature would usually determine the strength of the shot."

Joe Godfrey reached into his pocket, retrieved a business card and placed on the table. "Ed, could this be the same man you've been talking about? Has your friend Dominguez ever used the name Alverez?"

"I don't think so, but I'm not sure. It wouldn't surprise me, though."

Joe asked, "Do you know where I could get a phone number, or an address? We checked the address and phone number on this card, and they're both phony!"

"His number in Austin is probably unlisted, but I think he gave it to me when he asked about visiting Hidalgo Disposal. Just a minute, and we'll get it for you." Ed called to his wife and asked her to locate Sergio's phone number. He said he thought he'd written it on a Rolodex card.

Martin was exhausted and hungry when he and Joe returned to the County Courthouse building. They climbed the broad staircase to the Sheriff's Department on the second floor and Martin followed Joe along the seedy corridor leading to the squad room. He was reminded of a second-rate newspaper office: limited isle space, desks back to back with files, papers, notes, telephone books, and photographs piled on top of any available surface. Because of a dearth of closet space and coat racks, jackets and sweaters were strewn over the backs of the chairs.

Joe's reference to his space in the squad room as an "office," was a misnomer; it was a three-sided cubicle with just enough room for Joe to slide by the metal, navy gray desk to reach a matching metal tilt back chair. While he was making a fresh pot of coffee, Joe noticed that Tony Zedillo's office door was open. He led Martin across the room and knocked on the doorjamb. "Got a minute to meet Martin Leary, Tony?"

Tony jumped up, walked around his desk, and extended his hand. "Welcome, Martin! We're glad you could join us. We need all the help we can muster. Have a seat."

"I'm not sure how much I can help, Tony, but I'll give it my best shot. I just wish we were meeting under different circumstances."

Tony turned to Joe. "Find anything interesting at the disposal?"

"Martin located a spot that looks promising. Someone pulled off the road and parked there recently. It's only about twenty yards north of the disposal entrance. Forensics may be able to pull a tread cast." Joe patted Martin on the shoulder. "You've been here less than four hours, and you've already contributed."

Martin addressed Tony. "Joe said you wanted go out to dinner and talk about specific tasks. I'm for that idea. I'm hungry. I haven't had much to eat today. The meager snack the airline served wasn't enough to satisfy a mouse."

"We can take care of that." Tony looked at Joe, and said, "Why don't we go across the street?"

"Good idea. We shouldn't have a problem getting a table at this hour."

The clock hanging on Jake's wall read 5:15 P.M. when the three men entered. They moved to Joe's favorite table against the back wall. Although Jake's Restaurant could seat just 36 customers at eight wood tables, the place was busy all day long. Jake's wife had convinced him to create a warm, homey environment by placing four unmatched antique chairs at each table, and installing a wood floor to complement the furniture. She also decorated the tables with colorful tablecloths and napkins. Jake hadn't changed a thing after her untimely death two years earlier.

Jake came out of the kitchen to greet them. Joe said, "Jake, meet Martin Leary from Connecticut. He'll be helping us with the Acuna investigation."

"Welcome to my humble establishment, Martin." Jake's handshake was so strong, Martin grimaced a little. Jake patted Joe on the back, and said, "You'll need the patience of a saint to work with this character."

Joe Godfrey and Jackson "Jake" Perkins became close friends soon after Joe joined the Hidalgo County Sheriff's Department. Joe, a bachelor, would eat most of his meals at Jake's. Jake, a widower, would sit and talk with Joe when the restaurant was not busy. The twenty-five-year age difference didn't seem to matter.

"Will you be having dinner?"

Tony answered, "Yeah. We have a lot to talk about, Jake. We may be here awhile. Will that be okay?"

"Not a problem."

"Any specials today?"

"Your favorite, Joe. Chicken pot pie."

"Sounds good. How about you, Martin?"

"Okay."

Tony said, "Make that three chicken pot pies, Jake."

They remained in Jake's for over an hour, chatting about the progress of the investigation. Tony said that the District Attorney requested that Martin be assigned to his office for a few days to compile a dossier on the Sonora drug cartel. The dossier would be used if the case ever came to trial. Tony said that the DA had already made arrangements for Martin to meet with representatives from the DEA in San Antonio. "Before I let the DA get his claws into you, I have a more pressing assignment. When we sent pieces of Acuna's clothing to state forensics two weeks ago, they found traces of a plastique explosive called C-4 impregnated in the fabric. C-4 is used by the military, as well as the oil industry here in Texas. Since you'll be in San Antonio, I'd like you to visit with the ordnance people at Camp Bullis. Get a list of people who were stationed at the base during the last few years who may have had access to the C-4 supply. When you return, I want you to call the major oil service companies, to see if any of their C-4 is missing."

"How do I get on a military base, Tony?"

"You've been deputized. You can go anywhere as a representative of this department. Show your badge at the gate, and ask to see the officer in charge of ordnance. You may get bounced around, but don't let it upset you. Be patient." Tony removed a typewritten list of possible suspects from his shirt pocket. "Because of the drug connection, and the discovery of C-4 on Acuna's clothing, be especially alert to any mention of these names when you are talking with the DEA and the ordnance people."

The director of the San Antonio office of the DEA was extremely cooperative and provided Martin with extensive material about the Sonora cartel. The meeting with the San Antonio police reinforced what the DEA furnished, especially intelligence about Rodriguez. The information was so well organized Martin believed he could complete a report for the DA within a few days.

The commanding officer of the Camp Bullis ordnance depot was not as cooperative. He was reluctant to talk with Martin at first, but relented when Martin explained forcefully that he was involved in a murder investigation. Martin's first question about inventory shortages put Captain Raetz on the defensive.

"I'm embarrassed to admit, Mr. Leary, that three C-4 bars are missing from our inventory. I'm not sure whether our records are faulty, or that someone removed the bars illegally. We're checking."

"How difficult would it be for someone to walk off with the stuff?"

"If someone had access to the depot, and had friends that work here, it wouldn't be difficult. The bars aren't very big."

"Would you describe the bars for me, Captain? What should we look for?"

"The C-4 bars are pale white, about a foot long, two inches wide and about an inch thick. The stuff is like soft clay, easy to knead with your hands."

"Can you supply me with the names of personnel that may have had access to your C-4 stock over the past two years or so?"

"I'll ask my staff to get on that right away. It may take us a few days."

"Time is of the essence, Captain. Would it be possible for me to wait and review a list today, while I'm here?"

The officer fidgeted, but acquiesced. He summoned his orderly. "Go over to records, and retrieve the visitor logs for the past two years. I also want a list of personnel assigned to this depot during the last ten years. Tell the sergeant in charge that it's a priority request." He turned toward Martin. "Make yourself comfortable while you wait, Mr. Leary. There's coffee in the carafe, and," pointing across the room, "there are a few magazines inside the drawer of the end table over there."

After waiting for over an hour, Martin was able to begin the tedious job of reviewing the record of personnel assigned to the depot over the past ten years. Starting with the oldest record first, it didn't take long for Martin to spot the name of a Sergeant Sergio Dominguez, of Rio Grande City, Texas. Dominguez had been stationed at the depot eight years earlier. The search of the visitor logs went much faster. He only had to go back to June to discover that a Sergio Dominguez visited the facility. Unfortunately, the person who had signed him in had been transferred to Korea in August. There was no way to determine what he had done while he was on the base.

"Well I guess that's as far as I can go, Captain. This information will be very helpful to the investigation. If you decide that you can release copies of these lists, please send them to Sheriff Tony Zedillo." Martin handed the officer Tony's business card, and shook hands. "Thanks, Captain. I hope we can reciprocate some day. I'll call if we encounter those C-4 bars."

Martin reported that he'd been treated with respect when he visited with the DEA and the San Antonio Police Department. Both organizations provided him with valuable data about the activities of the Sonora cartel, and important background information about Rodriguez and Cisneros. "Those two characters are bad, Tony, especially Rodriguez. Apparently, he's a brutal son-of-a-bitch. He doesn't accept dissent within the organization. Offenders are either maimed, or eliminated entirely. The DEA suspects that the guy is responsible for at least three homicides."

"What did you find out at Camp Bullis?"

"The commanding officer was reluctant to talk with me at first, but finally relented after I explained why I was there. He admitted that a few C-4 bars are missing from his inventory. He said that either his records were faulty, or the bars had been removed without authorization. But here's the clincher, Tony. The personnel records show that a Sergio Dominguez was attached to his depot eight years ago. While he was assigned to the depot, he was classified as an expert with explosives. Dominguez visited the depot last June. It'd be easy to construct a scenario that says Dominguez stole a few bars of C-4 while he was at the depot. He sure as hell knew where to find the stuff."

Tony turned in his chair and looked across the courtyard to the windows of the judge's chambers. "It looks like our first order of business is to convince a judge to issue warrants to search Dominguez's apartment in Austin, and his vehicle if and when we find it. Can you get on that today, Joe?"

"It'll be the first thing I do after we break, Tony."

He turned back to face Joe and Martin. "Right now, unless we find something incriminating in his apartment, our evidence isn't strong enough to convince the DA to take the case to the grand jury. If the DA tells us we need an eyewitness, or a confession from Dominguez, we've got a problem. Besides, the guy we really want is Cisneros. That son-of-a-bitch probably paid his brother-in-law to kill the kid. Come to think of it, when you talk with the judge, ask him to include Dominguez's bank records in the warrant. We need to look at his checking account to see if he's deposited a large amount of money recently."

# 25

IT TOOK JOE A little over three hours to complete the drive from McAllen to Austin to meet with Jack Kelly. Joe poured himself a cup of coffee, and then got right to the point. "Ed Witnauer told me he's the one that arranged for Dominguez to visit the disposal plant three weeks ago. He corroborated the version DeWitt and Randall gave us. Dominguez concocted some bogus scheme about a new oil waste technology. Ed said that he doesn't know any Alverez, but it sure sounds like Dominguez is using Alverez as an alias. We're going to have to pin down the bastard's identity pretty quick." Joe went into a little more detail about his conversation with Witnauer, and then asked, "When do we meet with the students?"

"Two this afternoon. We'd better get moving. It's one-thirty now."

"If the students support the information I got about Dominguez/Alverez, we need a warrant to search Dominguez's apartment." Joe thought for a moment. "Come to think of it, to save time, why don't I meet with your DA while you're meeting with the students?"

"That would work. I'll have my supervisor introduce you."

"Any thoughts about how we locate Dominguez without alerting him?"

"Yeah. It might be time for me to enlist the services of one of Austin's best snitches, Donnie Scott. If Dominguez lives in Austin, Donnie will know where we can find him. I may be able to locate Donnie late this afternoon after I meet with the students."

The graduate apartment complex was comprised of four similarly designed two-story structures built in the early 1990's. When Jack made the appointment, he tried to be sensitive to the students' busy schedule—morning classes, and tutoring sessions with undergraduates in the afternoon.

Pat Duncan and Sonja Hyde lived together on the second floor. Climbing the stairs, Jack noted the cleanliness of the hallways and stairs, unlike his old dorm at Texas Tech. He guessed it was probably an indication of the maturity of the graduate students who occupied the building. Sonja Hyde welcomed the detective, explaining that Duncan had just showered and would join them in a few moments. "Any health complications from the explosion, Miss Hyde?"

Sonja answered with an obvious German accent, "No. I just had a big headache for a few days. May I offer you a soft drink, or a cup of coffee?" Kelly declined. He inquired about her plans after completing her doctoral studies. "I may return to Germany, Detective. I have a job offer from a firm in Bonn."

"Congratulations! What are Pat's plans after graduation?"

"Pat wants to teach. He's been offered a position assisting Dr. Gerba in the Chemistry Department." Jack Kelly was impressed with their goals, and maybe a little envious. During the past few months he'd wondered whether he'd made a mistake and left school too early, rather than pursue a Master's degree in some aspect of law enforcement.

When Duncan joined them, Jack reiterated the reason for the visit. He wanted the meeting to be informal and low-key; Duncan and Hyde still believed José's death had been accidental. "When Sergeant Godfrey and I met with Dr. Gerba last week he told us the precious metals extraction technology was proprietary, and the location of the test regime was confidential. We're not convinced. We have a hunch that others outside your group may have known about the tests. What do you think?"

Sonja and Pat looked at each other. They seemed to arrive at an unspoken agreement that Pat would be their spokesperson. "That seems unlikely, Detective. Dr. Gerba is paranoid about secrecy. I remember a Realtor guy dropped in on us at the Airport Industrial Complex just before we finished building the prototype. He said he was looking for industrial space for a client. He asked a lot of questions about the technology, but we didn't reveal anything. Do you remember him, Sonja?"

"Yes. He was persistent. José told him the technology was proprietary and that we couldn't talk about it."

"He finally took the hint and left." Pat thought for a moment. "You know, Sergeant, I think José did mention we'd tow the prototype to south Texas when we finished. Do you remember that, Sonja?"

"Yes, he did say that."

Kelly asked, "Can you describe this man?"

Pat answered, "As I recall the guy was a well-built dude, not quite 6 feet tall. He was dark, and had a Hispanic name. I assumed he was Mexican-American."

"Do you remember the first or last name, Pat?"

"I can't. How about you, Sonja?"

"No. I only remember that the man gave José a business card just before he left and asked us to call him when we set a date to vacate the space."

Jack remained quiet for a moment while he digested that information, and asked, "Does the name Sergio Alverez ring a bell?"

Sonja sat up and said, "Yes, sir! I'm pretty sure that's it."

Kelly stood up. "You've been helpful." He handed his card to Duncan and said, "If you think of anything else that help with our investigation of the accident, please call me at Austin P.D. If I'm not in, leave a message, and I'll get back to you as soon as possible."

A patrol car spotted Donnie Scott walking slowly along 6th Street, and immediately contacted Detective Kelly in his squad car. "Donnie is hanging out on the north side of 6th, near the Alcazar. Should we pick him up?"

"No. Just keep him in sight until I get there. Thanks, guys."

Jack spotted Donnie standing near a corner smoking a cigarette. He parked at the curb and approached Donnie from behind and announced, "Good to see you again, Donnie. What's new?"

As Donnie whirled around to face the detective, he removed a cigarette from his mouth, wiped his mouth and nose on his dirty sleeve, and replied, "Got a new job, Detective. I'm working in the kitchen over at the shelter from 9 to 4."

"That's fantastic, Donnie. What'd you do in the kitchen?"

He adopted a downtrodden look before answering, "Wash dishes."

"Somebody's got do it, Donnie. Might as well be you. Say, Donnie, I've got $20 for you if you can give me some important information. Interested?"

"I gotta watch out for my reputation, but I could use $20. What's the information?"

"What can you tell me about Arturo Cisneros?"

Before Kelly could continue, Donnie held up his hand. "Hold it, Detective. I want nothin' to do with that crazy bastard. He'd kill his own mother for a buck."

"Donnie, Donnie! I wouldn't put you in harm's way. I already know about Cisneros. I need information about his brother-in-law. Do you know him?"

"Yeah. Dominguez, he's a fucking punk. Thinks he's jack-shit. He's just a messenger boy for Cisneros."

"Where does he live, Donnie?"

"In an apartment on the corner of 4th and Grand. But don't be confused; the name on the apartment call box is Alverez."

"Thanks, Donnie. Here's your $20. You come see me if the job doesn't work out."

Joe Godfrey was working at a table in the conference room when Kelly returned to police headquarters. "How did your meetings go?"

Jack sat down on the opposite side of the table and said, "Donnie Scott said that Dominguez is a punk, nothing more than a messenger boy for his brother-in-law. He gave me an address, but told me to look for Alverez on the mailbox. I went over there and talked with a few neighbors. They confirmed that Dominguez lives there all right, but hasn't been around for a few days."

Jack removed his jacket and continued, "You know, Joe, I've been thinking. If we pick him up for questioning, he might break."

"You may be right. But, on the other hand if he doesn't break, we don't have enough to hold him, and then we could lose Cisneros. It's a tough call, Jack. I think we should wait until you've searched his apartment. Your DA said he'd have a warrant by tomorrow. If we find meaningful evidence in Dominguez's apartment, I think it may be time for us to meet with our county District Attorney, and ask him to convene a grand jury to indict our Mexican friend."

# 26

SERGIO'S NERVES WERE LIKE an open wound after he learned of Acuna's autopsy results. He wracked his brain to think of a way to deflect the murder investigation away from him. When he realized that the truth might be his best weapon, the pieces to the puzzle began to fall in place. He'd use the unique circumstances surrounding the student's death as the foundation for a diversion plan. By the time he arrived at Bustamonte's to meet with Arturo, he was ready to do battle.

Arturo sat quietly as Sergio began to brief him on recent developments. When he'd heard enough, he barked, "Okay, I don't want to hear no more crap. I got the message: things don't look so good. Now what the hell are we gonna do about it?"

"How about creating some kind of diversion? Like confusing the police."

"What the hell are you talking about? A diversion? Come on, Sergio, you don't know how to spell the word."

"Slow down and listen. I was thinking about the machine the college kids were building over near the airport. The disposal manager, Randall, told me the machine was designed to remove precious metals from brine. No wonder the professor, and that guy from Connecticut, were so interested in what the kid was doing." Sergio leaned forward for emphasis. "They were excited about the potential profits, Arturo! Think about it. Recovering gold, silver and platinum from brine! Shit, Arturo, that's news, right? Maybe we could get the Sheriff's Department to think someone was trying to sabotage the project because the technology was a threat."

Arturo showed little interest in what Sergio was saying. He fidgeted, raised his hand and motioned to the waitress. "What kind of a threat? I don't understand."

"A business threat. A process like that could be revolutionary. It could ruin a mining business. If you were in the business of mining precious metals, wouldn't you be concerned about someone producing that stuff from a waste product?"

Arturo slowly lowered his arm, turned and studied Sergio's face closely, looking for any sign that he was making light of the situation. Observing none, he asked, "How can we create a diversion? We don't know shit about precious metals, or where they're produced."

"Here's what I'm thinking. Suppose a precious metals mining company in Mexico hears about the technology, wouldn't they be a little concerned? They'd think the technology was a threat, and they'd go ballistic, right? Let's say we leaked a bullshit story like that to a newspaper, say in Corpus Christi, or San Antonio, and say the kid's death wasn't an accident." Sergio sat back in the chair. "How's that sound?"

Arturo stared at Sergio, and asked, "Why a Mexican company?"

"A couple of reasons. First, with your connections across the border, we might be able to screw up the sheriff's investigation by releasing a bunch of baloney leads. Second, if the sheriff believes a Mexican company is involved, his hands would be tied, wouldn't they? What could he do? He can't go after a Mexican company."

"How would this Mexican company hear about the technology?"

"I thought about that. Acuna was a student at the university, right? We could say their people heard about it from contacts at the university. You know, scientists talking to scientists."

Arturo was fully attentive now. "There must be some company in Mexico that produces precious metals. See what you can find out and get back to me tomorrow."

Sergio recognized how ill prepared he was to support his diversion plan. He'd never been taught to access the many information sources available on the Internet. He didn't even own a computer. In spite of not having visiting a library since his junior year at Rio Grande City High School, he decided the best place to start would be the Austin City Library.

Ms. Adams, the lead reference librarian, was intrigued by Sergio's admitted ignorance of library resources, and elected to help him with his research; she took it on as a personal challenge. She located a U.S. Department of State publication that confirmed the existence of a precious metals industry in Mexico, but the publication didn't identify specific private sector businesses. She next searched the Internet and obtained the name for the Mexican equivalent of the U.S. Department of Commerce, the Secretaría de Commercio y Fomento Industrial in Mexico City. She located its web site and found three mining companies that fit the criteria provided by Sergio—two Canadian firms, and a German company. She printed information about all three, and handed them to Sergio. "Why don't you sit at the table in front of my desk and read through the material. If you think you need more, I'll continue the search."

The printed material included important information about the location of Mexican properties owned by the three companies, described the metals mined, products produced, research activities, and management profiles. Sergio's confidence surged. After reviewing the documentation a second time, the details of a plan slowly began to evolve. He reread the information about the German firm, Hechmann & Co., KG, a third time. The material said that Hechmann, with headquarters in Bonn, was among the leaders in the worldwide production of precious metals. Their business included mining, research and development, manufacturing, and precious metals trading, especially the platinum group metals: platinum, palladium, iridium, osmium, ruthenium and rhenium.

Sergio slapped his hands together when he discovered that the German company had a research and development group in an area of Mexico he knew well, the southern section of the State of Durango. He felt he could make the case that it'd be highly unlikely Hechmann's scientific community in Durango, only a day's drive away from Hidalgo County, would ignore an important University of Texas sponsored precious metals research project in south Texas. Sergio rose from the chair, smiled at the librarian and reported, "I think the information you found will be enough, Ms. Adams. Thanks again."

"You're welcome, Mr. Dominguez. Glad I could help."

Sergio strode from the building with head high, confident his plan would work.

Cisneros sat back on a straight back chair at his kitchen table and nodded with satisfaction. He was surprised his brother-in-law was smart enough to originate such a plan. "Damn, Sergio, that's a great plan. I'm beginning to think it just might work. When will you call?"

"I'll call the *Corpus Christi Register* in the morning. When the *Register* story hits the streets, the other Texas newspapers will pick it up. The TV stations in south Texas should pick it up too."

Cisneros stood up and slapped his brother-in-law on the shoulder. "Damn, I love it, Sergio. Those hicks down there in Hidalgo County will be up to their asses in problems."

## ELSA

The call came into the switchboard at the *Corpus Christi Register* at 9:00 A.M., and was immediately shunted to Editor Peter Haven's extension. Haven's secretary answered the phone, "Mr. Haven's office."

"Peter Haven, please."

Haven's secretary responded, "Whom may I say is calling?"

"Tell Haven that that University of Texas college student who was killed in Elsa a few weeks ago, was killed on purpose. It was not an accident."

"Who'd you say is calling?"

"I didn't! And I don't intend to either. Now, lady, get Haven on the line before I hang up, and you'll be sorry you missed an exclusive story."

"Please hold."

The line went dead temporarily. Sergio smiled as he envisioned the secretary scurrying about trying to get Haven to pick up the phone.

"Peter Haven. What's so urgent that you needed to talk with me, mister, what did you say your name was?"

"I didn't. Remember that University of Texas student, the one who was killed at a brine disposal site in Elsa a few weeks ago? Well, the kid was executed. Do you want to hear about it or not?"

"Please, go ahead. I'm listening."

"The kid was working on a secret project to extract platinum from oil field brine. A German mining company got wind of the project, thought it was a threat, came up from their plant in Mexico and sabotaged the tests. They killed the kid. If you don't believe me, check with the university in Austin, and with the Hidalgo County Sheriff." With that announcement, Sergio hung up.

Haven sat motionless for a few moments. He shrugged his shoulders and mumbled, "Another damn crank call." He went back to reviewing the headline story for tomorrow's edition. He was having difficulty concentrating, however. Instead, his mind was consumed with the caller's claims. He turned to look out of his office window, and then called to his secretary. "Kimberly, please ask Bryan and Mondello to come into my office, and find the story about that University of Texas student who was killed down in Hidalgo County a few weeks ago."

Peter Haven recounted the content of the anonymous telephone call. "The caller's claims could be significant, or they could be bogus. Let's find out." Haven issued specific assignments: Ann Bryan was asked to contact the Hidalgo Sheriff's Department, and the University of Texas. Javier Mondello was asked to contact the Texas Railroad Commission, and identify the German mining company that was supposed to have operations in Mexico. "You should be able to confirm or deny the legitimacy of the caller's claims before the end of the day." Haven arranged to regroup with his reporters late that same afternoon.

"Well, people, what's the consensus? Do we have a story, or don't we?"

With a broad grin on her face, Bryan announced, "I believe we have a story. I drove down to McAllen and confronted the Hidalgo County Sheriff personally. After I badgered him, he finally admitted that the student was murdered." She giggled, and added, "He was really pissed, Mr. Haven. He said that he hadn't revised the accident announcement because his department is small and undermanned. He said he needed time to conduct a proper investigation, without incurring the normal distractions caused by the media. Things would have been a lot worse, he said, if the press had found out that the student was a doctoral candidate at University of Texas in Austin, and had family in Corpus Christi."

Haven leaned forward in his chair and rubbed his hands together. "Interesting! Very interesting. What did the university people say?"

"After a lot of waffling, the PR people at the university referred me to Dr. Ely Gerba, a chemistry professor. He was shocked by what I told him. He denied the story out of hand. He was angry to think that someone would float such an outrageous tale. The sheriff must have done a good job of keeping the lid on, and sucker the media. Dr. Gerba told me he was one of five founders of a new startup company called the Precious Metals Extraction Corporation. I asked for the names of the other four founders. I was surprised that he actually gave me the names." Referring to her notes, she read them off: "A fellow faculty member, Dr. Robinson; an Austin attorney, Richard Hammil; a south Texas oil field waste disposal operator, Roy DeWitt; and a gentleman from Norwich, Connecticut, Martin Leary. He also confirmed that Acuna was his top doctoral candidate."

Haven was obviously disheartened by that report. He leaned against the back of his chair, and frowned. "What's your report, Javier?"

Mondello straightened, and said that he was able to verify the existence of a German mining company in Mexico. "Hechmann & Co. is headquartered in Bonn, and has precious metals mining operations in numerous countries. One of their mines is in the State of Durango, Mexico. They also have an R & D facility there. When I attempted to talk with the plant manager about the story, however, I was rebuffed with, 'Sorry, no comment.'

"The next report may be the clincher, Mr. Haven. After four phone calls to various individuals within the Railroad Commission, I was referred to a Chief Inspector Travis Jenkins right here in Corpus Christi. I went over to his office and talked with him. He reluctantly admitted that the explosion was not the result of an accidental explosion. He said there was a strong possibility the student's death was a homicide. He indicated that the Railroad

Commission was assisting the Hidalgo County Sheriff's Department with the investigation."

"Damn! That was good work, people. Ann, I want you to call the sheriff this afternoon, and tell him we intend to run the story on the front page of tomorrow's paper. Tell him we are giving him one more opportunity to comment, if he wishes." Peter Haven stood up. "Javier, I want you to write the story. Make sure you run it by Ann before you give it to me. You must be very careful not to mention the name of the German firm, Javier. Until we have proof of their complicity, we sit on the name. You can write about a general theory of sabotage, without being specific."

Tom Snow, a reporter with the *Hartford Outlook*, was surfing the Worldwide Press website when a bulletin with a headline "Corpus Christi, Texas" captured his attention. The news service was reporting on a story published in the *Corpus Christi Register* about the untimely death of a University of Texas graduate student. The newspaper charged the student's death resulted from a botched attempt by a foreign mining company to sabotage tests of a new technology developed to extract precious metals from an oil field waste product. Snow's interest heightened when he read that a Norwich, Connecticut, man was listed among the individuals who served on the board of directors of the firm that owned the technology. He decided to print the report, and show it to the supervising editor of the news department.

"Look at this, Chief." The editor of statewide news for the *Outlook*, took the piece of paper from Tom Snow's hand, scanned the story until she arrived at a section highlighted by Snow.

"Hmm, Norwich. How did a guy from Norwich get involved with precious metals in Texas?" The editor looked up at Snow who was standing in front of her desk. "Are you suggesting there may be a story here?"

"It has the potential. Think about it: murder of a college student; precious metals research; industrial sabotage; international intrigue; and, now a local twist, a guy from Norwich on the board of directors of the company doing the testing."

"Go for it, Tom. Just keep me posted."

Snow called information to obtain the telephone number for Martin Leary in Norwich. The operator asked if he wanted Leary's home number, or the number for Leary Realty. "Hum, I'll take both numbers please." He called the home number first. On the sixth ring he heard the familiar recorded message of a voice mail service, and decided not to leave a message. He disconnected and dialed the number for Leary Realty. "Leary Realty, may I help you?"

"Martin Leary, please."

"Whom may I say is calling?"

"Tom Snow from Hartford."

"Mr. Leary is not in the office today. He's out of town. I don't expect him until the day after tomorrow."

"Is Mr. Leary in Texas?"

"Why, yes. How did you know?"

"I'm a reporter with the *Hartford Outlook*. Do you have a number where I can reach him?"

Snow called the Hidalgo County District Attorney's office and asked to speak with Martin Leary. Martin was tempted to ask the secretary to take a message; he was working against a deadline to complete the report on the drug cartel and didn't want to be disturbed. But, he thought the better of it, and picked up the instrument. "Martin Leary speaking."

"We've never met, Mr. Leary. My name is Tom Snow. I'm a reporter with the *Hartford Outlook*." Martin's skin tightened, and he sat up straight. He wondered why a newspaper reporter from Hartford would be calling him?

"Are you a member of the board of directors of the Precious Metals Extraction Corporation?"

"Yes. Why are you asking?"

"Does your company have a facility in south Texas, and did you experience a fatal explosion at that location recently?"

"No and yes. We were running tests of a new technology at a brine disposal plant, but we don't own the plant. A University of Texas graduate student was killed accidentally two weeks ago. Why all these questions, Mr. Snow?"

"Do you wish to comment on the *Corpus Christi Register* story that claims a University of Texas graduate student was killed during a failed attempt to sabotage tests of a new technology?"

Martin was stunned. How could that be? Not thinking, he shouted, "That's bullshit! That story has got to be a fabrication. Acuna's death was drug related!" Martin knew instantly that he'd made a serious blunder. He sank back into his chair and tried to recover. "What I should have said is that the police think the death might have had something to do with drugs." Snow, an experienced reporter, weighed the significance of Martin's outburst, and concluded he may have stumbled onto a story.

"Why do the police think the death may have been drug related?"

Martin lamented, "I shouldn't have said anything about drugs. Hey, I'm sorry, you'll have to excuse me. I have to go to a meeting."

Before Martin could hang up, Tom Snow took a chance, and asked, "Why don't you believe the Corpus Christi newspaper story about industrial sabotage?"

Martin quickly decided he'd better tell the truth or he'd dig a deeper hole for himself. "Because I know the facts. I'm helping the Hidalgo County Sheriff's Department with the investigation. Check out the story that appeared in our local Norwich newspaper last week. Listen, I'll be late for my meeting. Nice talking with you, Mr. Snow."

Snow looked at the telephone instrument in his hand, placed it softly in its cradle, and contemplated his options. He could forget about the story and not pursue further inquiries. After all, the kid was killed in south Texas. How many of the newspaper's subscribers had ever heard of south Texas? On the other hand, there was something fishy about Leary's responses. *What the hell did he mean when he said the kid's death was drug related?*

Snow decided to check out Leary's claim that he was part of the homicide investigation first. He went back into the Internet and searched for the *Norwich Daily News* homepage. Sure enough, the story was true. Snow thought it strange that a commercial Realtor would be chosen to work with law enforcement to solve a murder, and decided he'd look into it after he talked with the Corpus Christi newspaper.

Tony Zedillo read the newspaper story for the third time. He slapped the newspaper down on his desk, and remarked, "Son of a bitch! I can't believe the paper actually went ahead and printed this cockamamie story. Unbelievable!" Martin looked over at Joe Godfrey for some indication of how to respond to Tony's outburst. "The story is already creating serious problems for us. We're up to our ass in Texas media. They've inundated this community, trying to out-due one another. Whoever invented this story, and then convinced the *Register* that it was true, must be a genius. If we ever find out who floated this cockamamie story, we'll probably find our perpetrator."

Tony leaned forward and said, "This could be way out of our league, Joe. What if the story is true? Maybe Acuna's drug habit had nothing to do with his death? I think you'd better talk with Dr. Gerba. Between the two of you, maybe you can shed some light on the damn story."

"I'll call him as soon as we break."

Tony turned and looked out the window. It was obvious he was worried. He said, "You know, this fucking story may convince some of the County Commissioners to back away from the investigation. Let's face it, they're politicians first. They're more interested in protecting their political asses than they are solving the murder of a college student, especially since the kid wasn't even a resident of the county in the first place." Tony turned back to face Martin and Joe. "They'll be all over us to close out the case, one way or another. That would be a huge mistake, so we can't let it happen. Which means we can't be wrong about our conclusions. Let's review the evidence."

Joe summarized the evidence collected at the site of the explosion, what they'd learned about Acuna and his relationship with Cisneros, Dominguez's bomb making experience, and his groundless visits to Hidalgo Disposal. "I believe the evidence is solid, but I have to admit, it's circumstantial."

"I'm convinced, Joe. But unfortunately, you're singing to the choir." Tony stood up. "This damn newspaper story worries me. Our little department can't withstand an assault from the press. We need time to get Dominguez to talk, some way, some how." Tony hit the desk with the palm of his hand. "Damn it! We can't compromise. We've got to proceed with the investigation as if the newspaper story had never been published. With a staff of only ten people, we'll have to hunker down and wait for the press to lose interest in that ridiculous story."

"You're right, Tony. We need to buy time, somehow. We need to delay and neutralize the press. But, how the hell do we do that?"

Martin told them about the phone call he'd received from a Hartford reporter. "If the sabotage story is already news in Hartford, it won't be long before the jackals from New York take an interest in the story."

Tony said, "Gentlemen, we're gonna have a serious public relations problem on our hands."

Martin said, "Joe told me that your man Collins is quite a jokester. He said Collins could lie to his mother and be convincing. Why don't you use him as your spokesperson?"

Tony brightened. He looked over at Joe, and nodded his head. "Martin, I think you just came up with one tremendous idea! Collins is the biggest bullshitter in south Texas."

"I agree. That's a great idea. How come we didn't think of that, Joe?"

At 5'5", 140 pounds, Dave Collins was the smallest deputy on the ten-man Hidalgo County Sheriff's Department staff. Joe Godfrey speculated that Dave must have worn elevator shoes and eaten a bunch of bananas when he applied for the deputy position; the listed height and weight qualifications for a deputy were 5'6", 150 pounds respectively. Sheriff Zedillo must have ignored the man's physical limitations, and responded instead to Dave's jovial and upbeat attitude. Tony probably thought that Collins would have a positive effective on the morale of his department.

People passing Dave on the street wouldn't notice him. But if they did, they might label him as an ugly loser. He inherited a large nose and a narrow face from his mother and an overbite from his father. He had the irritating habit of combing his right hand through his blond hair when he talked. Offsetting his unattractive features, Dave possessed an infectious grin. Despite his small stature, Dave was fearless. Sheriff Zedillo was never concerned about Dave's loyalty to the department, or his commitment to protecting his partner when on duty.

To the casual observer, Collins was probably way over his head in the publicity ring, but the casual observer didn't know the man like Joe and Tony did. When informed of his new assignment, Collins decided early on, that he'd adopt his family's creed, "You can't bullshit a bullshitter, but you can bullshit everyone else."

Based on that strategy, It didn't take long for Collins to feel comfortable fielding all kinds of stupid questions from reporters who hung out in the hallways of the County Courthouse looking for news, any news. He'd monopolize press briefings with stories about growing up on a pig farm in a rural west Texas town. He described his home town as "a gas station struggling to be a town."

Dave's favorite stories involved his father and his father's friends. The senior Collins and his buddies would congregate on the front porch of the general store/gas station, and use it as a community-gathering place, town hall, and some instances, a makeshift courthouse. He'd talk about how his "old man" would collect inoperable vehicles and stored them in the front and back yards of his rural home, believing someone, someday would need parts. Dave claimed that his redneck daddy needed to be recycled because he was white trash.

A typical question from a reporter: "Sergeant (Collins received a temporary promotion to impress the media), you'll have to identify the foreign company that was involved in sabotage eventually, so why not now?"

A typical answer: "You guys are unbelievable! Can't you appreciate the sensitivity of the situation? The Sheriff's Department can't ignore our national security. If the State Department approves, I'll provide a name. Until then, be my guest and speculate."

"The State Department? You can't be serious."

"Why not?" argued Collins. "Think about it: a German firm, doing business in Mexico, sabotages a sensitive American precious metals project and kills an American graduate student. This thing could be so big, the President may have to get involved."

# 27

SYLVIA MOSCOSO STAYED WITH Rebecca Acuna for a few days after her son's death, keeping the house organized and cooking until Rebecca could get back on her feet. Sylvia continued to check on her friend periodically after moving back to her own home. She made it a point to telephone each night. But, telephoning was not very reliable; Rebecca wouldn't answer the phone half the time. When Sylvia heard about a bake sale at Rebecca's church, she convinced her friend to participate in the sale by baking her specialty: raisin scones. Sylvia believed baking might be the spark that would reignite her interest in living.

Working alongside her friend in the familiar surroundings of her own kitchen, Rebecca began her recovery. She actually smiled when she learned that her scones were the hit of the sale. Participating in the bake sale also seemed to rekindle Rebecca's spirituality. She reactivated her practice of attending daily Mass, one of a handful of comforting activities she'd allowed herself.

The morning that the sabotage story appeared in the Corpus Christi newspaper, Rebecca began the short three-block walk from church to her home after Mass. Sylvia Moscoso called to her from her front porch as she approached. "Good morning, Rebecca. It's nice to see you out walking. Returning from church?"

Rebecca was not in the mood to talk. She turned her head toward Sylvia when she responded, but continued to walk. "Yes. I started attending 7:30 Mass again."

"That's wonderful." Sylvia stood up, descended the porch stairs, and walked toward Rebecca. Sylvia said sympathetically, "The latest news about your son must have been shocking."

Rebecca stopped walking. "What news?"

Taken aback, Sylvia said, "The story in the paper this morning. About his death."

"What're you talking about? What story in the paper?"

"Please come up on the porch, Rebecca." Sylvia grabbed Rebecca's elbow as she ascended the stairs to the porch and led her to a chair. Sylvia picked up the newspaper from an end table, and was about to read the headline but thought better of it. She handed the newspaper to Rebecca and said, "Please read this, Rebecca."

As soon as Rebecca saw the bold headline: *U. of T. Student Murdered*, she took the paper with a shaking hand and read the sub-headline, *Sheriff Admits Students Death Not Accidental*. Rebecca's eyes watered. She dropped the paper to the floor, put her hands over eyes and began to sob, uncontrollably.

"Rebecca, I'm so sorry. I thought you knew."

Dick Hammil signed in at the reception desk on the first floor of the chemistry building and was issued a visitor badge. The receptionist called Dr. Gerba to alert him that he had a visitor.

"Yes, Alice, what is it?"

"Mr. Hammil is here to see you, Dr. Gerba."

"Send him up to Lab #2."

"Take the elevator to the third floor and turn left. Dr. Gerba is in the third lab on your right, Lab #2." Hammil turned left as instructed, and passed six laboratories, three on each side of the hallway, before he reached Lab #2. Ely was standing next to a bench holding a test tube over a Bunsen burner. Dressed in a long laboratory coat and wearing safety glasses, he looked like a mad scientist from an old B movie back in the 1930's.

"Dick, what a pleasant surprise."

"I was in the vicinity, Ely, so I thought I'd stop by."

"I'm glad you did. We have a lot to talk about. Have a seat, I'll be with you in a minute."

"Have you heard about the sabotage story that appeared in the Corpus Christi newspaper yesterday?"

Ely placed the test tube in a rack and removed the safety glasses. "I haven't seen the Corpus newspaper. One of their reporters called yesterday and told me that her newspaper received an anonymous telephone tip claiming that José was killed during an aborted attempt to sabotage the development of our technology. She asked for my reaction. I insisted that the claim was false. Couldn't be true, I told her." Ely sighed. "Why can't people accept the fact that José's death was an accident? I suppose the next call that I get will be from the White House."

"Ely, please be serious. The story appears to have validity; at least it had enough validity to motivate a newspaper to publish the story."

"I'm sorry, Dick. I've been under a lot of pressure." Ely sat down heavily. He sighed, sounding like air being emitted from a tire. "Maybe the newspaper has it right. That would mean that the chemistry had nothing to do with José's death and that would be a good thing. I was suspicious of the Railroad Commission's osmium gas explosion theory from the beginning."

"I'm concerned about the project, Ely. Can we salvage it, or are we about to lose our investment?"

"We lost a brilliant young scientist, $5000, a lot of time, and maybe technological confidentiality, but the prototype is intact and stored in a safe place, and the technology hasn't been compromised. Our major problem is not the technology; it's the damn Railroad Commission. We need to get them off our backs."

"For what it's worth, I've filed our appeal. We just have to wait and see. If they agree that brine is a raw material, we may be out of the woods."

"I'm tired of being the last one to find out about what's happening. While you're here, let's call Sergeant Godfrey and get some straight answers."

Joe Godfrey cut Ely off before he could launch into an angry tirade about the Corpus Christi newspaper story. "I suspect the press has contacted you about the sabotage story. Am I correct, Dr. Gerba?"

"Yes, Sergeant. The Corpus Christi newspaper contacted me before they ran the story. I'm very confused. Please help me sort this out."

"I know you're upset and rightly so, but please don't be concerned about the sabotage story, Doctor. It's a fabrication. Acuna's death was deliberate all right, but it was not the result of sabotage. I can't reveal the details of the evidence we've collected, but you can be assured, we'll make an arrest. We wanted to keep the killer, or killers, off balance until we were ready to make our move. We thought we could buy time by not correcting the original accident theory." Changing the volume and tone of his voice, Joe added, "I hope we'll be able to provide you with the results of our investigation soon. In the meantime, don't let the press rattle you. Be strong. Respond with a 'no comment' when they pressure you. Keep responding 'no comment' until they become sick and tired of asking."

Returning to the parking garage after a short trip to the bank, Sarah Bernard turned on her car radio and tuned into the 1:00 P.M. news. Her concentration waned at the conclusion of the international news. Her attention was rekindled, however, when the newscaster reported on a story out of Corpus Christi, Texas. The local Corpus Christi newspaper was reporting that a German mining company sabotaged the field tests of a privately funded precious metals research project in south Texas, and so doing, caused the death of a University of Texas graduate student. Apparently, the incident occurred two weeks ago, near the small community of Elsa. Before placing her purse in a desk drawer, Sarah buzzed her boss, Assistant Secretary of State John Wilkins.

Sarah summarized what she had heard on the newscast, and tactfully suggested that it might be appropriate for him to verify the story and, if true, contact the German ambassador.

"Good work, Sarah. Call the Texas newspaper and ask for the managing editor. If he's in, I'll speak with him."

John Wilkins introduced himself and explained the reason for his call. Editor Peter Haven told him about the anonymous phone call he'd received, and how his reporters had confirmed the claims made by the caller. "We believe we've identified the company allegedly involved in the sabotage, Mr. Secretary. A German precious metals mining company with a R&D facility in Durango, Mexico, seems to fit the caller's description. We realize our findings are tenuous, but it does seem logical the company's research scientists could have recognized that the tests were a technological threat, and decided to sabotage them. It's only a day's drive from their facility in Durango, to Hidalgo County, Texas."

"How confident are you that the student was murdered, Mr. Haven?"

"Very confident. However, the Hidalgo County Sheriff is not accepting the sabotage scenario. He believes the story is a hoax."

"Are you saying the local police don't believe the student's death had anything to do with testing a new technology?"

"That's correct. The police claim that a bomb, packaged to look like it had been mailed, killed the student instantly when he tried to open it. The killer was very clever. He or she made the bomb look legitimate by putting the student's name and address on the front and placing a University of Texas return address in the left-hand corner. The sheriff has evidence that the murder may have been a drug related execution. However, the police may be wrong. They admit that they can't prove the drug connection, nor can they disprove the sabotage theory. Our newspaper may be between a rock and a hard place on this."

"Can you tell me the name of the German company that may fit the caller's description?"

"Hechmann. Please understand, Mr. Secretary, we don't have proof. The information I've given you is speculative. It won't be creditable until we have proof."

"I understand, Mr. Haven. I'll keep your information strictly confidential. However, I believe I should have an informal talk with the German Ambassador, and ask him to research the allegation before it becomes an international embarrassment. Will that be acceptable?"

"Yes, but please be sensitive to our position here at the paper. We've been very careful not to identify a specific company."

"Has anyone from Hechmann, or any other foreign company or organization, attempted to contact you to comment on your story?"

"No."

"Well, thank you for your time, Mr. Haven. Please call me if you are able to validate the sabotage report."

Wilkins buzzed his secretary. "Sarah, please locate Ambassador Schremph at the German Embassy. Tell his secretary that I need to talk with him for about ten minutes. It could be very important."

"Good afternoon, Mr. Ambassador. I appreciated the opportunity to talk with you last week at the Danish Embassy."

"Thank you, Mr. Secretary. I too, enjoyed our conversation. Please accept my congratulations again for your promotion. We are pleased you are now in charge of the European desk."

"Thank you, Mr. Ambassador. I look forward to working with you and the other EU ambassadors." Wilkins took a deep breath and asked, "Mr. Ambassador, have you heard about a story published in the Corpus Christi, Texas, newspaper about a German mining company?"

"No, Mr. Secretary, but please elaborate. My curiosity has been stimulated." Secretary Wilkins recounted his conversation with Editor Peter Haven. "That is unbelievable! The paper did not identify the company?"

"No, sir. The published story didn't name the company. But, it did assert that the company has operations in the Mexican State of Durango, without being specific. Mr. Haven told me that the newspaper suspects Hechmann, but lacks proof. I'm as shocked as you are, Mr. Ambassador. I would suggest we both investigate the allegations to determine the accuracy, and then discuss appropriate remedies, if any are required. You may want to tap into the newspaper's web site."

"Thank you for taking time to report this unfortunate situation. I will attempt to determine what German mining companies fit the newspaper's general description, and as discretely as possible, make specific inquiries about Hechmann's operations. I will call if anything materializes."

Without placing the telephone instrument in its cradle, Secretary Wilkins buzzed his secretary again. "Sarah, please contact FBI Director Richard Covey. If you can't reach him, ask to speak with the next highest ranking official in the department."

Within fifteen minutes Sarah buzzed Wilkins. "Sir, Mr. Covey is in California, but I have Assistant Director Albert Houston on line two, and he'll speak with you."

"Good!" Pressing line two, Wilkins said, "Mr. Houston, thank you for accepting my call. I know it's somewhat unusual for an Assistant Secretary of State to be contacting the FBI, but I need advice, and I need it today." Wilkins proceeded to chronicle the events surrounding the south Texas explosion, which led to the story published in the Corpus Christi newspaper. "Would it be possible for you to ask someone stationed at your south Texas office to make inquiries and report back as soon as possible?"

"I'll call our Corpus Christi office today. I should be able to report back tomorrow morning."

"Thank you, Mr. Houston."

# 28

SERGIO KNOCKED ON THE door frame of Oscar Tatis's office. "May I come in?"

"Sergio! What the hell happened to you the other day?"

"I wasn't feeling good. I'm sorry."

"You haven't changed, Sergio." Oscar chuckled, "You're as unreliable as you were in high school. What brings you back today?"

"I'm on way to Austin. I just stopped by to apologize." Sergio tried to act casual as he sat on a chair in front of Oscar's desk. "Did you hear about the story in yesterday's Corpus Christi newspaper about the death of that college boy?"

"Yes. Dr. Arnett told me about it this morning. Dr. Arnett said that the District Attorney was very upset and plans to respond to the story at a press conference after lunch today. Let's go across the street and grab something to eat and then come back for the press conference."

Oscar was one of those rare individuals who could remember all sorts of details about childhood experiences. He had Sergio laughing for the first time in days. Sergio was able to push all thoughts of the Acuna investigation from his mind. At the conclusion of their lunch, Oscar glanced out of the coffee shop window and observed that the District Attorney was preparing for his press briefing. "It looks like the DA is about ready to start. We'd better ask for the bill, and get over there."

Sergio's unease returned and it showed on his face. Oscar noticed the change, and said, "You don't look so good. Are you okay, Sergio?"

"I'm fine."

Oscar led Sergio across the street to a spot to the right of the podium, facing the assemblage of media personnel. The DA held up his hand for quiet and began, "This briefing will be short and sweet. We want to make it crystal clear that Hidalgo County rejects the story that appeared in the *Corpus Christi Register* yesterday. The recent death of a University of Texas graduate student at the Hidalgo Brine Disposal Plant was not the result of sabotage. The evidence that we've uncovered, points to a drug related assassination. The young man was...."

Blood drained from Sergio's face, and he began to feel faint. He was on the threshold of a panic attack, practically hyperventilating. "I don't feel so good, Oscar. I'm gonna have to leave. Thanks for lunch." He abruptly exited the area, and walked slowly to his car with eyes focused on the ground to avoid attracting attention. It seemed like everything was turning against him. He was so alarmed he had trouble concentrating. Instead of creating the chaos he'd expected, the Sheriff's Department had deflected every probe by the media about the alleged sabotage, and now had successfully convinced the Hidalgo County District Attorney that the sabotage story was a hoax.

Sergio hurriedly drove from the courthouse and out of McAllen. He stopped at the first gas station he encountered. While the attendant filled his tank, Sergio purchased a copy of today's newspaper, and found more disturbing news. The *Corpus Christi Register* had retracted its earlier report with a front-page story headlined: *Sheriff Rebuts Sabotage Story.*

Sergio's primary concern now was survival. He pulled away from the pumps and parked behind the building to review his options. Sergio's stress level was so high he had to close his eyes and force himself to concentrate. Only two people knew that he'd been to Hidalgo Disposal before the explosion and could recognize him, Ben Jack Randall and Ed Witnauer. He'd have to eliminate both. Witnauer would have to go first because his testimony could be more damaging. Ed knew Sergio by his real last name, Dominguez, whereas Ben Jack knew him as Alverez.

"Ed, it's Sergio."

"For Christ's sake, Sergio, what shady deals are you involved in now? The police are asking a lot of questions."

Concerned, Sergio replied, "What police?"

"Sergeant Joe Godfrey of the Hidalgo County Sheriff's Department, that's who. Godfrey stopped by the office the other day and asked a bunch of questions about you."

Thinking quickly, Sergio attempted to deflect the conversation away from him. "Shit, Ed. My brother-in-law must be up to no good again. Do I need to say more? You've met my brother-in-law."

Witnauer countered, "Godfrey didn't mention your bother-in-law, only you. You make me nervous, Sergio. If I find out you have been lying to me, I'll kick your ass." Somewhat mollified, Ed continued, "Was that your 'new' technology that blew up the other day?"

Sergio relaxed. He could tell from the tone of Ed's voice that the man had settled down. He could also tell that Witnauer hadn't heard the news report that Acuna's death was drug related. He smiled to himself. *Ed never did read newspapers, or listen to news broadcasts.* "No, that explosion had something to do with chemicals that were being used by a group of graduate students from the university. But, you were right about the other technology. It was bullshit like you said. Thanks for arranging the visit to the disposal a few weeks ago. I'm sending you a gift. I was in Matamoros on business the other day, and found something I know you'll like."

Pleased by the gesture of good will, Ed chuckled, "You didn't have to do that. I was glad I could help."

"Thanks again. Enjoy the gift. I'll talk with you later."

# 29

THE CONCERN IN DETECTIVE Jack Kelly's face was clearly evident. He'd just entered Sergio Dominguez's apartment in Austin and discovered that Dominguez had emptied his closet and bureau drawers, apparently leaving for good. Using his cell phone, he reported to his superior first, and then called Joe Godfrey in McAllen. "Joe, it looks like Dominguez split. His clothes are gone, the neighbors haven't seen him in days, and they don't know where he is. He must've been in a hurry. The apartment's a mess."

"Damn!"

"Were you aware that Dominguez has two residences? The neighbors told me he owns a home in Rio Grande City, and rents this apartment in Austin. They said that his wife, Rosa, stays in Rio Grande City most of the time, and only visits Austin occasionally. Apparently, Dominguez has been splitting his time between Austin and Rio Grande City."

"Witnauer told me about the home in Rio Grand City. That explains why he could move around south Texas so easily."

"Dominguez must be a stupid bastard, Joe. He deposited $10,000 in his checking account a few days ago. Must be his payoff for killing the kid. We also found plenty of bomb making paraphernalia in a concealed section of his walk-in closet. I think the stuff we found confirms our suspicion that the guy knows how to make bombs."

"Have you called in forensics to go over the apartment?"

"Yeah, they're here now. They've already recovered hair from his bathroom. The hair samples should help with a DNA match."

"Based on the bomb making stuff you found, and on what Martin Leary learned up at Camp Nullis, I think I'd better pull together the evidence and ask our DA to call an emergency meeting of the grand jury and request an indictment. We'd better issue an urgent all-points bulletin requesting his arrest, and emphasize that Dominguez could be armed." Joe hesitated. "Here's a thought, Jack. If the bulletin were to originate from both the Austin P.D. and our department, it'd carry a lot more weight. Can you check to see if we can do that?"

"Yeah, I'll check on that right away."

"We've got to notify the Border Patrol first, especially the Matamoros and the Reynoso crossings, and the customs people too."

Jack said, "If Dominguez has heard about your District Attorney's announcement that Acuna's death was drug related, he might panic, and try to harm someone else."

Joe sat up straight. "Holy shit, Jack, you're right. Ed Witnauer's life may be in danger! Ed knows Alverez is Dominguez, and can testify that Dominguez was at the disposal plant just before the explosion. Dominguez may go after that young manager, Randall, as well. I'd better get in touch with both of them before something happens, or I'll regret it the rest of my life."

"Do you think Dominguez might come back here?"

"If he intends to kill Witnauer and Randall with an explosive device, he might. On the other hand, if he's as expert at bomb making as the evidence suggests, he could buy the materials anywhere and make a bomb in a hotel room. Better keep a 24-hour watch on the apartment in case he does try to come back. Listen, I've got to go, Jack. Thank goodness Martin Leary is still here. He can help me track down Randall and Witnauer. Call me later."

Joe rushed over to the County DA's office. "Martin, drop everything. I need your help." Godfrey summarized the conversation he'd just had with Jack Kelly, and explained his deep concern that Dominguez would go after Ben Jack Randall and Ed Witnauer. "Drive over to DeWitt's Disposal Plant and warn Ben Jack and Roy. While you're doing that, I'll track down Witnauer."

"Good afternoon, Mrs. Witnauer, may I speak with Ed. This is Sergeant Godfrey with the Hidalgo County Sheriff's Department."

"Ed isn't here, Sergeant. He's down in Starr County picking up a load of brine. I can reach him on his truck radio if it's important."

"Yes, Mrs. Witnauer, it is very important. Please ask him to call me right away." Godfrey gave her his office and cell phone numbers, and his beeper number. "Tell Ed I will wait by the phone until I hear from him." Within ten minutes, Ed returned the call.

*ELSA*

"I'm glad you called right away, Ed. Have you heard from Dominguez since you and I talked?"

"I just talked with him a few hours ago. Said he wanted to thank me for advising against the investment he'd been considering. He said he purchased a gift for me in Mexico and would mail it in a day or two. I told—"

Alarmed, Joe Godfrey interrupted. "Please listen carefully, Ed. We believe Dominguez is responsible for the explosion and death of the college student over at Hidalgo Disposal. He may be desperate. Don't, under any circumstances, open a package mailed to you from him. That's how he killed the student, a prepackaged bomb! Your life is in danger, Ed. You're one of only two people that can tie him directly to the killing at the disposal site."

"Holy shit!"

"Ed, I'm gonna ask the Laredo P.D. to keep an eye on your office and home. Please be vigilant. Tell your wife to be extra careful too."

As usual Ben Jack exited the office trailer as soon as he heard the noise of a car approach. The noise of a diesel truck was a common sound to his sensitive ears, but not the sound of a car.

"Martin, what brings you out here? Did you come for a cup of my coffee?"

"I'd love a cup of your coffee, Ben Jack. Is Roy here?"

"No, sir, he ain't. He drove over to Rio Grand City see the people at Texaco. They's about to haul to a different disposal, and he's gonna try to change a few minds. Hey, I just heard about the story in the Corpus paper. Is that right, the tests was sabotaged?"

"No, Ben Jack, that story is untrue. Forget it. The Corpus newspaper retracted that story this morning." Adopting a more fatherly tone to his voice, Martin said, "Ben, I need to have a serious talk with you. Can we go inside? Your assistant needs to hear this too."

Martin reviewed the status of the investigation into Acuna's death, emphasizing the drug connection, the use of a prepackaged bomb, and the District Attorney's reaction to the sabotage story. "We believe we have identified the perpetrator, one Sergio Dominguez, alias Alverez."

Ben Jack's mouth dropped open. "That bastard!"

"What I'm about to tell you is very, very serious. We think your life may be in danger, Ben Jack. You can identify Dominguez as the phony Realtor that came to the disposal a few weeks ago. We believe he may attempt to kill you with another bomb. Don't, under any circumstances, open any packages that have been mailed to you. Tell your wife and Roy the same thing. Don't open any packages!" Looking directly at Ben's female clerk. "That goes for you too, miss.

"If Roy has any questions, have him call Joe Godfrey at the sheriff's station. Call his voice mail, or his pager number, and he'll return your call immediately. Unfortunately, the sheriff doesn't have the manpower to send someone over to stand guard, so please be careful and cautious. Call the sheriff's station immediately if you receive a package in the mail, or a package delivered by a delivery service."

Tony Zedillo placed the forensics report on his desk and declared, "Well, gentlemen, this DNA information from the state forensics lab is the final piece. I think we've assembled enough evidence to convince the grand jury to indict Dominguez."

Martin said, "I'm not clear about what the DNA report says, Tony. Could you explain it?"

"DNA is a short abbreviation for, please excuse my pronunciation, deoxyribonucleic acid. It identifies a person's unique genetic makeup. It's become an important investigative tool of law enforcement, especially for little guys like us. There's a growing database of DNA profiles of felons, kind of like the fingerprint files the FBI maintains. We recently discovered that the state forensics people had DNA information on Dominguez. Apparently, he was arrested a year ago for punching out a guy in a bar, and was charged with battery. The charges were dropped later, but his DNA information was retained.

"When Joe searched the spot where we think Dominguez knelt or sat, he found a few fingernail clippings and a clipper. The state forensics lab recovered enough DNA from the clippings to match our friend's DNA stored in the database. Then, they analyzed the hair from Dominguez's bathroom, and it gave them a three-way match. That was the clincher, Martin. Dominguez was the person who watched Acuna get blown to bits." Tony paused, and added, "Can you believe that? The bastard just sat there in the grass, clipping his nails while he waited for his bomb to explode."

Martin said, "It's beginning to look like this case may be winding down."

Joe responded, "Yes and no, Martin. We all want the son of a bitch to burn. But convincing a jury here in south Texas that one of their own is a killer will be a tough sell."

The Hidalgo County District Attorney convened an emergency meeting of the grand jury. He and Sheriff Zedillo reviewed the evidence against the suspect, Sergio Dominguez, alias Sergio Alverez, and requested that the jury indict Dominguez for the murder of José Acuna. In less than an hour, Tony was back in his office and requested that his secretary locate Joe Godfrey and Martin Leary.

When everyone was seated, Tony announced, "The grand jury just indicted Dominguez."

Martin reached over and patted Joe Godfrey on the shoulder. "Well done, Joe."

"Thanks, Martin. But, that may be the easy part. Now we've got to catch him, and then go after the big fish."

Tony said, "Joe, I want you to go over to the DA's office and request an arrest warrant. Wait there until you get it, then fax it up to Jack Kelly. Follow that up with a telephone call. Ask him to check with his snitch, and ask around his department to see if anyone has any ideas about where we might find our Mexican friend."

Armed with the jury's indictment and the arrest warrant, the Hidalgo County DA requested an all-points bulletin be issued simultaneously from both the Hidalgo County Sheriff's Department and the Austin City Police Department, instructing law enforcement agencies statewide to apprehend and arrest Sergio Dominguez. The bulletin stipulated that Dominguez could be armed and dangerous, and that he might attempt to flee across the border into Mexico. The bulletin also gave a detailed description of the suspect, and suggested that he might be driving a red Chevy Malibu, with Texas plates.

# 30

THE EXPERIENCE THAT ADAM Leary gained from running on rural roads enabled him to recognize vehicle sounds when they approached from behind. He'd even made a game of it, attempting to guess whether the sound emanated from a small car, a big car like an SUV, or a truck; they all had distinctive sounds. Adam generally ran against traffic. He wasn't as concerned about vehicles approaching from behind, because they were traveling on the opposite side of the road. He couldn't see them until they passed, but he could hear them when they approached.

Adam had been running for over an hour and was heading for home on Route 160 when he reached his favorite section of the road, a flat, straight stretch only a few miles beyond the city limits. He saw Mrs. Ambrose descend the stairs to her front porch and make her way toward her roadside mailbox. She waved, and he returned the gesture.

Adam thought he'd show off a little, and began to accelerate. He also wanted to see what kind of a finishing kick he had. As he passed the mailbox, he heard the sound of a vehicle approaching from the rear. He thought, *Here comes another one of those gas-guzzler SUV's.* Suddenly, Adam had an uneasy feeling that the sound was directly behind him. When the sound changed, like tires running over gravel, he dove to his left. But, he wasn't fast enough. The high bumper of the SUV caught both his legs while he was in midair.

Mrs. Ambrose was grinning with admiration as she watched Adam's graceful strides. Her smile quickly turned to one of surprise and shock when she saw an SUV veer to the left, cross over the centerline and hit Adam while he was in midair and threw him like a rag doll into the high grass. She screamed. Adam rolled a few times and landed against a tree. She ran as fast as her seventy-year-old legs could carry her back into the house to call 911. "This is Dorothy Ambrose on Route 160. Adam Leary was just hit by a car in front of my house. Send an ambulance right away." She hung up the phone and hurried back to help Adam.

Adam lay on his right side with his back against a tree trunk. He tried to move his legs, but couldn't. He realized that unless he could sit up, he wouldn't be able to attract the attention of a passing motorist. He tried, but failed. His head fell back against the tree, and he passed out. When he regained consciousness, he saw Mrs. Ambrose running across the road toward him. She kneeled down, and told him an ambulance was on the way. Adam squeezed her hand, but couldn't talk. He fainted again. When he came to, he was in an ambulance racing toward Putnam General Hospital.

Sheriff Zedillo's secretary, knocked and then pushed open the office door. "Mr. Leary, you have a telephone call on line two."

"Thanks, Gloria. I'll take it at your desk." Martin excused himself, walked out of Sheriff Zedillo's office and picked up the phone. "Martin Leary."

Between sobs Shirley announced, "Martin, Adam was run off the road by a hit-and-run driver. He's in Putnam Hospital." Martin reached out and grasped the desk so he wouldn't fall. He had trouble breathing and couldn't speak for a moment. Shirley shouted, "Martin, did you hear me? Someone tried to kill Adam!"

Martin recovered and asked, "How bad is he?"

Shirley was able to calm herself. "Both legs are broken. He has a broken nose and lacerations on his torso and face."

"What do the doctors say?"

"He'll recover, but he'll be on crutches for awhile."

"I'll come home right away."

"I'll be with Ruth when you get here." Shirley sighed and added, "Ruth talked with a Mrs. Ambrose who lives out on Route 160. She saw it all. She believes it was deliberate. I'm frightened, Martin. What will those people do next? I don't want you to go back to that awful place."

"I'll take the redeye. I should get there early tomorrow morning."

Martin slammed down the receiver and stomped back into Zedillo's office. "Cisneros just had my son run off the road. Both legs are broken, and he's cut pretty bad." Joe Godfrey and Tony Zedillo looked at each other. Tony said, "I don't know what to say, except that we're sorry."

"I've done everything I can to help with the investigation. I've told you everything I know about Cisneros. A draft of my report for the DA is in the computer under the heading 'Sonora cartel.' I'm going home." He began to walk out of the office, but stopped. He turned around and announced, "This has gotten to be personal, gentlemen. You'd better arrest Dominguez and Cisneros before I do something drastic." He took a deep breath and added, "I'll be back."

It was midmorning when Martin arrived at Putnam General. He asked the receptionist to call the nurse's station on the fourth floor. He was told to come right up. Shirley was waiting for him by the elevator. Without saying a word, they embraced, and held onto each other for a few moments. Finally, Shirley pulled away, "Adam's okay, Mart, but it was scary for awhile." Shirley's lips began to tremble. "I'm sorry I was angry with you before you left for Texas."

Martin reached out and took both her hands. "I understand, Shirley. I love you, you know."

Shirley leaned forward and placed her head against his chest. "Thanks, I needed that. I love you too." They hugged again.

Shirley explained that an orthopedic surgeon had inserted a pin in Adam's right femur, and set a bad break in the upper portion of his left tibia. Martin could feel his anger resurface as he visualized his son lying in a bed with two broken legs. He realized, however, that he'd better calm down before he upset Shirley again.

Shirley said, "Let's go in." Martin held the door for Shirley and nodded to a nurse who was leaving. Adam turned toward them, and said, "Dad!"

With tears blurring his vision, Martin said, "Is that my son under all that spaghetti?" Skirting the apparatus supporting Adam's right leg, Martin leaned over and embraced his son. As he stepped back, he wiped away a few tears with the back of his hand.

"That's me, Dad, the bionic man." Pointing to his femur Adam added, "The pin is so big it'll probably set off the alarm when I try to go through an airport screening station."

Martin pulled up two chairs. "Tell us what happened, son."

Adam detailed the circumstances surrounding his injury, and the timely arrival of Mrs. Ambrose at her mailbox. "You remember her, don't you, Dad? Her husband died last year? Her family has been fixture in Putnam for over four generations. She lives alone in the old family farmhouse, a few miles out of town. Mrs. Ambrose called 911."

"Were you able to see anything when the vehicle hit you? Make or model, color, anything?"

"No, only the sound. But, Mrs. Ambrose saw the whole thing." Adam took a sip of water and added, "She told the police the vehicle was a white SUV. She recalled two numbers on the license plate, a 6 and a 1. The Putnam police are calling it a hit and run."

"What do you think, son?"

"Either the driver fell asleep, or I was hit on purpose." Martin glanced at Shirley. She returned his look, grimaced and stood up. She announced she needed to use the rest room, and walked out of the room.

"Why is Mom upset, Dad? Does my being hit by a car have anything to do with your latest trip to Texas?"

"I don't know, Adam. But I think I'd better have a talk with Chief Pierson in Norwich tomorrow morning."

Promptly at 8:30 the following morning, Martin entered the lobby of the Norwich Police Station, and asked to see the Chief. He was immediately escorted to Pierson's office. Walter stood up, and walked toward Martin with hand extended. "I'm dreadfully sorry about what happened to Adam."

"I'm mad as hell, Walter. I know it wasn't your fault. I blame myself as much as anyone. I guess we all overlooked the fact that Adam trained on rural roads and would make an easy target. Did you tell Shirley you thought it was a hit and run?"

"Yes. I received a full report from the Putnam police this morning. As soon as I got the report, I called the Groton Police Chief and asked him to check out Caldera's car. I'd bet my pension that the SUV the witness saw was his car. Just to be sure, we're also searching the motor vehicle records. While you're here, let's call Groton."

While they waited for the Chief's secretary to place the call, Martin provided Walter with an update on the Texas investigation. Martin was about to tell him about the grand jury indictment, when Walter's secretary buzzed him. "Chief Maxwell's on the phone, sir."

"Felix, thanks for taking my call. I have you on my speakerphone. Martin Leary, the father of the injured runner, is with me."

"Good morning, Mr. Leary. Sorry about your son. Will he be okay?"

"Two broken legs, Chief." Martin summarized Adam's injuries and the surgery that followed. "Have your people been able to check Caldera's car?"

"We have, Mr. Leary. He drives a white Ford SUV. It has Connecticut plates, HHT 6165. My guess is he's our hit-and-run fellow. Walter, do you want us to pick him up for questioning?"

"What's your opinion of the man? Will he break?"

"As I told you before, he's nothing but a two-bit hoodlum, who's been trying to get into the drug trade. We've been watching him closely the last couple of months. I think we can make him talk."

"Then go ahead and pick him up."

"The Putnam police will have to be involved, Walter. Would you call the

Putnam Chief and tell him that I'd like to have first crack at questioning the man? If he agrees, urge them to send a representative down here right away."

Martin said, "Before you hang up, Chief Maxwell, I have a request. I have a personal stake in this investigation. May I listen in on the questioning session if I promise not to get in the way?"

"Well, it's a little out of the ordinary, but if you're on the other side of the glass, I guess we can work it out."

"When should I come down, sir?"

"We've had a surveillance team on Caldera since Walter called. It looks like he intends to work in his deli today. I can pick him up and bring him to the Main Street precinct within an hour."

# 31

SERGIO DROVE BLINDLY BACK and forth across south Texas for two hours contemplating his next move. As he approached the outskirts of Alice for the second time, he settled on a plan: he'd eliminate both Witnauer and Randall with two, simple but deadly mail bombs.

He checked into a motel near a shopping center where he purchased the required materials, and worked most of the night building the bombs. The motel room looked like a chemistry laboratory when he finished. He looked at his watch, 7:30 A.M. Ignoring the mess, Sergio sat back and admired his work. He calculated that he had just enough time for breakfast before the post office opened. He'd clean up the mess in the room when he returned, and maybe he'd even have time to squeeze in a little sleep before he started his trip to the border. His plan was to arrive at the Laredo crossing during rush hour traffic, and then continue south to Monterrey. Working backward, he estimated one hour to mail the packages, one hour to clean up the mess he created then shower and shave. Even if he slept for three hours, he'd still have plenty of time to get to the border between 5:00 and 6:00 P.M. He'd have to pay extra for a late checkout, but the added cost would be well worth it.

Driving across south Texas from Alice to Laredo, Sergio's thoughts shifted back and forth, negative to positive, positive to negative. He regretted the failure of the sabotage story, not understanding what had gone wrong, but he was proud of himself for not procrastinating about building and dispatching the two bombs. He started to sing along with the radio, stopped in mid-lyrics. He frowned and banged his hand on the steering wheel. *Shit! I didn't tell Rosa. She'll be a basket case when she finds out I split for*

Mexico. *His frown was quickly replaced by a smile. If I promise to send for her later, it might soften the blow. Come to think of it, I really don't give a shit what she thinks. Rosa's been a pain in the ass lately. If she doesn't want to join me in Monterrey, Arturo can take care her.*

His thoughts segued from his wife to Arturo. Sergio decided that he wouldn't contact Cisneros either, at least not until he was settled in Monterrey. He'd demand that Arturo send a money order for the remaining $10,000 to a new account that he'd open at the Banco de Monterrey. Sergio reasoned that if Arturo refused to send the balance of the money, he'd call the sheriff and tell him that it was Arturo who contracted for the murder of Acuna. A threat like that should be enough incentive for Arturo to wire the money immediately. *Come to think of it, I'd better call the Austin bank tomorrow and arrange for a wire transfer of the first $10,000. Ah, $20,000. I can get a good start on a new life in Mexico with that kind of money.*

An all-points bulletin was received at each Texas/Mexico border crossing between 2:00 and 3:00 that afternoon. It attracted an extraordinary level of attention because it'd been issued simultaneously by two cooperating law enforcement agencies from south Texas, and it targeted a south Texan who grew up in Rio Grande City. Supervisors "red flagged" the bulletin, produced copies, and distributed them to all the border guards on duty, as well as the guards scheduled for duty within the next several days.

Chuck Grimshaw clocked in at the Laredo station at 4:00 P.M. He picked up communiqués, bulletins and instructions from his message box. He read through the instructions first, and then reviewed the law enforcement bulletins. He reread the bulletin about Sergio Dominguez a second time, wondering if that Sergio could that be the same guy he worked with in the oil patch years ago. *This guy's from Austin, but the name's the same, and it says he grew up in Rio Grande City. Don't jump to conclusions, Chuck; Dominguez is a popular Mexican name. Regardless, I'd better be alert.* He mentally reviewed agency procedures regarding the apprehension of a suspect wanted by law enforcement.

Grimshaw was a big man; a former college football tackle who'd played for Texas A & M, in the seventies. Although he'd developed a noticeable paunch, he retained his muscle tone by exercising regularly at a Laredo gym. As he waited patiently for the next vehicle to approach his station, he checked the time: 5:25 P.M.

A red '89 Chevy Malibu rolled to a stop. Grimshaw and the driver experienced instant recognition. Grimshaw bent forward, resting his left arm on the sill of the open driver's side window while he pressed the button on a beeper like device attached to his belt. "As I live and breathe, Sergio

Dominguez. Haven't seen you in years. How the hell are you?" Blood drained from Sergio's face. His mouth dropped open, but he couldn't speak. He just looked at Grimshaw. The latter identified the panic signs, and continued to lean over and look directly into Sergio's eyes. "Are you still working in the oil patch?"

Sergio responded meekly, "Good to see you, Chuck. Didn't know you were working for the Border Patrol."

Chuck continued with the general questions in an effort to delay and keep Dominguez off guard while his fellow guards responded to his alert. "Where are you headed, Sergio?" His question elicited no reaction from Sergio. The latter appeared to be traumatized. "How far into Mexico are you going?"

Sergio mumbled an answer, "Monterrey."

"Good choice. Probably the best town in the whole country."

Grimshaw's delaying tactics worked. Guards on foot approached from the rear and from both sides of Sergio's car. Vehicles took up positions in front and behind the car to block any escape attempt. Observing that his backup was in place, Grimshaw straightened, stood back from the vehicle, removed his firearm from the holster, and ordered, "Sergio, please get out of the car. Don't cause any trouble. I wouldn't want to hurt you." The normally aggressive Dominguez remained traumatized. He opened the door reluctantly, and passively stepped out onto the pavement.

Joe Godfrey placed a call to Jack Kelly in Austin. "Jack, the Border Patrol picked up Dominguez fifteen minutes ago. He was attempting to cross into Mexico from Laredo. Laredo P.D. officers are holding him at their headquarters. Dave Collins and I are leaving momentarily to pick him up and bring him back to McAllen. Can you come down and help with the interrogation?"

"I've been looking forward to that opportunity, Joe. I'll check with my supervisor. But I'm sure he won't object. I'll call if there's a problem."

"Call the graduate students, Duncan and Hyde, and ask them to drive down to McAllen sometime tomorrow. The DA wants them to identify Dominguez while he's in a lineup." Joe hesitated a moment, and then speculated, "I'd bet my next month's salary that there are two more bombs floating around out there somewhere. While I'm in Laredo, I'll contact Witnauer at his home and suggest that he continue to remain vigilant, in spite of the arrest. Martin Leary will drive over to Hidalgo disposal and tell Randall."

A Laredo P.D. patrol car pulled up in front of the Border Patrol Administration building twenty minutes later. When the officers entered the building they encountered a cuffed Dominguez sitting on the floor in the middle of the room, surrounded by two Border Patrol guards. The Laredo P.D. officer in charge smiled at the scene. "We'll take over so you fellows can get back to work. Good job, gentlemen. The Hidalgo County Sheriff is on his way."

Dave Collins and Joe Godfrey arrived at the station just after 7:00 P.M. They were driving a new patrol car equipped with a reinforced steel cage-like screen that separated the front seat from back seat, creating a mini-jail cell. After introductions were completed, Joe thanked the officers for their cooperation, processed the required documents, and commenced securing the prisoner in preparation to leave when Laredo P.D. Chief Manny Ramirez walked into the room. "If you can spare the time, gentlemen, I suggest you drop by the Border Patrol station and thank Chuck Grimshaw. He's the one that spotted your man, and alerted the entire station."

# 32

TWO PLAINCLOTHES DETECTIVES DESCENDED on Luis Caldera's deli in Groton just before 4:00 P.M. They used an outstanding warrant for a series of parking violations to arrest Caldera and bring him into the station for questioning.

Martin sat on a bench opposite the booking area with his designated escort and observed the booking of the arrogant Caldera. Martin hadn't seen the man before. When Caldera came to Martin's home to pick up the shipment of cocaine that José had conned Martin into carrying in his suitcase, Shirley was the one who gave him the package. Booking completed, the detectives led the suspect past Martin and up a back staircase to an interrogation room on the second floor. As Caldera walked by, Martin clenched his fists and stared at the man with hate in his eyes. He wanted to pounce on Caldera and hit him hard in the face, but he was able to control his emotions.

Martin showed his "Special Visitor" bag to the uniformed officer at the base of the staircase and was allowed to follow his escort up the stairs and into a small observation enclosure adjacent to the interrogation room. The observation area was small, not much larger than a closet and devoid of furniture. Occupants were forced to stand and watch the proceedings through a one-way mirror/window.

Three people were waiting for Caldera when he was led in for questioning: a detective from Putnam, a detective from Groton, and a Groton Assistant District Attorney. Martin was pleased that the sound system worked perfectly; he could hear every word that was spoken. Caldera sat in a straight back chair facing the observation glass. The Groton detective placed his foot on a chair, leaned forward within inches of Caldera's face and said, "Mr. Caldera, let's get right to the point. Do you own a white Ford SUV, license number HHT 6165?"

"You already know the answer. Why are you asking me?"

"Do you, or don't you?"

"Yes."

"Where were you two days ago, the 12th of October at 7:00 A.M.?"

"I was at the deli, preparing the lunch menu."

"That's bullshit, Caldera. We already know you didn't get to the deli until after lunch. I'd advise you not to lie to us."

"Okay, I wasn't at the deli. I was home screwing my girlfriend. Ask her."

Martin mumbled, "You lying son of bitch." He practically climbed through the window to attack him.

"We will. What's her name, and where do we find her?"

Caldera provided the information about where the Groton police could find his girlfriend, and then asked, "What's this shit all about, anyway? What do you want from me?" The Groton detective removed his foot from the chair, and introduced the detective from Putnam. Martin noticed Caldera flinch; the arrogance that he'd displayed earlier seemed to crumble.

The Putnam detective sat in the chair in front of Caldera and studied the man's face. "You weren't in Groton on the morning of the October 12th, were you?" Caldera began to perspire, and could only stare at the detective. He didn't know what to say. The detective continued, "I'll tell you where you were. You were on Route 160 outside Putnam attempting to kill Adam Leary with your SUV. We have a witness that saw you run him down."

The interrogation went on for an hour. Martin was spellbound by the interaction between the interrogators, and especially by their tenacity; they wouldn't let up. Finally, Caldera broke. He placed his head in his hands and started to weep. He admitted he'd run Adam off the road, but claimed he didn't mean to hurt Adam, just scare him. Caldera said that he'd miscalculated the distance between Adam and his vehicle.

Martin asked his escort if the interview was being recorded. Assured that it was, he requested the escort go into the interrogation room to encourage the detectives to question Caldera about why he'd tried to run Adam off the road.

When asked, Caldera refused to answer. The Assistant District Attorney sat down opposite him. "Mr. Caldera, we suspect that you were following orders. Is that correct?" Caldera didn't respond. "Okay, here's the deal. If you tell us who issued the order the DA will consider reducing the charge from attempted murder to manslaughter. But, we want specifics, Mr. Caldera." The DA sat quietly for two long minutes, staring at Luis. "I'll give you one more minute. After that, I'm leaving, and you'll be charged with attempted murder."

Caldera mumbled, "My cousin, Arturo Cisneros, asked me to do it."

"Louder, Mr. Caldera. We didn't hear you."

"My cousin, Arturo Cisneros, from Austin, Texas."

Martin slapped his hands together, and growled, "That's it, Cisneros. We're gonna fry your ass."

Martin telephoned Chief Pierson from the Groton police station and summarized what had transpired during the interrogation and asked him to submit an official request for copies of the audiotape of the interrogation. "I want to take a copy to Texas, Walter. That tape may help convict Cisneros for the murder of José Acuna."

Martin thanked the Groton Chief of Police for allowing him to observe the interrogation and for a copy of the audiotape.

Martin played the tape for Shirley, and closely watched his wife's reaction. She became visibly agitated when Caldera implicated Cisneros. While Martin rewound the tape, Shirley remarked, "That man Cisneros is an evil person, Martin."

"I know, Shirl. I'm more committed now than I was before Adam was injured. I know it's still a reach for you, but I think you're beginning to understand why I feel strongly about this. If people like us don't step forward and try to stop people like Cisneros, who will?" Martin sat down on the couch next to his wife, reached out to take her hands in his. "I plan to take the redeye back to Texas tonight. I'd like you to come along. Adam is in good hands at the hospital, and Ruth will be okay for a few days without us hanging around. Claire agreed to cover for me at the office until I get back."

Shirley hugged Martin. "If you really want me to go, I'll go. But I don't want to get in the way."

"You may get bored, but you won't be in the way. It'll give you the opportunity to meet the Sheriff Zedillo and Joe Godfrey."

Martin telephoned Godfrey and asked if it would be possible to hold off on the start of Dominguez's interrogation until he arrived. Joe agreed. Martin and Shirley packed, and headed for Bradley Field to catch the 11:30 P.M. redeye flight to Houston.

It took the Learys eight hours to reach McAllen. They were exhausted when they checked into the Holiday Inn; Shirley was asleep within minutes. Martin showered, grabbed a cup of coffee from the desk clerk, and drove to the County Courthouse in a car he'd rented at the Harlingen Airport.

He was greeted with an enthusiastic handshake from Joe Godfrey. "Glad you could make it, Martin. You look tired. Are you going to be able to stay awake?"

"You're right, I'm tired, but I'll make it. Before you start the interrogation, I want you, Tony and the DA to listen to a tape of Caldera's confession. I'm not sure it will help prosecute Dominguez, but it could help prosecute Cisneros."

At the end of the tape, DA Tom Berringer sat back and said, "Mr. Leary, for someone who doesn't have any law enforcement experience, you did a hell of a job."

"I can't take credit for the audiotape, Tom. I just arranged to have the tape copied."

Joe Godfrey and Jack Kelly strolled into the interrogation room at 1:00 P.M., and sat opposite Sergio Dominguez at a small conference table. Martin was again relegated to the role of an observer, behind a one-way glass.

Jack Kelly posed the first question. "Well, Dominguez, how's the bomb making business?"

"Shove it, you bastard."

"Now, now, Sergio, old man, don't get belligerent. Is that any way to talk to an officer of the law?"

Assuming the role of the "elder statesman," Joe Godfrey said, "Dominguez, we know you built the bomb that killed young Acuna and you're the one that placed it on his work bench at the test site. We also know you were paid $10,000 to carry it out. By the way, your checking account has been frozen. You're out the $10,000." Sergio's jaw dropped when he heard that news. "Do you want to tell us who issued the contract to kill the kid, or are you planning to attend a quiet execution, with you in the starring role?"

"Forget it! You can't prove anything."

"Oh?" Godfrey leaned forward and looked into Sergio's eyes. "Jack, I don't think our Mexican friend here understands that we have him by the gonads. Why don't you spell out the evidence against him?"

"Tell you what, Dominguez, I'll write it on the blackboard. That way you can fully appreciate the evidence." Kelly moved slowly to the blackboard and began to write. "First, we have a DNA match from fingernail clippings you left behind when you watched the kid get blown to bits." Kelly turned and asked, "Did you enjoy watching the kid go flying threw the air, Sergio?" He slowly wrote: "DNA match." Jack turned back and a looked at Sergio. "When the state forensics folks finished matching the hair we uncovered from your bathroom with your fingernail clippings, you became dead meat, Sergio." Jack stood quietly next to the blackboard for a moment, to allow his last statement to sink in. "We also have a cast of your footprint that we recovered from your observation spot." He wrote "Footprint." Turning toward Joe, Kelly said, "I think our Mexican friend is beginning to pay attention."

Jack continued, "You carelessly left bomb making materials in your apartment. We found the stuff in a sealed off section of your closet." Kelly wrote slowly for effect: "Bomb making materials."

"Next we have the C-4 residue. Is that the same C-4 you stole from Camp Nullis? That's probably enough evidence to fry your ass, but believe it or not, there's more. The final piece of evidence is like frosting on a cake. We were able to recover a cast of a tire tread. It looks like it's from your car." Jack slowly wrote: "Tire tread."

"We also have witnesses who will testify that you were at the crime scene a few days before the explosion." Kelly wrote "Witnesses" even more slowly.

Dominguez dropped his head into his hands, and whispered, "I want a lawyer."

Joe said, "That's fine, Dominguez. Make a call, we'll wait."

"I can't afford to pay for a lawyer."

Godfrey looked surprised, "You mean your Mexican drug friends aren't willing to pay your legal fees, or supply one of their own attorneys?"

Dave Collins knocked on the door, opened it enough to announce, "Joe, you have a call. The guy says it's important."

"Okay. I'll take it. Ask him to hold for a minute." Turning back to face Dominguez, Joe said, "When I get back, we want an answer. Should we contact the public defender's office?"

Godfrey left the interrogation room and approached the first available phone. "Sergeant Joe Godfrey, may I help you?"

"Sergeant, Ed Witnauer. I just received a package from Sergio."

"Don't, I'll say it again, don't attempt to open that package. I'll call the Laredo P.D. and ask them to send over a bomb specialist to disarm it. In the meantime, leave the package where it is, and don't let anyone else near it, okay? Thanks for being alert and diligent, Ed."

Sergio's eyes were riveted on Godfrey when he reentered, this time accompanied by District Attorney Tom Berringer. Joe stood for a moment and stared at the suspect. "Well, Dominguez, another one of your devious plans just went awry. That was Ed Witnauer on the phone. He received your package, and fortunately for him, and I guess for you, he didn't attempt to open it. The Laredo P.D. bomb squad will disarm it within the hour." Joe walked to the middle of the room, and sat down directly across the table from Dominguez. Looking at the prisoner, but speaking to Kelly, Joe said, "I guess we can expect a call from Ben Jack Randall next. Isn't that right Sergio?"

District Attorney Berringer said, "The Drug Enforcement Agency provided us with damaging information about your brother-in-law's organization, Dominguez, but we want a lot more. If you cooperate with us, and agree to testify against your brother-in-law, we won't seek the death penalty. But, we expect specifics from you; names, addresses and places."

Sergio's eyes glazed over and he looked down at his hands. "I want to make a deal. Call the defender's office."

Public Defender Frank Fermin was summoned. He and Dominguez were ushered into a separate room for a confidential conversation. Before Fermin could sit down, Dominguez blurted, "I want to make a deal, Fermin."

"What kind of deal, Mr. Dominguez?"

"A light sentence in exchange for fingering my brother-in-law, Arturo Cisneros. He paid me to eliminate Acuna. I'm willing to talk about his drug business too, if it'll help me."

"You'll be arraigned before Judge Delgado tomorrow morning at 9:00 A.M. We'll talk about a deal after your arraignment. Now, tell me about this brother-in-law, Mr. Dominguez."

At the arraignment, Public Defender Fermin pled not guilty for his client. The judge set a trial date, and because Dominguez was a flight risk, ordered the accused to be held without bail.

Fortified with the Dominguez confession and the audiotape Martin Leary gave him, District Attorney Berringer convened another emergency meeting of the Hidalgo County Grand Jury. Less than two hours later the DA marched into Sheriff Zedillo's office waving an arrest warrant.

Sheriff Zedillo exclaimed, "That was quick."

"I think we may have set a record today. It took the jury a little over an hour to indict Cisneros for the murder of José Acuna. I played the tape Martin brought from Connecticut. The jurors were shocked that Cisneros could reach as far as Connecticut to harm someone. They want him stopped before he kills more innocent people."

Tony said, "Joe, we've got to get you up to Austin with this indictment. Who do we know with an airplane?"

Dave Collins responded, "How about asking Travis Jenkins if he'd give Joe a ride on the Railroad Commission plane? The only other way would be to drive over to Harlingen and wait for a Southwest flight."

When contacted, Travis Jenkins was pleased to learn that Dominguez had been arrested, and Cisneros was about to be arrested. "We'll provide whatever you need, Tony. I can have our plane at the McAllen airport within the hour. It's a six-seat Cessna."

"Thanks, Travis. I owe you one."

Before Godfrey left for the airport, Tony instructed him to allow the Austin Police Department to take the lead role in Cisneros's arrest. "They've been following him for days and know his every move." Tony insisted, however, that following the arrest Joe was to bring Cisneros back to McAllen for questioning. "If anyone objects, call me right away. I won't have it any other way."

## ELSA

Joe responded, "I understand, Tony. I'm confident we won't have a problem. Jack Kelly said he'd fly back to McAllen with us. If Martin comes with me, we should have enough manpower to guard the prisoner."

## 33

ARTURO CISNEROS LIVED WITH his wife Vincenta at the back end of a cul-de-sac in an upper middle class, affluent neighborhood on the west side of Austin. Their red brick home was situated on a well-maintained, landscaped yard. Married for over fifteen years, the couple elected not to have children. In spite of Arturo's unusual work schedule, home most of the day, out most nights, his neighbors would have wagered he was a successful entrepreneur, specializing in the export/import business. He was considered "rough around the edges" socially, but the neighbors were pleased that his property was conscientiously maintained. Arturo was friendly when he worked in the front yard, but he was more comfortable in the back yard; he treasured the privacy. The back yard was enclosed on three sides by a six-foot wood fence. He loved to cultivate flowers, delicate roses in particular, and occasionally experimented with cross breeding in a small green house he'd constructed.

Vincenta opened the kitchen window and called to her husband. "It's 5:30. If you want to get to Bustamonte's by 7:00, you'd better come in and shower. I'll pour a glass of Chardonnay if you want."

"Okay. I just need a few more minutes, and then I'll come in."

Joe Godfrey and Austin Detective Denny Pimental were in the front seat of the unmarked patrol car parked at the entrance to the Cisneros's cul-de-sac. Martin had been relegated to the back seat. Detectives Jack Kelly and Art Cuomo were stationed in another unmarked car a block away. Approximately an hour after they'd begun their surveillance, Pimental radioed that the suspect had just exited his house, and was backing his dark blue 1997 Seville out of the driveway. Jack acknowledged receipt of the message, and prepared to follow when the Seville turned the corner and passed their location. The detectives were concerned that Cisneros might try to bolt if he suspected he was being followed, so they exercised caution and masked their tail by not following directly behind the Seville.

Cisneros pulled into a parking lot on 6th Avenue adjacent to Bustamonte's. He greeted a friend by draping his right arm around the shoulders of the man, and both entered the restaurant laughing. Jack Kelly waited until Cisneros was inside the restaurant before he pulled into the same parking lot and parked his patrol car two rows from the Cisneros vehicle. The second car driven by Joe Godfrey remained on the street across from the restaurant.

Suspecting Cisneros might be armed, Kelly radioed his superior at the police station to discuss his arrest options. He was told not to attempt an arrest inside the restaurant. Instead, he was instructed to exercise patience, and wait to see anyone else joined the group. An arrest would have to be made in the parking lot after Cisneros left the restaurant.

The supervisor directed Cuomo, who'd been equipped with a miniature camera before leaving police headquarters, to stealthily enter the restaurant and attempt to take a picture of the group Cisneros was meeting with. His mission accomplished, Art returned to the vehicle. "I think I got a good shot of the group. Just as I was about to leave, a new guy arrived. I got a shot of him too."

"Good work, Art. I guess we just sit and wait now."

At approximately 8:30, Javier Lopez, a friend and associate of Cisneros's, entered Bustamonte's through the front door, and marched to the back as if he owned the place. He pulled up a chair and sat down next to Arturo. "Cisneros, I just received a phone call from Brownsville. Your brother-in-law was arrested last night for murder and is being held in the Hidalgo County jail." Cisneros, who had just put a piece of steak in his mouth, spit it across the table onto the shirt of Juan Suarez.

The latter jumped up and yelled, "What the fuck are you doing, Cisneros?"

Sheepishly, Arturo responded, "Sorry, Juan." Turning to look at Lopez. "What'd you say, Javier?"

"Your brother-in-law was picked up attempting to cross into Mexico from Laredo. He was taken to McAllen last night, and arraigned this morning. He was charged with the murder of a University of Texas student back in September. Word from our contact in the Sheriff's Department is that he's cutting a deal with the DA."

"What kind of deal?"

"Shit, how would I know? I hope you weren't dumb enough to hire that stupid son-of-a-bitch to kill someone. If you did, I suggest you do whatever is necessary to protect your ass, and ours. You'd better call Rodriguez and have him send an attorney to McAllen as fast as he can. You realize, Cisneros, if your brother-in-law sings, you're a dead man."

Cisneros abruptly stood up and hurriedly moved to the front of the restaurant so that he could make a cell phone call. It took only a few moments to contact his sister Rosa in Rio Grand City. "It's Arturo, Rosa. Do you know where your husband is?"

"No, and I'm worried. I haven't heard from him in three days. It's not like him not to call."

"Shit! Thanks, Rosa. If I hear from him, I'll call. You do the same, okay?" With one hand, Arturo closed the phone with a slap motion. He began to perspire. Santiago Rodriguez would react brutally when he found out Dominguez had been arrested and was singing to the authorities. Unless he could figure a way to silence Sergio, Cisneros recognized that his life wouldn't be worth a plug nickel. He walked back to retrieve his coat, and without saying another word, briskly walked out the front door.

Art Cuomo sat up straight. "Uh oh! Guess who just walked out of the restaurant."

Jack hissed, "Shit! Notify the others." Art practically shouted into the mike, "Go!" Jack opened the car door and jumped out, banging his knee in the process. He mumbled, "Damn it!" He crouched down as low as he could and limped toward the Seville from the rear.

Martin heard the radio command, "Go," and opened the rear door to get out. Godfrey hissed, "Martin, you stay in the car."

Fortunately for Jack and the other detectives, Cisneros didn't start the engine when he reached his vehicle. He sat motionless in the driver's seat with the cell phone pressed against his ear. When Jack was only a few feet from the Seville's trunk, he said a silent prayer that Cisneros wouldn't look in his rearview mirror.

Pimental and Godfrey crouched down and cautiously moved forward. They approached the Seville from behind on the right side while Kelly and Cuomo moved in on the left side. When Kelly was comfortable everyone was in place, he signaled for all four to move forward together.

His adrenaline flowing now, Jack crept up to the driver's door. Holding his revolver in his right hand, he raised his left and quickly opened the driver's side door. He grabbed Cisneros around the neck and with a strong, quick jerk, forcefully pulled Cisneros from the seat onto the pavement.

Cisneros landed hard on his side. The cell phone flew under the car parked in the next space. Joe Godfrey and the other two detectives bounded forward, landed hard on Cisneros, pulled his arms behind him, and engaged the handcuffs. Kelly took a deep breath, stood, and with his knee throbbing, announced, "Arturo Cisneros, you're under arrest for the murder of José Acuna, and the attempted murder of Adam Leary." Joe pulled Cisneros to his feet and Kelly began to read him his rights.

Martin opened the rear door of the patrol car, slid out and walked quietly toward the group. When he was within a few feet of Cisneros, he rushed forward and sneered. "You bastard." He hit Cisneros full in the face with as much strength as he could muster. In spite of being held by two detectives, Cisneros's head bounced off the roof of the Seville. Martin hit him again, this time square on the jaw. Cisneros slumped to the ground, unconscious.

Joe wrapped his arms around Martin and shouted, "No! No more!" Martin didn't resist. He let his arms fall to his side. With tears in his eyes, he looked down at Cisneros and said, "You're lucky I didn't have a gun, you bastard."

Joe wrapped his strong arms around Martin's chest and lifted him off his feet. He carried Martin off the side, away from the others. "That wasn't very smart, Martin."

"I know. I'm sorry." Martin looked at his hand. "I think I broke it."

Joe's frown turned into a smile. He grabbed Martin by the elbow and led him back to the group. "Gentlemen, that incident never happened, okay?" The three detectives nodded. Joe looked at Jack Kelly and said, "When he comes to, ignore any attempt to talk about what just happened." Joe squatted down and gently slapped Cisneros on the cheek. "Wake up, Cisneros."

When Cisneros opened his eyes, Joe looked up at Kelly and said, "When he comes to, I guess we'd better read him his rights again."

As the suspect slowly regained consciousness, he looked around and spotted Martin. "I'll get you, you son-of-a-bitch!" Joe made eye contact with Martin, frowned, and shook his head. Martin turned and walked toward the patrol car.

After Jack repeated the suspect's rights, he said, "Help me get this character into the car."

"Sheriff Zedillo, may I help you?"

"It's Joe, Tony. We picked up Cisneros a few minutes ago. I'm calling from the parking lot of an Austin restaurant."

"Good job. Any trouble?"

"Not really. Jack pulled him from his car before he could do any damage. But it could have been a lot worse. We found a .38 in the glove compartment. You'll love this, Tony. Martin went ballistic and punched Cisneros in the face, twice." Joe chuckled, "He may have broken his hand. Outside of that little incident, it was a smooth arrest."

"Speaking as a father, I don't blame Martin. I might have done the same thing." Tony changed the tone of his voice, and counseled, "Got to make sure we do everything by the book, Joe. We don't want this guy to walk because of some damned technicality." Tony sighed, "Travis told me his pilot will stay with the airplane until he hears from you. Call him on his cell phone and let him know when you'll be ready to leave. It looks like we'll have a long night ahead of us."

Within minutes of the airplane's arrival at McAllen airport, a handcuffed Cisneros was led away to a waiting patrol car and driven to Hidalgo County Courthouse for booking. Meanwhile, Dave Collins drove Martin to the emergency room of the McAllen General Hospital. X-rays confirmed that Martin's right hand was broken. An emergency room physician set the break, wrapped the hand securely, and immobilized Martin's arm with a sling. "When do you leave for Connecticut, Mr. Leary?"

"Tomorrow, I hope."

"I want someone to look at the hand before you go. Call me, and we'll make arrangements for one of the residents to check it."

Martin looked at Dave sheepishly as they exited the hospital. "At least I feel as though I partially avenged the bastard's attempt on my son's life." Martin glimpsed down at the sling. "On the other hand, I've created a problem for myself. I'll have to dictate the final section of my report to the DA."

The following morning Cisneros was led into the one and only interrogation room at the Hidalgo County Sheriff's Department. Joe Godfrey joked, "Sheriff Zedillo, meet our guest, Arturo Cisneros. Tony, I know you may have trouble believing this, but Arturo here is the brother-in-law of Sergio Dominguez who just admitted to the murder of José Acuna. Isn't that interesting?" Tony didn't respond, just stared at the suspect as he moved to the side and sat down on a metal, straight back chair next to Martin Leary and Jack Kelly.

Joe sat down in front of Arturo, leaned across the table, and within inches of Cisneros, looked directly into the man's dark brown eyes. Cisneros returned Joe's stare but didn't utter a sound. "Arturo, my friend, your brother-in-law really blew the Acuna job, didn't he? You and your associates must be pissed. Sergio is singing an entertaining tune about you and your drug operation."

Joe noted a slight flinch, and smiled. From past experience he knew sarcastic comments would eventually take their toll on a suspect. Tony Zedillo slowly stood up, walked to the table and pulled up another chair. "Listen carefully, Cisneros. Your life is on the line. We know you engineered the murder of José Acuna and the attempted murder of Adam Leary up in Connecticut. Your arrest is big news. Remember, amigo, this is Texas. In case you've forgotten, Texas citizens favor capital punishment. You'll be sentenced to die." Tony didn't take his eyes off the suspect as he crossed his legs and sat quietly for a long moment. "We talked with the District Attorneys from Hidalgo County and the City of Putnam, Connecticut, and with a representative of the DEA last night. They were persuaded to offer you a deal. We'll reduce most of the charges against you, and add you to the federal Witness Protection Program in return for information about your drug operations in and around Texas. The DEA wants specifics about your operations in Austin, San Antonio, Houston, Corpus Christi, and the smaller cities. The DEA doesn't expect just general information, Cisneros. They want names. They want dates and places. We're ready to deal, are you?"

Cisneros spoke for the first time. "I'm not gonna listen to any more of your bullshit. You can go piss up a rope. I want legal counsel, now."

Trying to maintain the perception that he was the decision maker, Sheriff Zedillo said, "Sergeant Godfrey, please provide this man with access to a telephone. Let's see if he can wiggle his way out of this one." The interrogation recessed until after lunch to give Cisneros time to make a telephone call.

Martin called Shirley at the Holiday Inn to tell her about breaking his hand. Shirley snickered, and asked if it felt good when he punched Cisneros. "Yeah, it felt good in one respect, but hurt like hell in another, if you know what I mean." They both laughed. "I'll come over to the hotel in a few minutes and we can have lunch together. I'll have to return to the DA's office to finish my report. Please call Claire and let her know I should be back in the office by Monday morning."

"Hurry back. I'm bored. There isn't much to do in McAllen. I've seen every movie in town, and the librarian knows me by my first name. By the way, I'm proud of you, Martin Leary."

A drug cartel mole working in the Hidalgo County District Attorney's office sent an urgent and unsettling message to Santiago Rodriguez notifying him that Arturo Cisneros had been arrested, and that the Drug Enforcement Agency was offering him an opportunity to enter the federal Witness Protection Program in return for his testimony against the cartel. Within minutes, Rodriguez summoned Matt Wish, senior partner of Wish and Solomon. Wish had represented cartel individuals for a variety of drug related offences, but nothing on the scale of a murder charge.

"I don't care what it costs, Wish, I want you to spring Cisneros. Bring the bastard back here. Tell him that his life won't be worth a peso if he accepts the witness protection deal. Remember, if Cisneros talks, heads will fall, including yours."

Wish arrived in McAllen in time for the arraignment. With Matt Wish by his side, Cisneros pled not guilty to all charges. The judge asked the District Attorney, "Have the people considered bail, Mr. Berringer?"

"We ask the court to allow the people to hold the prisoner without bail, Your Honor. The people consider him a flight risk. Mr. Cisneros has many friends in Mexico who'd be more than willing to protect him from the people's prosecution."

Matt Wish objected. "Your Honor, Mr. Cisneros can't be a flight risk. He's not guilty of anything. If you allow the prosecution to hold him without bail, you'll be incarcerating him without giving him his day in court."

Tom Berringer responded, "The evidence against Mr. Cisneros is overwhelming, Your Honor. We have his own brother-in-law's written confession that Mr. Cisneros was the architect behind José Acuna's death. May I remind the court that the suspect has also been charged in Connecticut for the attempted murder of Adam Leary? We recommend the court order the prisoner held without bail, and be remanded back to his cell."

The judge slammed his gavel on the bench and announced, "So ordered." Referring to his calendar, the judge set March 15, as the trial date.

Wish pleaded, "Your Honor, I've come a long way to represent Mr. Cisneros. May I have a few minutes with him before he's taken back to his cell?"

The judge looked at both Wish and Cisneros, and said, "You have one hour, Mr. Wish. Mr. Berringer, arrange for a secure place for an attorney/client conference." He left the bench and entered his chambers.

Thirty seconds into his meeting with Attorney Wise, Arturo was shocked to learn that Rodriguez already knew about the DEA's witness protection offer. "Rodriguez knew about it an hour after the DEA made the offer. Understand something, Cisneros. The cartel has contacts in most law enforcement agencies in south Texas. I'll say this once and as clearly and as succinctly as I can. You're a dead man if you betray the cartel and accept the witness protection offer. The best you can do now is to help me prepare your defense."

When he returned to San Antonio, Matt Wish gave Rodriguez a pessimistic report. "Strictly from the standpoint of evidence, the DA appears to have a strong case against Cisneros. Couple that evidence with his brother-in-law's confession, and the possibility of an acquittal is slim to none."

More as an afterthought than as a design priority, a small, eight-cell jail had been included in the original plan of the Hidalgo County Courthouse building; four cells on each side of a hallway on the top floor. With the arrest of Arturo Cisneros, Sheriff Zedillo was forced to relocate two prisoners to the far end of the south side so that Cisneros would be the only prisoner on the north side. Zedillo assigned armed deputies to guard Arturo around the clock. He directed that one deputy sit in the hallway of the jail twenty-three hours a day while Cisneros was in his cell. Another deputy would accompany Cisneros when he walked in the exercise yard every morning from 7:00 A.M. until 8:00 A.M.

Javier Lopez slowly walked around the courthouse building, inspecting it from various angles. *I'll have to go up to a second level if I want to see over the wall of the exercise yard,* he thought. He stood by the front entrance of the courthouse and studied the two-story building across the street. A coffee shop occupied one half of the ground floor. A hardware store occupied the other half. Javier suspected that the door in between the two establishments probably led to the second level. He crossed the street to have a closer look.

Two signs were attached to the wall next to the door; one read P. J. Castro, DDS, and the other read Ortiz Salon. Javier tried the door and it was unlocked. He climbed the stairs, and entered a small hallway. The door to the salon was on the left, and the door to the dentist's office on the right. He searched for a way to get to the roof, but was unsuccessful. He retraced his steps, and went around to the back of the building. Javier reached up, grabbed the ladder leading up to the fire escape, and climbed up to the roof. He discovered that if he positioned himself in the far left corner, directly over the coffee shop, he could see all but a small portion of the exercise yard. Satisfied, he descended the fire escape, returned to the front of the building, and entered the coffee shop to have lunch.

At 6:30 A.M. the following morning, Javier was back on the roof. He attached a silencer to his M-4, settled back and waited for Arturo to appear with a guard. The guard stationed himself on a chair by the entry gate, and began to follow Arturo with his eyes as the latter began to circle the yard.

Javier watched Arturo circle the yard a few times through the rifle cross hairs. *It should be an easy shot,* he thought. The distance was only about 50 to 60 yards. When Arturo turned the corner and headed toward him for the fifth time, Javier pulled the trigger. He watched Arturo's head snap back as the bullet penetrated the forehead and exited through the back of the head, splattering the man's brains like a projectile of vomit.

The deputy reacted with disbelief as his charge slumped to the pavement. He ran to the wall, and pressed an alarm button. By this time, Javier was already descending the fire escape to a vehicle he'd parked in the alley behind the coffee shop. Within three minutes, Javier was driving out of the city heading back home to Austin by way of San Antonio.

# 34

MARTIN CALLED BILL DAVIS from McAllen to tell him that Arturo Cisneros would never face a jury; he'd been shot dead by an unknown assailant. Martin provided Bill with a summary of how the assassin had picked Cisneros off while he walked in the jail yard. "I may have some exciting news to report, Bill, but I'd like to tell you in person. Our flight is scheduled to arrive tomorrow afternoon at 5:45. Can you and Lois meet Shirley and I at 7:00 at the River Inn?"

Martin handed his report to District Attorney Berringer. "With the death of Cisneros, my report may be superfluous, Tom. On the other hand, the report may help with the prosecution of Dominguez. At least I hope it will."

"I suspect you feel that it was a waste of time. Not true, Martin. Look at it this way. The report contains a lot more information about the Sonora drug cartel than we knew before. I intend to use it as a training tool. I'll make copies for every deputy in Sheriff Zedillo's department, and make it available to every law enforcement agency in south Texas."

"Any leads on the shooter?"

"No. But it's just a matter of time. We know who killed Cisneros, but that information, plus fifty cents, wouldn't get me a cup of coffee. We've searched the alley and the roof of the coffee shop, but haven't found anything yet. One good thing resulted from the Cisneros arrest. The DEA is really motivated now. We might see some action against the cartel. What are your plans, Martin? Are you heading home?"

"Shirley and I plan to drive up to Austin tomorrow morning. Dr. Gerba and I are scheduled to meet with the Railroad Commission's chief legal officer. Ely told me that Travis Jenkins interceded on our behalf, and convinced the RRC to reconsider our appeal. If things go well, we may be able to take the prototype out of storage and resume testing next week. I guess Travis convinced the Railroad Commission's legal beagles that the time I spent helping you guys, had to be worth something."

Berringer added, "He wasn't the only one who stood up for you. Sheriff Zedillo flew to Austin yesterday and met with the RRC Director and the State's Attorney General. I made a few phone calls myself. You have a lot of people in your camp, Martin."

Martin was a little embarrassed. "I didn't know that." He changed the subject. "What about Dominguez? Can't you get him to testify against the cartel?"

"Sure, but he's only a little fish. We want the big fish. However, I never can predict how things will turn out. Maybe we'll get lucky, and Dominguez will lead us to the big fish."

The Learys were seated at a table by the big bay window overlooking the Connecticut River when Bill and Lois arrived. It was obvious to the Davises that the Learys were excited about something. "Sit, you two. I have positive news for a change." When everyone was settled, and drinks had been ordered, Martin smiled broadly and announced, "We've been given permission to resume technology tests!"

Bill reached out with his palm forward and slapped Martin's hand. "How did that happen? Why the change of mind?"

"Some important people interceded in our behalf, Bill, especially Travis Jenkins, the Railroad Commission's top investigative supervisor in Corpus Christi, and Sheriff Zedillo. Travis wrote a letter to one of the more influential RRC commissioners emphasizing my contributions to the Acuna investigation. He asked the Commissioner to initiate a reevaluation of the Railroad Commission's decision to scrub our Elsa tests. The biggest surprise, however, was what Sheriff Zedillo did. He flew up to Austin two days ago to meet with both the Texas Attorney General, and the Railroad Commission Director. He convinced both to review our appeal in light of my contribution. Their review resulted in a lifting of the 'cease and desist' order. We'll be able to resume tests next week. There's one caveat, however; the RRC will monitor the tests. Ely actually welcomed their input. He thinks it will give us another perspective and improve the test regime. How about them apples?"

"You must be proud, Mart."

"I am, Bill. And I learned an important lesson in the process. My real estate business can function fine without me hanging around all the time.

Because of that, Shirley and I have decided to take an extended trip to Europe next spring."

The End